INTO THE FIRE

RACHAEL BLOK

HEAD
of
ZEUS

First published in the UK in 2021 by Head of Zeus Ltd
This paperback edition first published in 2021 by Head of Zeus Ltd

9 7 5 3 1 2 4 6 8

A catalogue record for this book is available from
the British Library.

ISBN (PB): 9781838931728
ISBN (E): 9781838931735

Typeset by Divaddict Publishing Solutions Ltd

Printed and bound in Great Britain by
CPI Group (UK) Ltd, Croydon CR0 4YY

Head of Zeus Ltd
First Floor East
5–8 Hardwick Street
London EC1R 4RG

WWW.HEADOFZEUS.COM

For my children

PART ONE

NOW

Prologue

LOIS

Pumpkins fill the kitchen and Lois's hand is bleeding. The thin carving blade bends in the orange flesh, snagging on her attempt at a goblin's eye. She tries to pull it out, rescue the design, but it's stuck, and even tugging won't release it. Abandoning the blade, she goes to the butler sink and stares out at the blue sky, lying heavy and low over the Hertfordshire fields, rolling down from the big stone house. The tiers of the Roman amphitheatre lie to the right, the ruins of its old stage still used in the summer. The scene is almost set.

Ebba had guessed they'd be back around six. They'd just have to make do with the pumpkins already finished, fat with their garish grins. She will light the candles once it's dark.

'Lois?' Iqbal says, entering the kitchen. 'The new catering staff are arriving soon. I'll hang the sweets in the garden and the tray of drinks is still out there. I'll bring it in once the helicopter has left. I think they've just taken off.'

'Let's take the pumpkins out in a minute. There're ten,

one for each of us. I've given up on the last one, so that can be mine – more mutated than ghoulish. Thanks.' She smiles. The house will be transformed, ready for the party's return.

She had almost gone with them today, but what with the letter, it hadn't felt right. Someone had to stay, and Ebba is better at selling than she is. She'll take more pleasure later, when everything is announced. The deal is almost done.

Sliding the brass tap handle to the right, the water is cold; a gush runs over her hand and the wound reopens, blood spreading into the water and turning it pink.

A crack sounds overhead and she leans forward, looking out over the sink up into the sky, searching. It's loud like thunder, or the heavens splitting.

A black mass is falling. Crashing down, spinning. It's so high up that at first she can't make it out, then a scream builds, spilling out of her throat like it's been cut.

'Iqbal! The helicopter!' she screams, running from the kitchen. Knives clatter to the stone floor and she slips on some pumpkin flesh, discarded and splayed on the huge flagstones, scrubbed and polished for the weekend.

'Iqbal!' she screams again. She runs out of the back door, out into the October air, past the coffee cups from earlier, past the tray of cocktail glasses, and she takes the steps in one leap, landing on the grass, her feet skidding from under her on the autumn wetness, which seems to have painted each blade.

'I'm calling 999!' Iqbal's voice comes from behind her and she gets up, drinking air, gulping it. Her chest is tight.

'Ebba,' she says, not daring to think. Her legs run again,

running ahead of her mind, which has slowed to a photo-frame image of her sister as a child.

The helicopter falls fast. It's almost down, dipping left, right. The pilot must be fighting hard and, for a second, she thinks it will land. Land hard but squarely.

The air is fast with the spin of the blades and just as it looks as though it will finally settle, next to the stone ruins of the Roman amphitheatre, it tilts, comes down wounded on its side, crashing on the old stage. The uneven stone makes for an uneasy bed.

The bang is loud. She reaches the top of the path, overlooking the outdoor theatre's low stone walls, the circle at the centre, the grassy rises. Ebba, Filip, Aksel, Richard, Sarah, Marieke. The people who helped her build Archipelago. The people who, yesterday, were drinking champagne and laughing. So alive. But she can only think of Ebba. She stands and screams.

Smoke rises, black; the helicopter lies, a felled bird, its heart still beating, sounding out the last pattern of its wings.

BEFORE

FRIDAY, TWENTY-FOUR HOURS EARLIER

1

Lois

'I can see a car!' Ebba's shout is loud from up on the landing. She runs down the wide wooden staircase, sweeping its curve to the main hall. Her blonde hair is tied in a loose bun and she wears a blue dress.

Breathe, Lois thinks, trying a calming mantra, but her brain is fizzing with fear. So much rides on this weekend and glossy social situations make her want to bolt.

Ebba springs, poised, almost leaping the last step. Landing like a cat.

Lois had changed last minute from jeans into a vintage tea-dress. It's laid-back, but a step up from her usual T-shirts. How to look prepared and ready, not as though she's taken her eye off the ball. She'd had to check it with Ebba. She's only really used to jeans.

Breathe, she thinks again, running her hands down the thin material of the skirt, coarse, with tiny beads. Her heart races. They've spent two years waiting for this; they're introducing the new game and the franchise agreement at the confidential press briefing tomorrow.

Thoughts of Helen edge in, of how decisively Lois had been dumped. Helen's face, bored with her, any trace of affection gone. In some ways, the deal has demanded so much of her it has helped with the heartbreak. But the wounds are still raw. They snag open and weep when she's not looking.

'We're almost there!' Ebba spins her round, kissing her hard on the cheek and pulling her into a hug so tight Lois feels airless. 'Can you believe it? All your work. All your *talent*!'

'Us, our work. Our talent,' Lois says, grinning. 'I might have the ideas, but that's all it would be without you. You made it fly.'

'We. We made it fly.' Ebba laughs. 'I could scream right now!'

'Don't!' Lois glances nervously at the tray of champagne glasses, fizzing near the main door, sitting on the metal ledge of a white console table that rises from the floor in a large O. The hall is a mix of vintage and modern design, pieces bought from Europe during their negotiations. Their house has only recently been reclaimed, and they've worked hard to exhibit part of their history and their future. 'We're ready. I think.'

'I'll take the guests into the drawing room.' Iqbal appears at her elbow and Lois nods.

'Thanks, Iqbal. You've been a star, as usual. How are the others working out?' Lois frowns, thinking of cracked glass, the strangeness of caterers in the kitchen.

'Good. It's all good.' He smiles, stepping backwards, winking. 'I'll direct the luggage to the rooms. You can both relax. Please. Let me take care of it. Let me organise the weekend; remember I'll be avoiding the small talk where possible.' He pulls a face.

'Iqbal, I can't believe you pulled off all the organisation for this weekend! You could go into wedding planning. You'd make millions.' Ebba smiles.

'Just doing my job. We've got this covered: I'll organise, you're people focused, and Lois is the tech. We're on it. I'm going to be all over the details. Just leave it to me,' Iqbal says, and Lois thinks again how lucky they are to have him on board. He's taken on so much recently, but they'd all agreed it was important, and didn't want to trust the organisation to people lower down in their team. Ebba, the florist of the house, has planned flowers for every room as well as running the contracts and the agreement. Lois has worked on the tech presentation with Iqbal, who has planned everything else.

Ebba opens the main doors, tall and heavy. The cold air of the autumn day rushes in like a fan. There's the smell of rain, but it's dry at the moment, holding out, as though it knows.

Lois smiles at her sister, checking as she always checks, flushing with pleasure that Ebba is riding high on the weekend and that the stress hasn't become too much. Ebba had been with their dad when he died. She'd called the ambulance and sat with him. Lois isn't sure she's ever really got over it. Since the death of their father, stress has been something that stalks them, like a predator. But Ebba's been soaring on this deal, carving herself out in stone instead of sand.

'It's just the police,' Ebba says. A half laugh of anticlimax falls from her mouth.

'We'll stay outside, ma'am,' the officer says, turning naturally to Ebba. 'We're on duty all weekend. We swap shifts later and a senior officer is visiting.'

Lois can hear them talking to Ebba as they move outside. 'The house was checked first thing. Nothing to worry about, just a precaution. There'll be someone along later this evening.'

'Lovely, thank you so much,' Ebba says, and Lois can hear her coming back up the steps.

'Are we stupid to go ahead, when Marieke is still receiving threats?' Lois asks, knowing they've already talked about it, but doubt races her to the finish line.

'We're sticking with Plan A,' Ebba replies. 'We've done all we can. It wouldn't do to uninvite her, at this point. You know what she's like! Courage, Lois. We can do this. I know crowds make you nervous, but you're on home ground here. The deal is done. You just need to smile.'

Leaning back against the oak-panelled wall, Lois nods. The threatening letters Marieke has been receiving, warning her to stay away from Archipelago, scare her – it's the unknown quantity that's frightening.

Ebba puts her arms around Lois again, leaning close. 'For Dad,' she whispers.

Ostle House sits on the edge of St Albans. The cathedral rises in the distance. They moved back into their childhood home, surrounded by two acres of land, two years ago, buying it with every penny they had; filling it with all the designs, plans and dreams for Archipelago. The family home had been lost when they'd lost their father. Everything had gone. The memories had called them back. It had been hard to lose so soon after their father's death. Something he had invested in needed to remain. They'd agreed immediately.

'Imagine how proud Dad would be today.'

Lois's design studio is still in the attic of the old nursery upstairs, which had been their playroom when they were children. Now they have factories, staff, and an office near King's Cross. Archipelago is bigger than she ever thought it would become. It's exhilarating and terrifying. Only a couple of days away from announcing their agreement, launching her game: her tech baby.

The thought of it, factories in Holland and Norway, springing open like buds, scattering handsets and games globally. Lois couldn't face breakfast that morning, nerves in the form of nausea coming in waves. Twenty-four hours to go.

2

MAARTEN

'Nic, what about this one?' Maarten hunkers down to look at the costumes, aisles full of witches and ghosts. He pulls out a purple mesh outfit for a ten-year-old; a cape flares at the back with shiny stiffness.

Nic rolls her eyes. 'I'm not six, Papa.'

Standing, exhausted with looking, Maarten stares at the rows and rows of polyester, thinking his daughters would do well to stay away from naked flames. 'Well, you need something to wear at the weekend. Sanne's all sorted and we can't have you with no costume. Should we try somewhere else?'

As well as trick or treating, there's the station party on Saturday. As DCI, he'll have to go and take the whole family. They're all dreading it, even Liv, who is good at these things. She'd known the names of his team almost before he did. She has gifts, has made up bundles of sweets for children, hand-printed cards with the kids for all his team. But last night an arrest had vomited on him and he feels like staying as far away from the station as he can.

There's a noise; the sound of a familiar voice. It's soft, but clear, like a wind chime. The ring floats lightly on the air and he knows before he looks up that she's standing before him, as if a ghost from one of the hangers has sprung to life.

It must be twenty years.

'Maarten?' Her face mirrors his shock. She stands at the end of the aisle, just over a metre away. The burn on his cheeks matches her colour. And he feels confusion, his fingers hot as they rise to rub his mouth. He can still feel the stain.

She recovers first and steps forward, leaning in to kiss his cheek. Smiling. Her scent is a memory, coloured in reds and pinks, softness. The darkness of a past buried stirs; shadows quickly widen. The night in the rain. Adrenaline sharp, the taste of beer. A bunch of flowers in his hand. A man, laughing. Her voice, *Maarten! Stop!*

Something pulls on his hand and it takes him a moment to realise that it is Nic, calling him.

'Papa?'

He can't look down immediately, can't turn his eyes.

'Maarten! It's been so long.'

He's never one for small talk, but right now all his words have left him.

'The same old Maarten,' she says, eyebrows rising, and he stumbles over whatever he was going to say, thinking of a secret, which she knows. Only her. And it rushes at him, with edges tacky and torn.

'Marieke,' he manages finally, and Nic pulls again on his arm.

'Papa, that costume over there?' She points, ignoring Marieke, and Maarten wishes he could step into the folds of the red and black costumes, retreat and take cover.

'Sorry,' he says, 'we're shopping and we don't have much time.'

It's a coward's way out. But she brings back a host of unwanted memories.

He allows Nic to pull him away and he can feel Marieke's eyes on him.

'Papa, why have you gone so red?' Nic asks, as a string of questions sit waiting, collecting, ready to pour out. Things he hasn't thought of for years.

'I'm hot, Nic. It's so hot in here. Can you pick something and we'll go home to Mama?'

The breath of perfume is still hanging close to his mouth, and he feels heady. In a second, he will recover, but the ghosts lift themselves for All Hallow's Eve and he feels himself untether. Adrift.

'Maarten!'

The shout from the super sounds across the floor and, still reeling from his encounter with Marieke, he tries for a wink at Sunny and Adrika, with whom he'd been going over a case.

'Best answer that one,' he says.

Adrika smiles, as Sunny pushes his blond hair off his face and glances at his reflection in the window. Sunny has a new girlfriend and he's been taking his appearance seriously.

Maarten forces himself to smile back. Thinking of what

the super will want, his stomach is still in knots. He knows, with the dread of premonition, that this meeting will be about Marieke.

What a coward he'd been, running this morning. He thinks of all the things he wishes he'd said. Replays the meeting, a version where he greets her like the old friend she is.

'Afternoon, ma'am,' he says, entering his office, where the super is waiting. 'How are you?'

She nods, moving past pleasantries, smiling brightly. 'Good to see you, Maarten. I have a job for you this afternoon, if you don't mind.'

A cold hand grasps him somewhere below his diaphragm. It can be no coincidence after seeing her earlier.

'There's a politician staying in St Albans this weekend, from Holland. I believe she lives in Rotterdam, where you're originally from?'

He nods. It's the only part of his body that moves; the rest of him is lead heavy. He thinks back to Rotterdam, twenty years ago. He doesn't recognise himself. He'd been a child, fresh out of university. He'd thrown himself into his job, which demanded attention to detail, observation. Then Marieke had come along.

'Her name is Marieke Visser, and she's causing controversy in Holland. She's pushing for all Dutch companies to eliminate modern slavery in their supply chain. If it goes through, it will cost some businesses millions. She's been receiving death threats and, as a courtesy, I've agreed to staff a PC at the house for the weekend. We'll give it a sweep. It's low risk.'

She pushes a file at him and he picks it up, skimming: rape threats, Twitter trolls, death threats. And now anonymous letters telling her to stay away from a business deal with a company called Archipelago.

The super is still talking: '...offering security will be good for relations. I was due to head over and shake hands, offer a reassuring word or two – show face. But,' – she screws her face up – 'I've been asked to head up some meeting this afternoon, which will run over. It's little more than a polite hello. I know it's not really your favourite thing.' She glances at him, a question on her face.

'Ostle House,' he reads. 'Archipelago? They're the gaming company?'

'Yes. They've given a lot of money recently to the St Albans community, particularly local schools, so it's good PR all round.'

It hangs in the air. He clearly can't say no. He scrambles to think of a hospital appointment or something, anything, but he can't grab hold of an excuse quickly enough and he can feel himself nodding.

'Great. There's a dinner invitation too. Liv might fancy it. Thanks, Maarten. I owe you one.'

She checks her phone as it beeps. 'The social media threats seem to come mainly from right-wing men claiming to protect the free market, but, for my money, probably just don't like a woman with power. It's assumed the letters come from angry business leaders. And she seems to rub people up the wrong way. You know what social media is like nowadays, you're villainised or angelicised. No middle ground. Particularly for successful women. But she has a reputation for being prickly. Be charming.'

He nods. 'Archipelago – People Before Profits, right?'

'Yes, and they make amazing games. They make the virtual reality one everyone is playing. My son is obsessed! And it seems they've signed a deal with Hollywood for some superhero VR game. We're lucky they're local. It's a big press weekend.' She smiles. 'Hopefully a quiet weekend for you, though. Enjoy dinner!'

The door slams behind her.

Maarten looks at the file.

He can still feel the rain on his skin, the anger in his mouth, and later, the guilt. It was twenty years ago and the memory of what happened with Marieke sits with him. He'd always known it would bite him at some point. But here? In St Albans? He'd thought that by leaving Rotterdam he had left it all behind. He'd thought secrets couldn't cross the sea.

He will need to tell Liv about Marieke and what happened. If he is going to be talking to Marieke again, he will need to tell Liv everything. It wouldn't be fair to her not to.

Kak, he thinks. *Kak*.

3

Filip

Still cursing as he thinks of the row that morning, he swears under his breath. It will look weak if she doesn't come and he'd told her as much.

'Bastard! Fucking workaholic!' she'd screamed in the huge reception area in their apartment in Rotterdam, the chrome lights watching silently above them, highlighting his shame. He winces as he thinks of it, shrinking even further into his seat.

'*Kak*,' he mutters, as the car turns from the M25, heading into Hertfordshire. There is a cabinet of booze in the back of the car. He pours himself a tumbler and knocks it back, the tinkle of ice clinking as his throat burns. He can take his drink, but right now he wants it to take him.

She had screamed at him that morning. 'I'm not coming! Why is it always me doing what you want? Where are the dinners? The weekends away?'

He had taken a breath, seeing the cleaner scuttle up the stairs. 'Sophie, this *is* a weekend away. We said we would go. They're expecting us. It's a beautiful house; it's a celebration. Please come.'

'Why? Why should I come? For you to parade me round like a trophy? For me to do all your talking for you, while you disappear to work? What's in it for me? Why is this my problem?'

'Sophie, please.' He had been able to hear the pleading in his voice and he wasn't sure why. Was it just embarrassment? Did he really want her to come? Maybe she was right, maybe he wasn't being fair to her. He had taken a step towards her and she had thrown her hair over her shoulder, fixed him with her gaze. 'Why is it that everyone else recognises my success, wants my company, and my own husband doesn't seem to care one bit? You don't lay a finger on me unless I make the first move. You might be one of the richest men in Holland, but I am a fucking *film star*!'

Under the lights – rose-gold dressing gown, blonde hair in waves – she had looked every inch the film star and he had stood silent, transported back to when he first met her. Back then, he couldn't speak a word in her presence; a smile from her would make him hot, make him nervous. He is still nervous around her. And she is right. She is a stratospheric success; she can hold a room. He can hide in a business deal, count money. Why are they still together? Why has she not left him? He can't hold a candle to her.

He taps a text: *Tickets booked on Eurostar, if you change your mind.*

It's shorter than he'd like – it sounds angry? He will have to tell them she's ill. No one will think twice probably, but the paper cut of embarrassment stings. She is a celebrity in her own right and he likes to hide behind her at these things. He'd known when he asked her to marry him that a tiny part of her charm was her ability to deflect attention from him, soak it all up for herself.

The reply zings to his phone. *I'll think about it.*

Fuck. She knows how to deal with people and parties far better than him. He's good at numbers, at plans. He was supposed to enjoy this weekend. He has been looking forward to it.

The car turns down a long private drive, trees bend, scattering leaves like confetti. This setting couldn't be more English. Or further away from the open-plan flats of Rotterdam. All these fields, with their fences and their trees. The waiting house is imposing, challenging. Nerves stir about the manners that will be expected and then he's irritated with himself. He is providing the money. Why should he be the one on the back foot?

There's another car behind him. It could be the other investor, the Norway money. How should he handle it? He mustn't seem like a pushover. He drinks again, not caring if they smell booze on his breath. It's only a fucking dinner.

Filip checks Twitter. Marieke has posted about the weekend. He smiles and taps out his own post: *Pleased to be attending this weekend!*

Marieke has been such a support. She's been behind this deal from the start. Archipelago's progressive conditions for all employees are right up her street, and it's big money. Having her around to talk to has been such a relief. She doesn't let people in right away, but when she does – unlike most people – she has no artifice. This makes her so easy to confide in – even about Sophie.

Closing his eyes, he feels the emptiness underneath it all.

That moment, months ago, like a flashback.

The ledge had been short and the wind had rushed up, sending him off balance. He'd shaken, been frightened. It had all spanned below him and, despite the weight, the crushing weight of it all, he hadn't been able to jump.

There's a pain in his head, sharp and then throbbing. A numbness, lurking beneath everything he does right now, settles in his chest.

Each movement towards the top had lifted his load a little. The idea of throwing it all away. Lessening the grind in his head.

But he hadn't. He'd found himself stepping back. Terrified.

He has everything. On the surface.

He has a wife who men look at, greedy. But his relationship with Sophie is torture. Every eye on her is like a needle. He sees the eyes of others on him, too, thinking it must be the money she has chosen.

And he can't satisfy her, can't come close. Each time is worse than the last. The inadequacy is killing him.

The drizzle in the air wets the colours on the trees and they look brighter. Perhaps getting out of Holland will bring a relief. He checks his phone again.

Lowering the window, he lets the damp touch his face.

He'd seen her first on screen, watching a film in his lounge. Halfway through, there'd been a scene where she'd sat in a park under a tree and sung. Her voice... And she'd stopped in the middle, laughing at the line from the other actor. She'd worn jeans and a T-shirt, bare feet; a silver bracelet on her left wrist, her eyes brown with flecks of green, her smile the widest he'd ever seen. She'd winked at the end of the laugh and delivered a line so deadpan he'd laughed out loud at home on his couch; and he'd replayed that moment over and over. She'd been so funny, so bright. When she sang, her voice... Her voice.

The car slows, driving over an old cattle grid. Filip pours himself another drink.

It had been easy getting tickets to an event where she'd be. She wasn't the headline invite. That had been a bigger star, over from England, but he'd bided his time and made a donation to the cause, so the organisers were falling over themselves.

When she'd been introduced, his heart raced. He knew he'd flushed red, made some remark about the heat in the room. He'd felt stripped, naked.

Everyone must have been able to see he was already hers if she wanted him. He'd been laid out for the taking.

Following up the evening with flowers: he'd researched her favourites, yellow roses and wolfsbane, sent bunches to her home each day; he'd invited her to the theatre: the best seats. The courtship was as lavish as he dared. Nervous every time he met her, he'd allowed his status and his money to speak for him.

After months when he'd not dared go too near her, when wanting her so much had paralysed him, she had finally touched him. He'd almost cried and she had been as calm as his breath had been quick. With even the first kiss, he'd been convinced she could see in his eyes how easy he was to take. To pluck. He'd been hers the first moment she held his gaze.

His phone rings and Ruben's name flashes up, his secretary.

'Filip, I've got some bad news. Are you there yet?'

'Ten minutes out,' Filip says.

'I've heard a rumour. There's info coming in that suggests the Norway deal might be slightly different. The upfront investment figure of fifty million GBP is the same, but our research suggests their distribution deal is significantly better.'

'Fuck.' Filip leans his head back. The threat of social niceties recedes as his brain processes the information. 'This is serious. I need all the details.'

'I'll look into it and call you back.'

'Thanks, Ruben. If this is true, I'll arrange a meet before we release the signatures on the contract. I'll confront them head on. I want this, but I'm no one's puppet.'

'I'll be in touch.'

The phone is silent and heavy; he drops it on the black leather of the seat. The car slows.

He pours himself another drink.

4

MAARTEN

'Are they terrorist threats?' Adrika asks, sitting down across the desk from Maarten.

The station is emptying over the lunch hour. People are walking the five minutes into town for last-minute Halloween chocolates for the weekend, for a sandwich. The sun is bright through the window. Warm enough to leave a coat at the desk.

He shakes his head. 'They don't think so. Here.' He puts the file down and shakes out copies. 'Overall, it's a mix of threats. She's been receiving Twitter abuse for a while; social media is bashing her. You know how vile and abusive that can be – but usually it's non-specific and it's ongoing. Most of the abuse directed her way is more general, or references her policies: she's become the populist scapegoat. These letters are different. For one, they arrive at her home and they also directly reference Archipelago and this deal. Here, a few photocopies.'

Adrika lifts three photocopies from the file. In a mash-up

of cut-out newspaper letters and thick black marker pen, the orders are spelled out in clear terms. She reads:

STEP BACK, BITCH. TAKE A MONTH OFF.
YOU'LL REGRET IT IF NOT.

TO THE WHORE,
THE RED DRESS YOU WERE WEARING ON
THURSDAY? I'LL WRAP THAT ROUND YOUR
NECK.

FUCKING WITCH. STAY AWAY FROM
ARCHIPELAGO.

'Are they all like this?' she asks.

'Seems so,' Maarten says. 'Quite vague. But vicious. Personal.' Maarten skims the file. 'They've set up a watch on her home and office in Rotterdam. They've no idea where they're coming from. Her home address would be very difficult to find – and she's careful not to share any details of her private life in the media. Working theories are that it's a Twitter troll taking things a step too far, or someone vengeful – a jilted lover possibly, or more likely someone she's forced out of business. She recently exposed two companies disposing of chemical waste illegally. Their businesses took a real hit from the fines.'

'What a nightmare! It's about time business was forced to be accountable: pensions disappearing, dumping of chemical waste. You've got to be rich to get away with it. It's shocking. We need more people like her.'

He thinks of Marieke. Seeing her that morning: an apparition. A ghost of Halloweens past. She'd been thinner than he remembers. Flintier. Something about her stance now had come across as defensive. The way she'd held herself, maybe? The rush of feelings had been overwhelming.

God, what he had felt for Marieke back then had been all-consuming. He hasn't thought of it for years, but shame stabs now.

'Have you ever met her?' Adrika asks, reading the file. 'It says here she was in the police force in Rotterdam, years ago. Did you know her then?'

Opening his mouth, the lie sticks behind his teeth. Instead, he says, 'I think she might have worked there when I started.' He touches his cheek, feeling himself colouring, and he buries his head, reaching into the drawers by his desk, pulling out his phone and looking at it.

A missed call from Liv.

'She gets a bad rep. Look. There's a story here about her kicking off at an environmental charity event. High-profile figures had flown in from all continents to support it, and in her speech she named every single one of them and the emissions from their flight. I bet that went down well!' Adrika grimaces. 'Look, another story – she's written an open letter to heads of companies detailing an estimate of their emissions each year. And I hadn't realised she was the one who called out that pop star who was campaigning for the environment but flew to every city in a private jet, then drove to the demonstration in a Prius! I'm not surprised she has haters.' Adrika drops the printouts. 'What do you want from me?'

'Hopefully nothing. You and Sunny are both on this weekend – if there are any problems, I'll call. We've got a couple of PCs watching the place. I think I'm basically window dressing. I'm going to the dinner tonight.' He pulls a face.

Adrika grins. 'I know how you love a dinner party.'

'Well, at least Liv's looking forward to it. She's packed the kids off to her mum's for the weekend.' He laughs, but it's hollow.

As Adrika leaves, he calls his wife. She doesn't answer but he listens to the full length of her voicemail answer message before ringing off, as though investing this time will make confession softer, later.

Why did he ever think leaving Rotterdam would leave it behind? He's been a fool.

5

FILIP

'I'll take your bags in, sir.' The driver heads round to the boot as Filip's phone rings.

'Sophie,' he says.

'Filip, I'm still not sure if I can come. I've just had Stefan on the phone. There's a drinks thing in Amsterdam tonight; he thinks it might be a good idea if I go.'

Unbidden, the image rises of his wife, naked, legs circling Stefan's back, his mouth on her skin. He can't shake it. He has no evidence. But Stefan kisses her cheek longer than he needs, every time he says hello.

'You're going out with Stefan, rather than me? Has he booked a hotel for you both over there?'

'Oh fuck, Filip, I'm not sleeping with him. He's my agent. These drinks are important, he says. Anyway, I haven't decided.'

There's a silence on the line. Filip can see the doors to the house open and Ebba appears, directing the driver with the luggage. He'd forgotten how beautiful she is, and he's hit with a flush of nerves. He lifts a hand, gestures to the phone.

'It's almost one. If you're going to catch the train in time for dinner, you'll need to decide soon.'

His skin crawls. He won't sleep a wink later if she goes to Amsterdam. He thinks of Stefan unzipping her dress, slowly, of her breath quickening. Does she want him?

'Aren't you going to say anything?' she says, and he holds the phone hard, wanting to manage to laugh it off, to offer an endearment. To ask her to come. But tears slide into the back of his throat.

'Let me know,' he says. It's all he can manage.

Where had it gone wrong with Sophie?

On their honeymoon? There had been moments of such sweetness he'd realised he'd not really been alive before. But some negotiations at work had been rising and falling, and just as he could feel his nerves slow, just as he and Sophie were beginning to feel real, the deal had nosedived.

He'd been busy: checking emails, on conference calls. He'd worked his way through it and pulled it back up.

After forty-eight hours of being locked away, he'd gone out to the pool finally, and she'd been lying on a lounger, wearing a yellow bikini, looking new and untouchable: he'd been floored. He'd stumbled an apology – his authority of only moments ago vanishing.

She'd ignored him to start with. Well, he'd been working, not focused on her for two days, so some payback was owed, he reasoned. But along came a James Bond contender, carrying a drink for her; and Filip felt his blood flood green.

Aksel Larsen. He'd briefly met him before, and his profile was everywhere. If he wasn't skiing in some high-profile charity race, he was sailing on the front of a magazine, and had even played hockey professionally, for about five minutes. As a major business figure from Norway, Filip knew of him, if he didn't know him personally.

Larsen handed her a drink and Filip could see her start to smile. By anyone's standards, Aksel was attractive. His middle looked like a Greek god had spent time sculpting the grooves of a six pack, firm and tanned. Filip had glanced down at his own frame: tall and skinny, pale; he'd rarely seen the inside of a gym.

Aksel had held his hand out to help her up and cracked a joke.

Filip had coughed and she'd introduced him: *my husband*, and he remembers the look on Aksel's face: mirth and derision.

'Don't worry, I've been looking after your beautiful wife,' he'd said, and he'd reached out, put his arm around her.

Filip was hit with two fundamental truths: he had more money; Aksel Larsen had more of everything else.

Like a crashing wave, he'd rolled with the crystal realisation that while he could offer all the gold and trimmings she'd need, he'd never be able to compete. He wasn't handsome, not like this. Nor funny – no easy quips. Others carried themselves with an ease he'd never possess. And through her eyes, he saw what he'd never minded before.

He'd ordered a couple of drinks and had stewed, silent

and churning on all his flaws, all his lack of grace. He'd answered her questions with silence. The intimacy he'd begun to feel, the secrets that had begun to flow between them, began to seal up.

When they'd lain on the bed later, he'd touched her and doubted himself. He wondered how his hands compared to others she'd known. Stuttering, he hadn't been able to hold himself back. It had been over quickly and he'd been too ashamed to give her what she needed; nervous he'd fail anyway. And while all he'd wanted was to please her, to touch her, he'd gone out to the balcony to check his phone. He knew he'd deserted her. His own inadequacy was finally apparent. She would go to bed dreaming of the hands of another man and his fate was sealed.

It had never really recovered. That had been little over a year ago. They were still newly-weds, yet he was wondering how long it would be until she left him.

The mists roll across the gravel drive. The door to the house sits ajar and he'll have to go in soon. He can't sit in the car forever.

He taps out another text: *Can you at least let me know if you're going to come? I should let the hosts know.*

Did that sound too pleading?

Sometimes, when his wife is out at another event with her agent, he thinks of their closeness, and wonders again about their honeymoon. When he had been ignoring Sophie and working, had she been with Aksel, finding all the pleasure he couldn't give her?

Filip has gone out of his way to avoid Aksel Larsen since. Not attending award ceremonies, business dinners, if Larsen was due to attend. It's getting harder. He's expanding his business empire out of Norway, widening his net.

Maybe it's Aksel Larsen Sophie is really seeing this weekend? Filip tries to breathe, to calm down.

He wishes Sophie would come. Be here with him. By his side. Fucking Aksel, peering into all his business, like a snake slipping beneath a flap in a tent.

At some point, Filip has lost his way. When he has had enough of answering his inbox, he sits in bed and watches TV he doesn't care about; he watches Rotterdam unfolding before the huge window that looks out over the city. The lights move around on the ground like guests at a cocktail party and he watches, like someone without an invite.

That moment. Weeks ago. When it had all built up to a towering wave of disappointment. When he'd felt small, weak, like he couldn't see the light anywhere. Step, step, step. The tap of his shoes on iron stairs. The rush of wind. The nothingness. He'd stood on the empty factory roof and considered it. But no. He'd shrunk back. Shaking.

Facing Sophie each day presents him with everything he loves and everything he hates about himself. He daren't initiate sex, he daren't touch her. Each time he fails. Can't finish. Each time he leaves her, walking away like he doesn't care. He is filled with self-loathing. He can't even look her in the eye, unable to read what must be written there.

Emptiness threatens to swallow him. Would it be better if he left her? But how does he leave Sophie? It would be like carving out his heart.

6

IQBAL

Steam rises from the hob and someone is shouting about asparagus.

'All OK?' Iqbal asks and there are nods in reply. 'Here, they'll get you a drink if you like,' he says to Filip's driver, asking to refill his water bottle before he leaves for London, but no one steps to help, hands full of pans and knives. Iqbal takes the bottle and does it himself.

The fairy lights in the hall are soft. The sisters stand waiting for Filip, who must still be on his call outside.

A soft ping of an email notification in his pocket.

He glances at his phone. He'd said no work emails for the three days. It's from one of the admin team; they've forwarded something. The header flashes up:

PERSONAL – For you, Iqbal?

He stops, ducking left into the snug. Always on alert in case there's news of Rajita, he opens it quickly. It's been sent to the email address on the 'Contact Archipelago' page of their website.

It's an email from Obaidur.

Skimming it, he falls against the door. His heart beats quickly and his knees buckle. He closes his eyes, opens them again. It's still there. The room vibrates around him, and his ears fill with a rush and a thump. A flash of the factory, of flames, leaps into vision.

Moving to the low sofa, he hangs on to the arm as he lowers himself.

Fingers trembling, he taps on the inbox, scrolling down.

Obaidur. The last time he saw him was nearly nine years ago. He'd been grey with dust, streaked red with blood.

Iqbal had worked next to him for four years, been to school with him. Obaidur had been his best friend, like a brother.

In 2012 the fire had happened. And all their lives had changed.

Afterwards, Obaidur had vanished. Rajita had vanished. Iqbal had searched for them both, but there'd been no trace. His home wasn't his home any more, not without his wife, not without his friend. He wakes to an empty bed. Their absence grew day by day. It ripped him apart. And they were nowhere. He looked everywhere.

Skimming the email too quickly, none of it goes in. He starts again at the top. It begins with an affirmation of their friendship. Iqbal feels tears warm his eyes, his mind spinning. The email is in Bengali, and he realises how much he has missed the rhythm of his tongue.

I can imagine your face, reading this. Surprise! It's been so long. I've wanted to write for years, but I had no idea where you had gone. I'm sorry. I know I disappeared too. But I'm leaping ahead of myself. I hope you are happy to hear from me.

I have so much to say to you. And to say sorry for. Before I go into all that, I must tell you I know Rajita disappeared. I spoke to someone the other day who has come back from a maid position in the Middle East. She works for a good household there, and she said that she spoke to Rajita a few years ago. She has not been so lucky. She is not working for such a good family. My friend said Rajita seemed frightened: she no longer has her passport. She heard that they moved on. Maybe even England?

At this point Iqbal puts his phone down. Thinks. He will need to speak to the liaison officer who is looking into Rajita's case. His head crowds with thoughts, they spin and weave. Picking up the email again, Obaidur's voice sails across the oceans.

And now I think you are in England too? You know I looked for you – Facebook, Google, everything. I know you've always hated those sites so I didn't hold out much hope. But then yesterday I saw your photo. I found a business magazine in a café, left in a pile. Can you imagine what I thought, when I saw you looking out? The article was in English so I could not read the details but it ran over four pages – you must be doing well.

I recognised another man whose photo was in that article,

and I wonder if you know him too? Just before the fire, I sold him an idea. Can you believe it?

Thanks to him, I had money and independence for a time. But I am back in the factories now. How strange that you have ended up working with him. But maybe it's no coincidence: did you meet him in Dhaka too?

Hot and cold, Iqbal reads and rereads. Obaidur goes on to explain a meeting with the man, a researcher, back before the fire.

His eyes wide, the email burns his fingers.

At the end, his palms sweat and his phone is damp to his touch: fingerprints mark themselves out on his screen.

There's a shout from the front step. People are arriving. He's needed.

So much information. So much he's still desperate to know. He has tried for years to find Obaidur.

And Rajita! If only she could be that close. This is not the first time there's been a whisper of England. There have been leads before, but he can tell from the last meeting with his liaison officer that everyone has given up hope.

And the information Obaidur details about the meeting with this unnamed man. If what Obaidur has said is true, then Archipelago could be sitting on shaky ground. Obaidur's account of how he'd been given the money, *why* he'd been given the money, stirs Iqbal's stomach.

Could one of the men coming here today really have been capable of such a theft, dressed up as a purchase?

One of the men coming to his home? One of the men investing in Archipelago?

There's a crevasse opening up before him. Rank and dark.

Had one of the men arriving today been in Dhaka around the time of the fire? If he can find that out, then he can work from there. He can't ask questions too directly: he can't upset this weekend. But he also cannot ignore this email. If it were revealed that someone at Archipelago was corrupt, the whole company could crumble. They have built themselves up as a beacon of ethical business. People Before Profits. Lois could lose everything.

Iqbal's legs are shaky. He will need to tread carefully.

Lois means so much to him.

And what does Obaidur mean, so much to say sorry for?

He thinks of Obaidur, back in those factories after his taste of independence. Iqbal closes his eyes, thinks of the endless shifts, the heat; the disproportionate way that business values lives.

Before doing anything else, Iqbal types an email and sends it to the officer who liaises with him over Rajita's disappearance. He copies the section from Obaidur's email about Rajita across and presses send. His heartbeat speeds. His wife. To have her back…

He misses the indent of her body in his. She slept deeply, her limbs would tangle into him. He would wake sometimes, lifting an arm carefully from his neck; ease away from a knee in his back. Her presence was solid, physical, even asleep. Now, he drowns in space. He wakes gasping for air, for *her*. The lack of her has untethered him, and he has not slept for years.

He closes his eyes.

'Iqbal?' Another shout from the hall.

He slips his phone back in his pocket. He'll need to spend real time on this later.

Swallowing, he looks out of the tall windows that take in the back lawn, the trees, the edge of the Roman amphitheatre. Lois and Ebba's home. His home.

Thinking again about Lois, he wonders if he should be honest with her, tell her of this now? But there's nothing concrete to say, and they are so busy this weekend.

Once the weekend is done, he will update her: he's been searching for Rajita for so long. He hears her laugh. She was always laughing.

There's something telling about the timing. If one of the investors had been in Dhaka around the time of the fire, why have they never said so? Iqbal's history is no secret. It is strange that they have never mentioned it.

If what Obaidur has said is true...

It feels as though the foundations are cracking.

Replying to Obaidur, he wipes his face with the back of his hand, roughly clearing the tears. He will be able to help him; joy bubbles and explodes like a shaken Coke can. 'Dear Obaidur, my friend...'

For a second, he lays his head back and allows the spinning to slow. The autumn weather is kind and the light is soft over the lawn.

Uneasy, premonition gnaws; the logs in the fireplace crackle.

Secrets burn, and Iqbal itches. Obaidur remains in the workshops and Rajita is still missing. Was Archipelago founded on a lie? Does someone know that? Someone arriving today?

Iqbal needs to stay alert.

7

Filip

'Welcome, Filip.'

Ebba sweeps him up with the Dutch four-cheek kisses. She hands him a drink and smiles, talking easily, dropping in a Dutch phrase she'd learnt recently, laughing at her own stupidity with languages, but her accent is clear and precise. Her dress is a bright blue, like a cornflower, picking out the vivid blue in her eyes.

Filip stumbles over a hello, looking at the floor halfway through his replies that his trip had been fine, that no, he isn't tired. He finds beauty in women disconcerting; her social ease unsettles him, highlights his lack. He makes a comment about the flowers. There are flowers everywhere.

Ebba calls to Lois, her hand warm on Filip's arm. 'I know you will be desperate to hear about the presentation tomorrow,' she says, as she passes him to Lois. And he is; a rush of relief she has handed him a topic to discuss.

'Filip! How lovely to see you,' Lois says, accompanying him into the drawing room. She walks apart from him, her arms stiff by her side.

Lois lacks the star quality of Ebba and he remembers he finds her easier to talk to. She looks like a student with her short straight fringe, cut bluntly across the top of her brow, and her hair hangs long and straight. Her glasses are square, clear frames. She looks eighteen, but she's around thirty. So like a student, it's reassuring. He often feels barely out of classes himself, despite his success. The boardroom he can handle, but he's as shy now as he was at nineteen, stumbling into university parties with a warm beer and lasting only five minutes.

Finding his tongue, feeling more comfortable, he manages, 'I'm so sorry Sophie can't make it – she's really not feeling too well. Maybe if she's feeling better later she will catch the train.' He can't look at Lois in case he blushes, and he fumbles with the stem of the glass, rubbing at an imaginary stain.

The apology is brushed away easily with hopes she is feeling better soon.

Uneasy, he looks at his toes; thinks of Sophie and where she is now. He realises Lois is saying something, but she's finishing as he looks up. Having no idea what she had said, he asks about the presentation. He can always talk about work.

'Anything new in VR development at the moment, any hints of what we're likely to see in the next few years?'

'Filip, it's so exciting!' Lois smiles. 'Major developments! I've something new to show you. It's a prototype. I've not even shown Ebba yet. Virtual Reality that interfaces with the brain – it's in its infancy, but the future – Filip, it's going to be huge!'

'Lois, that's cyborg territory!'

She laughs. 'You'll be impressed with the developments on our game; we'll show you all tomorrow, but the visuals are much sharper than the last time you saw it. And we've managed to develop the sound further – it actually slides over your head, completely immersive…'

Filip listens as Lois slips quickly into the technical detail. Usually so quiet, she speaks easily and quickly about the product, and he finds it relaxing, not being required to reply much. He nods as she speaks and he thinks again of Sophie, wondering if Stefan's hands are slipping beneath her clothes. Whether she is enjoying it. He thinks again of Aksel, of his open sneers, his arm around his wife; while Filip stood, mute in board shorts, pale and stuttering in front of Sophie.

He takes another drink.

Lois slows her speech. 'Anyway, top secret! And you'll get a full demonstration when we go to the London studio tomorrow. We've booked a helicopter for the journey. Fuel-efficient too! I think you'll be impressed. Sorry, I've been talking too much about the details. Nobody loves the games like you. How was your journey?'

Nodding, he says, 'Good.'

'Pleased to hear it.'

There's a pause a little too long and he looks out of the window. Finally he manages, 'Weather's not too bad.'

At the same time, she says, 'What do you think of the champagne cocktail?'

They both smile and then wait for the other to answer, and Filip can't think of anything else to say. He blinks and thinks of Sophie, naked, with Stefan. He rubs again at the stain on his glass, looks at the floorboards.

'Lois!' Ebba calls across the room.

'More guests,' Lois says. 'Back in a minute.' Smiling, she looks relieved, and he feels his shoulders sagging. He stares out of the window, wondering if the rain is coming.

Going to get a refill, Ebba smiles at him from across the room and his cheeks flood red. She and Sophie are friends. The last time they all met, they had drunk wine and laughed together on the other side of the room. He'd wondered what they'd been saying. Whether Sophie had told her about him. Had they been laughing about him? His inadequacies? Would Sophie have told her how he can't...

He shakes his head, wondering if he should just go to his room. He has drunk so much.

Intelligence in others he finds calming, but beauty throws him. People often think that because he has a beautiful wife, he must be comfortable with beautiful women, but it's not the case. Sophie can still throw him off balance with a sudden change of expression, and ever since the honeymoon, they're competitive, combative. But recently, as though she's planned a game change, there's a new nakedness in her eyes. She seems to momentarily see him, want him.

And he forgets who they are now. The other day: her hair piled up and her body shining, like it had been sprayed in gold. He'd been lost to her, fumbling in his eagerness, embarrassed by his wanting.

Their marriage has become a points board. She is way out in the lead and he's not sure of the rules.

Only yesterday, on the balcony outside their bedroom, she'd called to him. Rotterdam had lain beneath the balcony wall and she'd worn nothing as she'd leaned over it, legs slouched and eyes bored. The October sun had been hot behind her and he was sure the cleaners were in somewhere, that they could be watching – had that made it better?

He'd stared down at the heads on the streets far below. She'd called his name…

He still didn't get it right. He hadn't been able. The air had felt chilled. He'd frozen, unable to say a word. He'd looked away from her, down at the heads of those below.

It had been so unexpected – she's taken to ignoring him over the last few months. But he had fallen into her. And he'd been quiet, embarrassed afterwards. When she'd risen and walked away, he'd lain on a lounger, spent, empty. Inadequate.

He is such a disappointment, he reflects, as he stares out of the wide French doors over the Hertfordshire fields. So successful in work, he has allowed himself to fade into the image he has created for himself.

Lois returns, bringing with her Iqbal to say hello and another drink for Filip. Iqbal is talking: '…the helicopter will be amazing…'

Sipping, Filip smiles and throws in a laugh quickly, guilty that his mind is wandering back to Sophie and the feel of her skin. Desire rises and falls, and he swallows the champagne quickly, sharp to his tongue. Once again, he thinks that this will be his last big deal. That his company and the investments are sound and he can take himself out of this society; move to a farm somewhere, with only fields to plough. Maybe.

A shift in the room; a laugh, loud and confident. Every pair of eyes swivel to the door. The mood changes.

Bubbles catch at the back of Filip's throat and he coughs, liquid shooting down his nose as he feels the stab a second before seeing the Norway investor enter.

His heart races.

Aksel.

Of course it's fucking him – who else makes a room vibrate?

Every sense prickles. Fight or flight. Filip's fingers flex.

8

LOIS

There is some pleasure in seeing everyone arrive and settle in. Some pleasure and some trepidation. Lois believes in the tech, in the game. It's not doubting herself, but doubting that these dreams are real. They have wanted it for so long. It feels as though a disproportionate amount of luck has come their way and they will pay for it in the end.

Ebba moves quickly between the guests, introducing them.

'Filip, such a long time. Have you been busy in the gym?' Aksel holds out his hand, a smile on his lips, and Lois watches Filip bristle like a hedgehog, quickly retreating beneath his prickles. What is going on?

Aksel, as usual, arrived with fanfare. He had brandished a bottle of vintage champagne, which Lois knows must be worth over five hundred pounds. He had handed it to Iqbal to take to the kitchen, and Lois and Iqbal had looked at each other and rolled their eyes. Aksel's habit of treating anyone who didn't own a company like staff always rankles.

'What a beautiful home!' Aksel gestures round the room. 'These flowers! The candles! The wisteria! It's stunning. And you grew up here?'

'Yes.' Ebba glances round with pride. 'It keeps our secrets, doesn't it, Lois?'

Lois taps her nose. 'We know all the hiding places.'

'Yes! Even a secret panel. Where we used to steal chocolate from the kitchen and hide it for midnight feasts.' Ebba laughs.

Lois thinks of midnight feasts, and their father finding them at night, his mock shock. He'd been a gentle bear. She'd not been there when he'd died, when stress had bitten hard. She will always regret that. She didn't get to say goodbye. The blow of betrayal that killed him had been quick and decisive; his company had dived fast. But she trusts that Ebba said goodbye for both of them. Ebba had held his hand as he'd slipped away, and it had broken her.

Watching Ebba fall apart after his death had lain as heavy on Lois as grief for her father. She hadn't been there when they had both needed her. She'd been at a gaming conference in LA. And if she had been in London, been able to race to Ebba, then maybe she could have helped? Saved Ebba from the onset of sleeplessness, weight loss, the physical deterioration that showcased her pain.

Maybe that's why being alone scares Lois so much. She'd been alone when she'd lost her father and almost lost Ebba. Now, being alone makes her nervous.

Filip is still scowling, staring at his drink. Refusing to look at Aksel as Ebba tries to spark conversation. There's definitely something up with these two investors. Filip's wife isn't really ill; he had blushed scarlet when he'd spoken, announcing the lie, and his breath smells of spirits. But Lois doesn't care if Sophie Atwood comes or not. They didn't necessarily need a film star in the group, soaking up attention and detracting from the focus. Sophie never has any time for Lois. She veers straight to Ebba. They have the demonstration tomorrow afternoon, when everyone gets to play with the product, and it will blow all of their minds – there's nothing out there to touch it. Lois has never felt so completely elsewhere as she does when she's playing.

'Lois!' A liquid voice sounds behind her, like melted chocolate, and she is kissed on both cheeks by Marieke, her hands warm on her arms.

'Marieke, I didn't see you arrive,' Lois says, noting that Marieke travels well; she looks as though she has spent hours dressing rather than the morning on the Eurostar.

'I brought these.' Marieke waves a bag of masks coloured with all the shades of Halloween. 'I bought one for everyone! I stopped at your local costume shop – the driver took me.'

She looks as though she wants to say something else, but instead shrugs. 'I think we will look très chic, no?' Her eyes already look past Lois, scanning the room.

'Come,' Lois says, nervous as she always is with Marieke, her words tumbling out quickly. 'Let me get you a glass of champagne. And has Ebba told you there are police here?'

Marieke smiles at her quickly, saying, 'Thank you. I'm not worried about a few jealous, spiteful letters.' She rolls her eyes; but Lois thinks she looks paler than the last time she saw her, and thinner. She might talk as though she has nothing to fear, but relief had skimmed her face when Lois mentioned the police.

While Lois struggles to think of something else to speak to Marieke about, Marieke looks around her for Ebba, and raises her hand, stepping away from Lois.

Clumsy in Marieke's presence, Lois thinks again that clumsiness is not something Marieke has time for.

Ebba approaches, quickly embracing Marieke, talking easily, as though she'd only seen her an hour before. She walks her over to Filip, saying she will get him a refill.

'Filip's just asked me if there is any difference in the partnership agreements, between his and Aksel's,' Ebba whispers to Lois, filling the glass with champagne. 'I don't know what he's heard, but do you know anything? He wants to meet tomorrow, before we release the signatures.'

Lois shakes her head. 'They're both putting the same money in?'

'Yes.' Ebba takes a sip of her drink. 'But I don't want anything to derail us, which could happen if there are rumours – could be dangerous. He's no fool, he won't go ahead if there's any suspicion. I wonder what's causing it?' Lois watches her lift a nail to her teeth and not quite bite it, before lowering it again.

Lois's anxiety steps up; her arms start to itch and she blinks repeatedly, breathing and trying to remember the mantra she's practised. She needs Ebba to be OK this weekend; it's the only way she'll get through it. Lois looks at Filip: a tall man with thick dark-framed glasses on a pale thin face. Usually when he talks, he glances towards the ground mid-conversation, looking uncomfortable. He's talking with Marieke now and seems to manage to hold her eye. He's attractive in a geek-chic kind of way. He hunches slightly and his brown eyes are intent when he talks. He moves his hands when he describes things. He gives the impression of being worth the time, if you're prepared to invest it. Marieke smiles at him, touching his arm, and he laughs. For the first time since he arrived, he seems to be unwinding.

'I don't know what to do,' Lois says. There are sharks swimming around this deal: nasty letters, Twitter storms. She thinks of the house: they had borrowed over and above their means to buy it back, betting on the promise of the deal. It is inconceivable it will not go ahead. Incomprehensible that they could lose the deal, and with it, their house. It would be like losing their father, all over again.

She scans the room and for a moment doesn't see the huge bright works of art on the walls, the lime rugs, pale stripped-back wooden chairs, the bright velvet of the curtains. Instead, she see two girls, riding their bikes around the room on a rainy Sunday. Their father timing their races after he'd cleared furniture out of the way, pushing the old dark furniture to the side. Wistful, she remembers the smell of the varnished mahogany; they'd sold all of it when they'd lost the house.

'Ebba,' she whispers. 'What can I do?'

Ebba shakes her head slightly. 'Not here. We'll talk later. Let's find out what the rumours are first.' She steps towards new guests, but Lois's hands are clammy and the butterflies in her stomach are worse.

Richard and Sarah have arrived. As the original angel investors, they deserve a red-carpet hello. Ebba does not disappoint, smiling and laughing, paving their way in.

The room softens as the drink flows. Rain starts rattling the old windows, and the top of the amphitheatre disappears in the mist that settles over the Roman city. It's not too long.

Not too long to keep everyone smiling and to prevent any cage-rattling.

Lois bites her fingernails, as Ebba had almost done earlier. The rattling scares her.

9

FILIP

Looking out over the fields from his room, there's an old ruin in the distance and what looks like the remains of an outdoor Roman theatre; there'd been a mention of that in the invite.

Filip thinks of a run before dinner, but his blood is full of alcohol and his head is fuzzy.

Tiredness engulfs him. He kicks off his shoes and socks, untucks his shirt and unfastens the top few buttons. The thick carpet is soft and the room is warm.

There is a knock at his door.

'Hello,' he says, hoping it's coffee, wondering if it would be rude to call down for some.

'Filip? It's Marieke.' Her voice is familiar from the other side of the door.

'Marieke,' he says, smiling, and he opens the door, gesturing into his room. He can see the English couple further up in the long corridor and he waves a hand awkwardly.

'Come in. Can I pour you a drink?' He gestures at a silver tray on the side, which holds glass bottles of water and a decanter with a dark, expensive whisky.

Marieke sinks into the large plum velvet chair by the window. 'How are you feeling? You didn't seem too happy downstairs. Is it Aksel?'

He falls into the sofa opposite, immediately feeling better. This is why he likes Marieke so much. No matter how uncomfortable he is feeling, she is able to sweep it aside and pinpoint exactly what is bothering him. She's become such a good friend.

'Yes.' He shrugs. 'He comes into the room like he's already won.'

'You're investors in the same company now – it's not a competition,' Marieke says, smiling. She stands, reaching for the water and whisky, pouring them both a glass of each. A large vase of Sophie's favourite flowers sits on the table, yellow roses and wolfsbane. The sisters have thought of everything.

As she sits, Filip thinks again that she is so different to his wife. Whereas Sophie is tanned, hair in long waves like she's stepped from the beach, Marieke is tall, pale, with cropped dark hair and fierce eyes. Elegant and eloquent, she is intimidating, and the room becomes hers slowly when she speaks; she earns it gradually, by seeming to listen to others without simply waiting for it to be her time to talk. But he's always thought it a ruse. Marieke can be ruthless – crowds part for her. They'd not dare not to.

Sophie has said many times that his nerves around women are all because his mother was distant with him; she has declared loudly on a number of occasions, when the staff have been around, that he should seek therapy.

But he has no problems when he's at work. He's just no good at small talk. He returns quickly to the structure of the investment that is bothering him.

'No, it's not a competition, but I'm sure there's something going on. He's so… smug. I can tell, from the other side of the room. He's got something over on me.' He drinks his whisky, thinking he should have made a point of getting coffee instead, but Marieke has obviously come for a reason and she is more likely to tell him if he matches her.

She says nothing.

'And the threats?' he asks. 'I've heard they've increased.'

'The police are here for the weekend, the house has been checked.' She shakes her head and drinks the whisky, but she drinks quickly, and her hand clenches the glass with white knuckles. 'They're personal. Like someone hates me. The Twitter stuff I'm used to. These are…' She waves her hand. 'I believe in Archipelago. Change works fastest from the top down. Lois and Ebba are leading the field, as are you: signing up to the Visser principles on modern slavery, leading the charge. But I'm tired. I'm no whore, Filip, and I'm sick of being called one.' She drops her head, and Filip leans forward.

'Marieke, you're an incredible friend. You've made these past few months bearable for me. If I can find the courage to leave Sophie, to build myself back up…' He shakes his head. 'Well, it will be because of your support. I hate this. I hate watching you feel like this.'

'Filip! Stop! I'm receiving death threats – you're married to someone who you think is cheating on you. Our situations are not the same! How many times have you said you need to leave her? She plays games with you. She's rude! I have to wait it out; you have to act. It's time to act!' She stops, glancing out of the window. 'We've spoken of this so often. I'm guessing she's not here this weekend because you have begun the process? You have told her it's over?'

The whisky sits warm in his stomach; the October sun frames Marieke like a halo. Filip thinks of Sophie, of how he's always known it would be absolutely impossible to tell her it is over, despite how much he hates the person he has become as her husband. He's tied to her, in a thousand ways. It will be Sophie who cuts those threads. It will never be him.

'Marieke…' he begins, and the phone on the table to his left rings loudly. The vibrate is on and it rattles against the glass of the table.

'Please,' Marieke says, leaning back, sipping her drink.

He glances at the screen and Sophie's name flashes up. He feels caught out. He almost dismisses the call.

'Filip, darling, I miss you.' Her voice comes loudly through the phone. Marieke can hear every word.

He's nervous, uncomfortable. Their parting had been so angry. Is she coming? Is she with Stefan?

All this he thinks of as he opens his mouth to reply, aware that Marieke is sitting nearby.

'Sophie, how…' He wants to say how are you, because he really means it. They've gone wrong. *He's* gone wrong. He's made all sorts of promises… but it sounds so formal, and he switches mid-sentence. 'How are things?'

'How are things, Filip?' Her mocking sails down the

line, into the room. He glances at Marieke, who looks out of the window.

'Look, can I call you back in a minute? I've got someone here.' He walks quickly to the other side of the room. He wants to ask about Amsterdam, but he doesn't want Marieke to hear him pleading.

'Who?' she asks, her tone sharp.

'Someone from the deal. We're discussing the deal.'

'Who, Filip?'

'Marieke Visser,' he says, cursing himself for saying her name, bringing her into it. Glancing at Marieke, he thanks her silently that she doesn't look up. He steps to the side of the room. Tries to lower his voice; hopes Marieke can't hear.

'Can I call you back in a minute?'

'Filip, I have phoned to make up. I might be able to come after all.'

'Good,' he says, feeling caught out. The change in her tone is quick. He knows he's wrong-footed, feels uncomfortable; she'll be able to tell he's off balance from his voice.

'But if I'm going to come, I need a bit of effort from you. Remind me,' her voice becomes softer, almost a whisper, for which he is grateful, 'remind why I should come. Remind me how happy you can make me.'

He's sweating. What does he say?

'Shall I send a car?' he asks. 'I can send a car to bring you – the train could get you here for dinner? Or fly, it's only an hour to Heathrow.'

'Filip, look at me.' The phone switches to FaceTime; the ring sounds. He knows he shouldn't press the button as

Marieke is still in the room and he doesn't want to be rude, but he wants to avert a row. Also, Marieke can't see and he's sure she can't hear. He steps into the bathroom. He presses the accept button as he speaks, trying to answer quickly and get rid of the call. 'Can you give me five minutes? I'll call in five? I'll just finish with Marieke?'

The screen fills with Sophie on their bed at home. The room is filled with light, the curtains are wide open. She's undressing. One hand holds the phone, the other trails slowly across her stomach.

'Tell me how much you want me to come, Filip. If you can tell me properly, I might just make it.'

There's no sign of Stefan. He looks at Sophie's skin, the light catching her curves. He feels a wave of desire, heady; a wave of shame: to be on display, such pressure now, every time.

Marieke is in the room and he needs to say goodbye, to say he'll see her at the dinner. About to lower the phone, his heart rate quickening, he opens his mouth to speak to Marieke.

There is a slam of a glass on the table, the bang of a door. She has already left.

10

LOIS

Lois lies across Ebba's huge bed, sinking into the mattress. Her body feels thicker, more real. The waves of nausea have progressed. Her mouth tastes metallic and she can smell Ebba's perfume from the other side of the room. It reminds her of a thousand afternoons on this bed, talking school, friends, boys...

The rain has stopped outside and as she sits up to watch the sun tint the sky burnt orange as it begins to set, she sees Aksel in shorts, running hard back towards the house.

She had seen him and Ebba emerge from the room by the kitchen earlier, the wooden door opening slowly, Ebba's eyes glancing left and right quickly as they stepped out. Her cheeks had been flushed.

The idea of Ebba and Aksel getting together turns her stomach. Maybe it is that too, which makes her feel so sick, so churned up.

Lois's hand rests on her stomach for a moment: is her period coming? She can never keep track. It aches. She lifts a dress from the bottom of the bed, its folds light, like paper. Her sister's dress for the evening.

Ebba comes out from her bathroom wrapped in a robe. Her bright blonde hair is locked up in a white towel, tendrils escaping from the edges, curling with steam.

'Aksel is attractive,' Lois says, watching for Ebba's response, fingering the dress, which is red silk and floor length. The light changes the colour of the silk as it bends beneath her fingers.

'You think so?' Ebba sits on a stool and unpeels the towel, beginning to comb through her hair slowly, spraying oil on knots. 'He's OK.'

'I don't think it's up for debate. Six foot, dark, amazing eyes…' Lois thinks of him, of her distrust. 'But cruel eyes. You know he destroyed the last company he took over? Sacked everyone then replaced their jobs with AI. That's a lot of unemployment. And he's going along with our People Before Profits motto, but I think it's lip service.'

'I suppose so,' Ebba says, rubbing cream into her face now, patting under her eyes with her ring finger. 'I've not really thought about it. He's distributing the product, not buying the company. That's all we need him for.'

'Hmm…' Lois says, lying back on the bed and looking up at the ceiling. She tilts her head a little to watch her sister's face in the reflection of the mirror.

'I saw you two having a chat earlier, near the kitchen. You came out looking a bit pink. Not like you to blush around men?' Lois keeps her tone light, willing it not to be true. But the signs are there.

'Lois!' Ebba swings round on the stool and looks to

the ceiling. 'No! Nothing! You are the worst. Why do you always think I have love affairs going on, right, left and centre?'

Lois laughs. 'Well, you usually do. It's been a quiet week for you. Only the one date?'

'Well, I like the company of men. So, sue me,' Ebba says, and grins. 'I'm only twenty-eight; I reckon I've got a couple more years before I need to stick a pin in one.'

Lois smiles, sitting up, and lifts a lipstick from the bag of make-up that Ebba has left at the bottom of the bed. 'What about this for tonight?' She holds up a shiny lipstick, almost black.

'Yeah, alright,' Ebba says, winking at her. 'Wearing a thrash metal T-shirt too?'

'I wish. Ebba, be careful, you know I want to turn up in jeans.' She grins. Her thin arms wrap round her knees as she shivers, more to emphasise a point, waiting for Ebba to reveal the promised evening outfit.

'Just wait. You'll not want to wear anything else when you see the dress I've bought for you!' Ebba says. 'Here.' Ebba pulls out a dress, still in its cotton cover, and she unzips it. 'This is perfect. Spot on.'

Lois pulls a face. 'It's so short!'

'Yes, but you have great legs. You're straight up and down. This is high-necked, and it will surprise everyone to learn that you have legs at all.'

Lois unpeels the legs in question from beneath her. 'You mean I'm so flat on top, I may as well detract from that.'

'Definitely.' Ebba is deadpan. 'Anyway, you have to trust me on real-world stuff. You live for games and escaping reality. The moment life gets tricky, you disappear into those worlds you create. You'd turn up in sweatpants if it wasn't for me.'

'Seriously, though, is there something going on with Aksel?' Lois asks, looking out of the window. He is stretching against the wall, leaning his arms forward while he rests his weight on his back leg.

'No. Nothing.' Ebba smiles. 'Why? Are you into him? I thought you were hoping for another chance with Helen?'

'Nope, seems that was definitely the end. A fucking dumping at a conference in LA. Almost glamorous.' Lois tries to laugh but she sees Helen's face. Tears swell. She thinks of what happened the next day; she'd never told Ebba, felt too ashamed. Lois feels another stomach twist. She almost retches.

'Well, Helen doesn't know what she's missing,' Ebba says. 'But really, Lois. You need to learn to be alone. Don't think I didn't see a man's shirt in your room when I Skyped you the day after Helen dumped you. I know we all have rebound flings, but you cling to people sometimes. It's OK to be on your own, you're enough, you know?'

Lois thinks of Helen's last words: *You just try too hard, Lois. You're too... too pleased to see me!*

Lois lowers her leg, stares out of the window again. 'I'll find someone at some point. Someone...' She thinks of a distant figure, strident, funny. She'll know, she reckons, when she meets them.

'Only another thirty-six hours to go. Should all be over then. And then, man or woman, you can hit the dating pack with the rest of us,' Ebba says. 'Here, try it on.'

Lois steps out of her clothes, slipping the green dress over her head. It clings without being clingy. She looks most unlike herself, but she looks good. Even she can see that. The light is soft in the room and the mirror tilts away, stretching her shape, elongating her into someone taller, more sophisticated, distant.

'Here, try these earrings,' says Ebba. 'It's too short for tights, but I've got a tan we can rub in. It'll come off in the shower. It's got sparkle in it too. You look amazing,' she says, standing behind Lois, lifting the earrings. 'You'll dazzle them all,' she whispers.

Lois smiles at her. 'Thank you.'

Nausea swells upwards, her mouth fills with acid. And she knows she needs to run, saying, 'I'll go and get changed!'

She makes it back to her bathroom only just in time.

Exhausted, her head aching, she searches once she's rinsed her mouth. She's got one somewhere. She bought a pack for Ebba last year, after a scare. Here.

Lifting the packet, she skims the instructions. Her fingers shake as she peels away the sticky edge.

No, it can't be true. Like Ebba says, she can't even cope with being on her own.

Waiting the five minutes is torture and then, there it is. The blue line.

'Fuck,' Lois says, sitting on the cold porcelain of the loo seat. 'Fuck.'

NOW

11

Filip

Time winds down as Filip takes in the details. The helicopter is still in its ascent; it's not even been minutes. The lawn falls away beneath them, the Roman amphitheatre further away each second. The huge country house is now like a toy on the ground. The cocktail is still warm in his stomach and the blue of the October sky is vivid.

Inside the helicopter, sound ricochets like bullets. Fright ignites the air, which burns with screams and cries: cacophonous, dizzying. Filip looks round; time slows further before him. The faces of the passengers are locked in screams like a slow-motion sports playback, as though unfolding slowly, shouting for a goal.

Another scream from Ebba, further up towards the pilot, and Filip turns, blinking, the action unreal. It's all so unreal. Marieke clings to her seat, white with fright, as Richard reaches for Sarah's hand. Her mouth open in a cry that's lost in the noise.

Aksel stands and falls back against the pilot's seat, the helicopter lurching like a bird hit with a stone. Ebba takes off her seat belt, shouting at Aksel and reaching forward. She stands too, screaming, hanging on to the seat. 'Aksel!' But he's out of her reach.

The pilot is shouting, 'Sit down! Sit back down!'

What's happening?

Aksel stumbles towards Filip, who grabs him as he tips to the side. They all sit in two long rows, facing each other, and Filip is towards the rear. Aksel's eyes are red and he's bent double, clutching at Filip's hand. His breath burns hot in Filip's ear as he mutters.

Filip knows this is important and he tries to piece the words together, sticking them to a mental wall, but already they are a jumble of sounds, rattled inside the can of the metal bird, as fear rises like bile.

Falling again, in a jolt, the helicopter shakes them all, and Aksel flies backwards.

Reaching out for him, Filip sees Aksel's eyes close as he slips from his grip and falls back on to the pilot.

Ebba must have done up her seat belt again because when she reaches for Aksel as he sails backwards – like a perfect six dive, a graceful arc – she can't reach him. He falls past her fingertips, crashing into the pilot's seat.

Everyone is screaming.

Filip's hands burn. Desperate. Aksel's words echo in his head, tumbling.

And now they spin in descent, plummeting, whirling. Down, like a falling stone.

BEFORE

FRIDAY

12

Night falls into the colours of the day like drops of midnight paint spilling into water. As they pull up to the house, Maarten stares back at the winking fairy lights woven into the thinning wisteria. Candles sit in glass lanterns on each of the steps that rise up to the huge front door.

He'd pay money to stay in the shadows tonight.

'It's beautiful,' Liv says, unclicking her seat belt and leaning forward. 'What a house!'

'More British,' Maarten says, 'than real Britain.'

No one lives in these kinds of houses any more; this is Hollywood's England. The huge manor house, with its tall wide windows edged with velvet curtains, is imposing. Up close, it's even bigger: three storeys, with two wings that step forward at either end. Small trees in glazed pots mark a perimeter, sitting beneath the windows that rise taller than doors. Each tree is perfectly round, perfectly placed.

It knows more than me, Maarten thinks, imagining the years of secrets hidden in the walls. Is he grand enough?

He's wearing black tie. It tightens round his neck; he pushes his finger in and around the collar.

He's half told Liv about Marieke. He needs to finish. He's sweating. She hasn't said much the whole way here, putting in earrings and fastening jewellery. The moment the dinner invite had been mentioned, Liv had raised her eyebrows. 'Ostle House?' she'd said, as though he'd said Buckingham Palace.

'So, this Dutch politician who has been receiving the death threats,' he starts, wanting to just say it. He has no idea why he doesn't.

'Let me guess. She's an old girlfriend?' Liv asks, still gazing through the window at the house.

'Yes,' he says, and then wonders why he can't say the rest.

'Maart, I had boyfriends before you. We've been married fourteen years. It's OK that your ex-girlfriend will be at dinner. I promise not to catfight.' She grins.

'Yes, but could you not mention it?'

'What, that you went out?'

Silence again. He picks his words carefully. 'It wasn't public knowledge. It was kind of a secret.'

Liv laughs. 'Maart, was she married? Were you her bit on the side?'

He could just leave it there, but he never lies to Liv. It would feel like a lie, if he and Marieke held this secret between them, in a room with Liv. It would tighten the secret, turn it into a tie. Liv needs to be on the inside.

Then why does she still not know? Why isn't he just telling her?

He tries again. 'She wasn't married, but she might have had a partner, we didn't really talk about…'

Liv looks at him, waiting.

'She was my boss at the time, though. And, well…' He picks up his wallet, pulls the keys out of the ignition. The engine is quiet now. Liv has her hand on the door handle.

'Well, it got in the way of work once, and so I asked her not to say anything. Please, I wanted you to know. It's obviously all over now. It was short-lived and it was years ago. But it wouldn't do any good for anyone else to know.'

Liv looks at him. 'Maart, you have a secret you have never told me. I'm not sure if I mind, or if it's wildly sexy.'

He coughs, the sound flying out of him like a pebble he's been choking on. 'Neither!' he says. 'It was a long time ago.' He glances at her sideways.

He's been so ashamed, for so long. It's harder than he thought.

They climb out of the car. The sky is now a deep black velvet, stars like sequins. The evening is unusually warm for October. Liv's not wearing a jacket and her arms are bare; she wears a backless black jumpsuit. Her blonde hair is curled up, pinned, and she's a few inches taller in heels.

'I can't believe you didn't want to come,' she says. 'We never get dressed up. I know it's work, Maart, but I can't wait for a grown-up night out without the kids. Archipelago are major now. I bet the bubbles will be the real stuff.'

Still hesitating, he watches her climb the stone steps, thinking she looks caught out of time against the vast green door with its ornate brass knocker. There is something out

74

of time about the evening. Talking to Liv about Marieke has brought the past hurtling forward, colliding with the present like atoms in a reactor. His head vibrates with the sound of his blood quickening, beating at his temples.

Maarten! Stop! The rain, heavy that night. His mind fogged but frantic. A wilting bunch of flowers still in his hand. He'd thought Marieke would be pleased with a surprise visit. But the pitying look on her face when he had burst into her apartment... And then he'd run back to his car. When the work call came through...

They had both stayed silent for twenty years. There's no reason to think that will change tonight.

'Come on, Maart! What are you waiting for?' Liv smiles at him and he stirs himself.

They are greeted by a young blonde woman, her hair lighter than Liv's – almost Scandi, whereas Liv has hints of brunette beneath the sun's highlights. This woman is sleek in a long red dress, and her eyebrows are raised in a question as she leans forward to greet Liv with a kiss on each cheek, finding her name quickly and smoothing their way in; handing Maarten a glass of champagne as he steps on the antique rug that lies across the huge hall.

'Ebba Munch,' she says, as Liv moves forward and it's his turn to be embraced, lightly. 'It's DCI Jansen, isn't it – how lovely. We'll all feel much safer knowing you're here. So good of you to take this seriously.'

She smells expensive; her dress drops low at the back. He'd wondered briefly if Liv would be overdressed for dinner when she'd come down the stairs earlier into their kitchen, which had been wet with the papier mâché of Sanne's Halloween mask; Nic slouched on a chair, her face covered with an iPad. But no. Liv blends into the room like a shell on a beach and he curses his shabby dinner jacket. No one defers to the cheapest suit in the room.

'Filip Schmidt.' A man appears at his elbow and Maarten recognises the name.

'Maarten Jansen,' he replies.

'Police? Is that right?' Filip's eyes scan the room quickly, returning to Maarten.

Unsure of how much Marieke has said about her police protection, Maarten bats it away lightly, nodding, and recognising Filip's accent, he replies in Dutch. 'My wife told me we had to come for the champagne.'

Filip smiles, though his eyes stay on the ground. 'Where are you from?'

'Rotterdam,' Maarten says, 'originally.'

'Me too,' Filip says, and glances at his glass. 'Well, I'm no connoisseur. One glass tastes much like any other, but I guess this is expensive. It seems nothing has been spared.'

They stand quietly for a minute.

Maarten looks across the room. It is heavy with velvet, but the colours are bright. Modern meets yesteryear with large paintings, but all abstract in vibrant colours, rather than dark oils. One wall has a Banksy-style graffiti painting of a figure wearing headphones, looking at a tablet. The rugs look thick and heavy, expensive, but also bright. Maarten sees Liv's designer eye darting everywhere. It feels very *tech*, very fresh.

There is a man at the far end, talking to Marieke. He's tall, though not as tall as himself and Filip, who are both about the same height, he would guess. Maarten is six foot six. It's refreshing not to peer down at everyone. To feel less distinct.

The man at the far end of the room has black hair and he is handsome, with a clean, strong jaw. Maarten recognises him from somewhere but can't place him – until he realises he is a dead ringer for a man he's seen on a poster at the airport, advertising a watch that costs more than his annual salary. He has a beautiful but dangerous quality to him, Maarten thinks, like he could suck the air from the room with a smile.

Beside him, Marieke's dark head is bent forward, catching his words, and he feels a flash of jealousy, like a reflex. She once was his. He's surprised by himself and he looks for Liv.

He finds her; she is nodding to the tall, slim, brunette girl with the blunt fringe, who stands with her back to the wall like she wants to be somewhere else.

The atmosphere is... tense? Marieke and the dark-haired man stand close together, but Marieke holds herself back, slightly stiff. Filip is staring at them too, with an expression of dislike on his face.

'When did you arrive?' Maarten asks.

Filip begins answering, his eyes turning to Maarten slowly.

'Only today.'

'Who is everyone?' Maarten asks. He's got a fair idea from the file, but everyone looks different in the flesh.

'Well, that's Aksel Larsen. Let's say he's the headline invite.' He gestures across the room, and Maarten feels the air vibrate. 'Aksel owns a huge chunk of the tech manufacturing and export business in Norway. He'll buy up anything for a profit; he doesn't care about the product. This new game we're investing in is amazing. Have you seen it?'

Maarten shakes his head.

'There's a demonstration tomorrow afternoon. We're taking a helicopter to their VR studios. I'm sure you could come? The whole game is based on full immersion. You can play with others, either in the same room or from somewhere else entirely. And Lois has added a sensory element – you'll see if you come. But it adds the feel of rain, of wind, of fire. She's built it all in – with brain interface next, it seems! There's nothing on the market like it.'

'Isn't that a bit creepy?'

Filip laughs. 'Maybe. I don't think they're talking next week. There are only a couple of major VR names out there and this new game will pull Archipelago right up. They've secured a contract from a superhero franchise – major money. They won the contract mainly by flagging up their commitment to limit their slavery footprint – it's all over the contract. We're all betting on it.' He pauses, seeming to want to say something more, then changes his mind. He rubs his jaw, as though he's unused to speaking so much. Maarten can smell alcohol on his breath. He wonders how much he's had to drink: there's a drunken, rambling feel to his conversation – and an undercurrent of anger. It doesn't bode well for a relaxed evening.

'There she is, Lois Munch. She's the brains behind Archipelago.'

Maarten looks at her again. 'She came up with all this?' She looks terrified, he thinks.

Filip smiles. 'I know. Don't be fooled by how quiet she seems. It's an amazing achievement. Ebba over there looks about ten years her senior, but she's the younger one of the sisters. She organises rooms like she owns them. People are her game. Most people in here are putty in her hands. Me included, possibly.'

Maarten wonders what Filip means. There are jibes beneath the surface of his sentences and he feels like he's missed a page. Filip's voice is tinged with awe when he speaks of Ebba and he clearly hates Aksel. His eyes are bloodshot. He's drunk.

'Their parents were originally from Norway. Their mother died very young, and they came over here when the girls were tiny. The father died soon after the 2008 crash. There was a leak at his company about an issue with a financial product, and everything went in days. The shock killed him.' Filip quickly drains his glass, which is filled discreetly from the left by one of the servers. 'To be honest, I hate these kinds of things. If I could have just signed the contract and been done with it, I would. I was going to, but then...'

His eyes cloud, his mouth tightens. There's definitely something afoot. 'Yes?' Maarten prompts.

'Well, let's just say, the deal is not necessarily all I thought. Or maybe it is, and I've got the wrong end of the stick. Or the wrong stick. However that saying goes.'

He looks at Maarten again, up and down. 'And why am I telling you all this?'

Maarten laughs. He wonders if Filip knows quite how much he's revealed. 'We Dutch have to stick together. And don't worry, I know nothing about the world of business. Your wife is here?'

Filip shakes his head. 'She ducked out last minute.' He glances over at Aksel and Marieke again. 'She's the one out of the two of us at ease with these kinds of things.'

'My wife is talking to Lois,' Maarten says, 'and she's the same. She can talk to anyone.'

A laugh as loud as a saxophone riff reverberates and Filip glances back to Aksel, who is laughing at something Marieke says.

Again, he and Filip stare at the couple. Maarten begins to ask about his favourite café in Rotterdam, but there's a smattering of applause as another couple enter the room.

Ebba sweeps the two in, dressed in finery and blinking under the sheen of the room, like moles in the light. They are expensively dressed, but they don't carry it easily. Ebba is introducing them like they are royalty, announcing them to the room. 'Our founder investors, Richard and Sarah, who made all of this possible!'

The applause ends and Maarten sees his glass filled again. Has he already finished the first?

Filip leans in. 'And here are the original investors. The Arkwrights. They'll do very well out of this deal, and as silent partners they'll have no real concern over the day-to-day running. Come Sunday, we'll all be looking forward to huge wins. At least...' He drains his glass again, not finishing; his face twisting in a scowl.

Maarten lowers the arm he'd been raising to take another sip. Filip has had three glasses in the last half an hour.

There is something about this room, this night. There's something in the air.

Maarten needs to take a firm hold. He has his own secrets to be watchful of. And there's a tension, like the whine of an over-taut violin string, snaking through the air and the conversation.

Richard approaches them and Maarten nods. He knows he's too direct at times, no good at small talk. He feels a clutch of panic. Talking to Filip had been easy; it had been like sneaking a peek back at Rotterdam. Richard seems the kind of man who would hang out with his superiors on the golf course.

'Maarten, isn't it? Good to meet you. Ebba tells me you're in charge of making sure these nasty poison pen writers don't affect our weekend? Excellent! Now, I'll tell you what I would do in your position...'

Maarten keeps his face blank. Richard launches into a monologue on security measures for grand houses. Maarten is not required to say too much.

'That your wife?' Richard asks, gesturing to Liv, who is now speaking to Sarah Arkwright and Lois.

'Yes.' Maarten smiles.

'I'm sure I've met her before. Is she an interior designer, by any chance?'

'Yes,' Maarten says, surprised.

'I'm sure she did some work for the firm I'm with in London. A really great job. I'll go and tell her what we've changed since then. Good to meet you.' He shakes Maarten's hand.

'Nice watch,' Maarten says, seeing a leather strap and a watch face that even he recognises.

Richard's face softens, stroking the glass quickly with his thumb. 'My daughters bought me this for my fiftieth birthday present. They saved all their earnings from their summer jobs.' Pleasure and pride light his face.

Maarten smiles, ready to forgive Richard's earlier hectoring. 'That's impressive. I'm not sure my two would even manage a cake.' He thinks of Nic and her furious early pre-teen angst and Sanne, almost eight, singing in the mirror to the latest Disney fairy-tale high school musical.

'Kids, eh?' Richard claps a hand, heavy, on Maarten's arm.

As he watches Richard approach Liv, Sarah and Lois, Maarten sees Aksel lift his hand in a wave of acknowledgement. Richard flinches. There's a twist about his mouth. And even from only the back of his neck, Maarten sees Richard's colour flare red and angry. He pauses en route, hands remaining firmly by his side, ignoring the wave, and continues forward. Determinedly.

Aksel, it seems, is hated. Interesting.

'This is something else,' Liv whispers, slipping her arm through his as they walk towards the dining room. From the high ceilings drip tear-drop bulbs, at uneven lengths.

The paint colours that wash the hallways are light and fresh. Heavy velvet everywhere, in plum, apricot, vanilla.

'This is my dream home,' Liv says, touching the edge of three words written in italicised thin, fluorescent neon light bulbs: *People Before Profits*. 'This must have been a commission.'

Maarten has held back, stepped outside to have a few words with the PC. He looks around.

'It is?' he says. 'Having fun?'

'Not sure "fun" is quite the word. I got stuck with Richard Arkwright telling me why I should have used damask cushions instead of silk when I worked with his firm. But it's a bit of an insight. And the money in this room – the dresses, the jewels. Sarah Arkwright is wearing earrings that must have cost thousands. And her dress! I'm sure that's Gucci. I've seen it in *Grazia*.'

'Me too, never miss a copy.'

She laughs. 'Your ex-girlfriend is pretty intimidating. She's got that older woman, power-carrying, sexy vibe going on. Edgy, though. Not so friendly. She asked what I did, but I'm not sure interior design is her thing. She walked off halfway through my answer! Anyway, I've seen you looking at her.' She winks at him.

Maarten feels himself flush. 'Liv…'

'Oh, I'm only winding you up. Of course you'll look at her. If my ex-boyfriend was in the room, I'd be all over the details. Don't worry, Maart. This whole house is a revelation. Is she really in danger?'

'Marieke?' Maarten pauses to look at a painting. Huge swirls of blue and green take up most of it. It's stunning.

'Yes, I think so. The fact that someone knows her home address in Rotterdam is bad news. But they can't reach her here at Ostle House. This place is clean.'

A red-haired woman in a caterer's uniform steps aside to let them pass. She smells of cigarettes, and carries a silver tray with champagne; Liv lifts one. 'I've had far too much already, but we rarely go anywhere like this,' she whispers to Maarten as they pass her. 'Lois takes a while to warm up, but her job is fascinating. I'm not surprised they're successful, they have the best parental controls in the business. They run programmes to help kids manage the addiction, *KnowLimits*, they've called it. We should try to get Nic on one, she's always on a screen.'

'What do you think of the others?' he asks.

'Powerful! The Norwegian, what's he called?'

'Aksel.'

'He's gorgeous. Drop-dead. Looks like an older male model, or film star, but to be honest, I'm a bit afraid of him. He's what, forty-eight? Worth millions. But there's something about him. He's a bit over-intimate with Marieke. Rude too. Like one half of a divorced couple. Bit different to the quiet one you were talking to. Lois was telling me he's a self-made billionaire and not even forty. He speaks six languages and he's married to that film star, Sophie Atwood. Is she Dutch? I never know. I think her mother's Canadian – I read an article.'

'Never heard of her.' Maarten glances back to the front door. Is he missing something? He feels like he is.

'Yes, you have. We saw her in that subtitled war film, remember? And she stars in a huge role in Hollywood next year. Lois said it's top secret, but Sophie talks about it loudly after a drink – she's really close to Ebba, so Lois gets to hear all the good stuff second-hand. They're not sure if she's coming tonight. I hope she does. I've never met a film star before. The girls will go wild when I tell them on Sunday.'

The dining room is looming, and he feels uneasy. 'Liv, I've got a bad feeling about this. Whatever happens...'

'What's going to happen, Maart?'

He shakes his head. He has no idea. Is it the death threats that are bothering him? Is it Marieke, or Aksel who inspires hatred in the guests, or the brewing anger that seeps from Filip like smoke?

'I don't know,' he says. 'It's only a dinner – I'm being ridiculous.' But he steps to the door to have another word with the PC.

'One more check outside?' he suggests.

The night is granite black; a werewolf moon has disappeared behind a cloud.

13

IQBAL

Iqbal is hot; the air in the dining room warming still as the guests enter. The musicians have relocated and it's not just the heat, but the noise. Laughter is louder, smiles are broader. Everyone looks filtered, like Instagram swept through: Clarendon, Juno, Ludwig, *#NoFilter*.

The room is beginning to give him a headache.

Lois has been so worried about the night. Is it going well? There's a lot of drinking; the guests becoming wilder, gestures ever grander. They have unpeeled their day selves; claws are sharpened.

The heat of the evening closes in. The candles, the flames. The heat unnerves him. The candles flicker their warning. He can taste pennies, which is always a bad sign. He hasn't had a panic attack for so long.

Aksel Larsen is interesting to watch. He drinks with the rest of them but seems less affected, touching most of the women when he talks to them, complimenting them, smiling at them. He pays attention. He moves assuming they won't mind from him what they may all mind from someone with lesser looks, less sophistication, less money, less confidence. He moves quietly, like a ship through water.

Men watch him, hackles raised.

If Iqbal is right about what happened with Obaidur, one of the men in this room could bring down the whole company. But which one?

Iqbal's not had contact with Obaidur for nine years and for most of that time, as well as working for Archipelago, he has worked tirelessly to find Rajita. With Obaidur's email arriving this evening, so has his thirst for Rajita. She always lives in his dreams. Tonight she smiles at him every time he closes his eyes. He thinks of the food she would make to feed the older women in the factories. They would often arrive with little, and Rajita would make her lunch, and more for others. 'Here, I have too much, please take it,' she'd say. He thinks of how she would hold his hand, when they sat talking at home, how she would touch his face. She cried when he hurt his palm in the factory. She had felt it more than he had. He touches his hand now, thinking of her warmth, touches his own face. Where is she?

The flames from the candles' wicks dance at the corner of his eye. It has taken time to train himself not to mind the flickering of fire, but tonight is harder.

Richard had been to speak to him, as he often did. For the first time, he mentioned that he'd visited Bangladesh years ago. He'd dropped it casually into the conversation, like you might throw a tissue in the bin. Iqbal's head spins. He'd asked him when, and he'd answered, 'Just before that terrible ordeal with the factory. The one that collapsed?

Awful. I was in Dhaka. Anyway, I'd like to visit again at some point. It was like nowhere I'd ever been.'

Iqbal had been light-headed. Could Obaidur have met with Richard?

Feeling hotter still, thinking of the heat of Dhaka, the humidity and the daily traffic jams that sprawl in the city like living beasts, Iqbal slips out of the back door to the stone steps that overlook the gardens, coated thickly with night. The air is still warm for October, but it's fresh. Out here, there is no scent of smoke from the tiny fires in the house.

Along with the reconnection with Obaidur, the warmth of Bangladesh whispers to him. The saturation of heat, of sun that digs beneath your bones. The sweat. The noise, the city that spills out in a scramble. He's avoided it for years. He'd been back regularly in the beginning to search for Rajita. But she'd vanished after the fire, disappearing under the dust as it settled, while he'd slept off his injuries. There's no sign of her. Now he works with different charities, authorities and the police to look for her. He's never lost hope.

Without notice, he finds himself crying and he puts out a hand to steady himself. The noise from the dining room rises and he chokes on a sob.

The moon reappears from behind a cloud and its round ball of whiteness casts a pale light across the trees, the lawns. There are tiny lights in the branches; flecks of bulbs flash like fairies. There is magic in this night.

The pennies. Metallic and sharp in his mouth. He falls to his knees.

The heat of the flames. Images of the factory in Dhaka flash, breaking up the present. They mingle like water and oil, moving together then separating. His head a jumble, slippery and wet.

Shaking, his eyes, open or closed, see only fire. Everywhere. There is fire everywhere.

Smoke, clagging and thick. So real he struggles to breathe here, his chest tight.

Fire! Fire! The shout had come from his left. Screams echoed like gunfire round the factory. Only moments ago, the buzz of the workers had been as usual: heads bent, fingers busy in the heat. The sound of the machines had been loud. As usual. All as usual. And then without any notice, a bang, loud like a car backfiring, and hot shards of metal flew through the air like shrapnel, felling all those they hit.

Like a war.

There'd never been a drill. Some countries rehearse for earthquakes. No one rehearses for an explosion from heat so quick it's like a bomb.

Sudden loud screaming for the door, a swell, a crush. Not enough exits. Many families worked in the factory together. Some could see they had already lost loved ones and instead of running away from the debris, ran towards it.

The fire had spread quickly at the far end of the factory, searing all it touched. Running, standing, crying, workers screamed for family, for friends.

The building had been six storeys high. For the fire to begin here, on the ground floor, meant that above them would only turn to chaos.

Time ticked urgently, both sped up and slowed down. A flood of feet from the building, like a landslide.

Rajita had been up ahead. Relieved she was getting out, Iqbal ran. Panic jolting him into action.

Screaming, shouting. The workers wore blue masks over their faces, bright orange covers for their clothes for work with electronics. They moved like lava.

But Obaidur, his friend, had crawled under a desk and wasn't moving anywhere.

'Obaidur, come out! We have to leave!' he'd shouted.

Obaidur had shaken his head, buried his face in his knees and pulled his arms tight around his legs. Moaning, saying something over and over.

The desks were knitted in closely. To get to Obaidur, Iqbal hadn't needed to move a step.

He'd grabbed Obaidur's arm and pulled, yanking so hard it hurt, dragging him behind him.

It was difficult to see. Dust, grey and opaque, saturated the air. Only the noise of the crowd and the light from the door pointed the way out.

The screaming, wailing – the sound of fright, like a physical force.

By then he'd lost sight of Rajita. He forged ahead, praying she was out.

Once out, the street was like a film reel sped up. Movement flickered, as his eyes got used to the light. People were running, screaming, bleeding. The midday sun, hot. The dust from the street kicked up. Groups of people carried makeshift stretchers, made with tools from the factory. Most of the floors were garment factories. The colours were bright from those workers with no uniform. Blood splattered skin indiscriminately. Children ran screaming.

But no Rajita. He saw the man who worked near her station and he grabbed his hand.

'Rajita? Rajita?' he shouted. But it was like he was speaking a different language. The man's face was covered with dirt, and blood was making its way down from his brow.

She was nowhere.

Hordes spilled out, crushed, some on the ground, trampled. It would be impossible to use the door. He picked up a stick and hurled it at a nearby window. The thin glass gave way immediately, already shattered in part, and he climbed inside, taking off his shirt and laying it over the broken glass, cutting his feet and arms.

The dust and debris from the building had permeated the air with impressive power. Moving was like swimming in a muddy sea.

'Rajita! Rajita!'

Minutes lasted years; his chest was choked, dizzy. The blurry air pressed heavy.

She was nowhere. Instead, he'd seen a white girl. A westerner. She'd gripped the wall, blinded by dust. He'd run to her, screaming, *We must get out!*

Toxic smoke, toxic air, burned his lungs. He wouldn't survive another five minutes.

He offered a prayer to Allah.

The sound of the foundations shaking came like thunder.

The intensity of the burning materials was acrid; the room span as he pulled her arm.

The rest he couldn't remember.

He'd woken in hospital over two weeks later. They told him he'd been wrapped up with the girl, his body protecting her from debris, when they'd found them both. Pulled them out just in time. She'd been conscious and when they took her to the private hospital, different to the ones they'd taken the workers to, she'd forced them to take him. Insisted on paying. He'd woken in his own room, sanitised and looked after. Money easing his recovery with food, water, no queues for treatment. The white girl from the factory had been by his bed when he'd woken. She'd held his hand. She'd said her name was Lois.

But Iqbal had always known that, in trying to save him, Lois had taken him out of every place Rajita might search for him. He'd not been on any of the lists from the state hospitals to which the workers had been taken. In trying to do the right thing, she had removed him from the world of his wife.

If Rajita searched for him, she'd have found nothing. Once he was able, he'd spoken to her friends. With the factory burnt, employment had vanished. They lived with no savings, their wages the only income. He heard that Rajita had thought he died in the fire. With nowhere to go, she'd been forced to take a job as a maid in a big house. There were always people to speak to, to arrange employment overseas: the Middle East, Singapore, Hong Kong, London. She'd been employed by the end of the week, still searching for him. No one knew where.

The trail for Rajita had gone silent.

He knew with that kind of job it all depended on the

employer. Some were kind, providing health insurance, providing holidays. Some took passports, freedom. Rooms that barely contained a single bed. Factory work might have felt like slavery, but you were free to leave. Being a maid wasn't always something you could walk away from. The line of freedom, he had learnt, is blurred.

His shaking slows; his breath calms. The garden returns, the chill of England. This air, so fresh and so clear. Standing, he pulls open the door.

With Obaidur's email, the secrets of that time are cracking open.

One of the men here cheated his best friend and could destroy Archipelago. He must find out which one. As much as he wants to remain here in the cold air, he knows he must go back inside.

Back into the smoke.

The air that reminds him of Rajita.

Rajita.

14

Lois

The dining room looks different. There're no piles of papers, no tech, no huge projection screen. Usually it's light-flooded, a room of space and air.

Tonight, curtains are drawn, candles are lit. Flesh is on display. Sarah, who Lois thinks of as dressed in jeans and a polo shirt, wears a dress that curves low. She is fiddling with it now as she enters the room.

'I honestly don't know why I bought it. My daughter watches some reality programme, set in London, and they're always wearing these kinds of things. Alice helped me stick it on firmly with tape, but now I can't leave it alone. I'm terrified it's going to fall open and I'll have to leave before dessert.'

Aksel had looked at her twice and made his way over to her earlier. He had left Ebba's side and touched Sarah's lower back as he greeted her. Richard had taken a step closer towards his wife, and Lois wondered if Aksel *intended* to make others jostle: was it just games? Ego?

Richard glances over at his wife again now.

'Well, I think Richard approves,' Lois says. She pulls at her own dress, feeling over-exposed, vulnerable. What is it with dressing up, offering their skin up for approval, for exposure? For attack.

'I've had two kids. This dress doesn't forgive that.' Sarah rolls her eyes, wriggling her shoulders, then throws them back. 'Well, I'm in it now. Maybe a few glasses of champagne will help. It's a celebration, after all. You look amazing, Lois. You're actually glowing.' Sarah peers at her.

Lois looks to the floor. The misery of her secret is crushing.

'Oh, Lois, come on. You're a star!' Sarah smiles, squeezing her arm. 'We're so lucky to have been in the right place at the right time. Richard's parents dying was so sad; but now we've done something real with the money, something that felt right for the kids. They've loved being a part of it.'

'Thank you. Sorry! I'm so nervous.'

'Don't be. Richard was nervous too, earlier. Something—' She shrugs. 'Well, something threw him off. Maybe it's having to wear the DJ. He's more at home in jeans.'

'Is there a problem?' Lois asks, nerves pulsing quickly.

'Forget I said anything.' Sarah whispers, 'You've got this, Lois. You've got this in the bag.'

'Iqbal, I'm barely coping,' Lois whispers; she hands him yet another undrunk glass of champagne and he hands her back the non-alcoholic fizz she'd nipped out to get earlier.

'I'm terrified. I'd forgotten how much Marieke scares me. I can barely say two words to her.'

'Ha! You're fine. Always the weather. Talk about the weather.'

'I can't even remember my own table plan. I think I might faint.' Lois is hot and cold all at once. The odds of surviving dinner feel higher than an Everest climb right now. She's never been more uncomfortable.

'You're up at the other end, opposite the main door. There are place cards out – Ebba did it earlier.'

'Thanks,' she says, looking at the round table, also elegantly dressed. 'Are you holding out as long as possible before you join us? There's loads of food, someone has organised some great catering.'

'You know I'm much happier on the edges. I'll join you all soon.' He winks.

Lois squeezes his arm as she makes her way to her seat. Iqbal is her partner when it comes to creating the games. Her right-hand everything. 'I'm not sure I'll get through this without you.'

The time they met: the heat, the flames. It never really leaves her. It's the most vivid memory she has. It had brought her Iqbal; he'd helped her realise her designs.

But meeting him… It had left them both scarred.

She knows she will lose him soon.

His tragedy, she thinks again, with the usual burst of pain, ever sharp, had ended up saving her. She tightens her hold on his arm, kisses him on the cheek.

'None of this would have happened without you,' she says.

He grins. 'Of course it would. Now, don't force me to sit down all evening and make small talk – let me organise things and then disappear out the back once it gets late.'

Going back to the table, she thinks of the money heading into Iqbal's account next week. But she knows he plans to leave once the deal is launched and their expansion complete. He works hard for the charities they support, speaking about his time in the factories, the hidden workforce.

Slipping into her chair, she paints on her smile, as thick as the lipstick painted on earlier. As she sits, the already short dress becomes even shorter; she quickly pulls her napkin out of the waiting wine glass and drops it over her thighs.

'Lois, I have the pleasure of you this evening?' Aksel says. He lowers himself in the chair next to her and, lifting up the water jug, fills her glass. He slides the edge of his hand down her bare arm.

Lois's body reacts for her, goosebumps rising, arm hairs standing on end. He creates a conflict in her like no one else here. They need him. They need him for the deal. But something about him makes her want to scream. 'Seems so,' she replies, not quite remembering why she had put him near her. She takes a sip of the water and looks at his hands, his expensive cufflinks, thinking how he speaks casually, implying something personal, private. *He really is attractive*, she thinks, of course Ebba is drawn to him. Ebba's heightened colour earlier when she spoke about Aksel makes Lois uneasy. She doesn't want Ebba to fall for

Aksel. It would become too complicated. Her sister, with this man… She feels her stomach twist.

As he looks at her, she feels herself blush, remembering what he might be thinking of.

'Here, let me refill your glass,' he says, leaning over her. He uses his arm furthest away from her, curling round into her; his breath touches her cheek as he leans in, coils in, slithers in.

She catches a glimpse of Ebba, her hand on Filip's arm, who glances down at the table, looking downright miserable. Is it his wife? Lois wonders. He had seemed so uncomfortable earlier. And he is drinking heavily tonight.

Aksel is talking to her and she still cannot face looking him in the eye.

'You look beautiful tonight,' he confides. 'I almost didn't recognise you,' he says. 'Almost.' And his eyes hint that he's always thought of her as beautiful and she can't even look past him now to Ebba. He's everywhere; panic stirs. She swallows hard.

She coughs, raising a hand in an apology and pushing her chair further back.

Aksel is still running through a list of praise: the house looks amazing, Lois's hair really suits her…

'Your dad would be proud of you both, you know,' he says.

'Sorry?' The slip into sincerity catches her off guard.

'Your dad. He'd have been proud. He was always proud of you both, but this would blow his mind. It's good to remember that. My dad died when I was young, but we didn't get on. I've spent my life trying to prove to him I was worth it. But he'll never know. And maybe I'll never stop trying.' He smiles, lifting his glass, taking a drink.

'I… I didn't know,' Lois says.

'Why would you? But you can do all this for yourself. Not just for a ghost. He was always proud. You'll find some relief in that. Remember it.'

And she nods as he moves to the deal. Aksel had worked for their father for quite a few years. He had been a protégé. They had known Aksel since they were small.

Lois looks at him again, thinking of him as a small boy, running after his father. Tears come quickly and she blinks them away. God, she's crying at everything at the moment. He's talking now about how much he was looking forward to the afternoon of games they'd planned for tomorrow.

There is a baby inside of her. Will it ever know its father? Will she cope? Can she be a mother?

The police officer – Maarten, she thinks – sits down on her left, and she excuses herself to Aksel, welcoming Maarten Jansen.

She's thankful to be able to look away. Aksel's beauty is a bit blinding but it's like a mask. And then flashes of what is on the inside. You can never read anyone.

'Thanks so much for the invite,' says Maarten.

'A pleasure,' she says, thinking how nervous the letters still made her, glancing quickly to Marieke. 'Everything looking safe?' she asks.

'I think so,' he says. 'A big night for your company?'

And she nods, pleased he doesn't say anything else. Aksel has turned to speak to Marieke, who sits on his right, and she immediately likes Maarten, who is gentle. He doesn't push his gratitude on her, as is the way of some people at the moment. She finds the more successful the company becomes, the more and more pleased people become at receiving her attention. It's quite overwhelming.

'My kids will go crazy when they hear where I've been,' Maarten says. 'My eldest loves your game.'

'Really? *Vertigo*?' Lois asks, and her interest sparks. 'What level's she on?'

'Level six. She's currently battling out of a zombie maze. Without much luck, so far. It's amazing you managed to scale the VR sets down for kids' games – amazing we can afford it!'

Lois laughs. 'How old is she?'

On more comfortable ground, Lois thinks about children playing her game, as Iqbal hits a gong and Ebba rises.

'Welcome, everyone.' Lois sees eyes from all around the table look to Ebba and glasses rise, ready for a toast. Filip stares at Marieke, who is talking to Aksel as her glass lifts in the air.

'Welcome,' Ebba says. Her eyes are bright as she looks round the table. 'It's taken quite a few years to get to this point, but I have to say, I'm liking the view!'

There is laughter, some glass clinking.

'Tomorrow, we begin the process of announcing our agreement. We commence work on producing the new game, and the US projection figures are more than promising. I couldn't be prouder of Archipelago, our fledgling company, about to soar like an eagle. And I couldn't be more pleased to welcome you all. To friends, to success, and to Archipelago!'

As Ebba lifts her glass, she smiles at Lois and mouths, 'To Dad.'

Dinner has begun.

NOW

15

FILIP

There's smoke.

He's still alive.

Sirens scream in the background, but smoke will be followed by spreading flames.

Filip's sure he can smell oil. A handbag has emptied by his head. He is almost flat in his seat, hanging to the side. A lipstick, a packet of tissues, a mobile phone screen – shattered. The everyday items take him aback. They don't fit with the twisted metal, the screaming.

'Come on!' he shouts, coughs, through the wispy grey. 'We need to get out of here!'

Marieke first; she was opposite him in the seat so she must be near.

'Filip?' Her voice is weak, but he can make her out. She hangs above him; her feet half kick and her head hangs. The helicopter has landed on its side, and her seat is raised high.

He releases the seat belt. There is blood on her face and he lowers her in his arms. A branch of a tree has smashed through to the left side, near her face.

'I'll get Aksel – he was near the front,' Ebba says from the side, or behind him. The disorientation makes him spin. Her top is ripped and her face is black with something. It looks like oil.

'Hurry,' he says. He doesn't notice Marieke feeling heavy, but his whole body aches as he carries her out. Through the grey, he sees Lois and Iqbal up on the edge of the surrounds of the Roman theatre. Lois begins to run. The smoke obscuring his view darkens; it's black and still thickening.

Iqbal emerges, running, holding Lois back, shouting, 'I'll get her! Stay put!'

'You can't save me twice, Iqbal!' Lois is crying.

Filip has to duck down through the twisted metal to reach the open air. He catches his arm on something and he knows he's cut himself, but he can't feel it. His body is slow, like he's under water. One step at a time. Marieke stirs in his arms; he manages another step, towards the blue-grey of the sky.

'Here, let me take her. Where is Ebba?' Iqbal has reached him and Filip feels Marieke lifted from his arms. From her hairline a trail of blood trickles and he panics. He wants to reach out and take her hand, tell her everything will be OK. It would reassure him, almost more than her.

'Where is Ebba?' Iqbal asks again, and Filip gestures behind him.

'She's gone for Aksel, I'll help them. You take her out.'

'Everything will be OK, Marieke,' he says, feeling instantly calmer, turning back into the burning wreck. 'Get her away!' he shouts over his shoulder.

The smoke, dense now, makes him cough and he is light-headed. A drop of blood falls into his eye and he smears it off his face with the back of his hand.

'Ebba?' he shouts.

She is dragging Aksel by the shoulders, but it's a slow task. He's completely unconscious. Filip runs forward and grabs his feet.

'Aksel? Can you hear me?' he shouts as he pulls. There is nothing.

'On three!' He counts.

They lift him and suddenly there are more hands appearing, taking Aksel from him and pulling him backwards, pulling him out of the wreck. Filip looks at the limp body, thinks of the words Aksel had said to him when he stood up on the helicopter. What were the words?

There's no sign of Richard or Sarah. Pulling from his rescuers, Filip runs back into the smoke.

BEFORE

FRIDAY

16

MAARTEN

Something's off. He doesn't know what.

Just as the food is being served, he nips back outside. It's not really his job to monitor the whole place. The PC is watching the doors for intruders; really, Maarten knows he's just here as a handshake. The threat based on the letters has been deemed small, even in Rotterdam. It's simply a PR exercise. Everyone knows.

But something's off.

'Sign of anything?' he asks the PC standing outside.

The night is still warm.

'No, sir. Nothing. We've had a call that a car is expected soon. Someone's wife, I think.'

Maarten watches with interest as a long black car pulls up. Out of it climbs a young woman, tall with blonde hair in waves down her back. He recognises her from something he'd watched on TV with Liv the other week. It must be the actor Liv mentioned. She is, according to Liv, on track to become stellar.

She climbs out of the car and looks long and hard at the house as the driver brings her bags round and lifts them up the steps. Someone from the house opens the door, takes the luggage, and, throughout it all, the woman has not moved a muscle.

Her poise, dress, make-up, hair... She looks as though she's about to step in front of the camera. She glistens. And it is interesting, Maarten thinks, that for all that, she looks far from home.

She thanks her driver, then lights a cigarette. She takes only a few drags, ditches it, walking up the steps. She walks with a straight back. But her fists are clenched.

She looks like she's going into battle.

He checks around the gardens and the drive. The air is still. The moon appears, disappears behind a cloud, and the shadows grow darker as he steps back into the house.

There's a great buzz coming from the dining room. The string quartet appear to have relocated to the far corner and the conversation levels are growing louder. They must be starting to eat now and he'd better head back in.

He pauses next to the young actor, who stands outside the room like she's waiting in the wings for her performance.

'Going in?' he asks, offering his arm, feeling suddenly more gallant, like the house has demanded he raise his game, step back in time. He speaks in Dutch, to offer some support, and she glances at him in surprise, then smiles, taking his arm.

'Thank you,' she says. 'I could use something to lean on right now.'

He allows her to step forward first and he feels a flash

of sympathy. This is a lion's den of a room into which to walk.

'All OK?' he asks, as they approach the door frame.

'I'll tell you,' she says, 'by the end of the night. Ask me then.'

17

LOIS

Lois sees her first, as she sits at the side of the round table facing the dining room doors.

The music has started up and it could be a mistake, Lois thinks. With all the drink being consumed, people are loud enough already. They raise their voices to be heard above the background of Mozart, and the energy in the room lifts a notch higher.

Aksel, to her right, has poured her glass of wine, passed her bread and is charming to his left and his right. Ebba's eyes glance his way more than once, her face becoming pinker when he appears not to notice. He finally mouths something at her and Lois sees Ebba shake her head, barely perceptibly. She mouths '11.30' at him and Lois feels on alert. Something is coming and it is not good.

To her left, Maarten's space is empty. He's not drinking tonight. Not drinking herself, she is more aware of it; she's both relieved he is on the job and nervous about the issues that demand his sobriety.

He'd said he'd be back in a second and she can see him now, coming in.

With Sophie Atwood on his arm.

People say 'dressed to kill' and Lois has never really thought much about the saying, but as Sophie enters the room, the air changes, the tone changes. Whatever had been going on, heightens. It's like a rattle of bullets has been fired upwards.

Many things happen at once.

Lois glances at Filip, who is staring across the table at Marieke, still talking to Aksel. Filip finishes another drink and, as Aksel sees Sophie and rises in his chair, saying, 'Sophie, how lovely,' Filip jumps, like he's been shot; his chair lands backwards with a thump. The music rests between pieces and, for a good few seconds, there is no sound. Filip stands, staring at his wife, and it is Aksel and Ebba, rising almost as one, walking towards her, who welcome her into the room.

Lois could swear, as Sophie leans forward to acknowledge their greeting, that her hands are shaking.

Ebba, after kissing each cheek, takes Sophie by the arm and leads her from Maarten to a space at the table, for which Iqbal has quickly made room. She and Sophie are good friends so this makes sense, but still Filip has not moved.

Instead, he stands, almost swaying, and Lois knows that he is drunk, but can't quite work out why he hasn't gone to greet his wife.

Aksel gets there before Filip. Pulling out her chair,

asking her about the journey, commenting on the trains, saying how well she looks.

She looks more than well, Lois thinks. Sophie wears a pale lemon dress, sleeveless and cut low. Triangles are cut out of each side of the bodice, so that it is straight to the waist in a v-section, and then it falls full length to the ground, spilling out in silk folds. She wears gloves, which adds a bygone glamour – on anyone else they would look like a costume, but on Sophie they are vintage Hollywood. Her hair is long and loose and her make-up light; her eyes luminous from the other side of the table. She shakes her hair over her shoulder and smiles at the room.

'Hello, everyone,' she says warmly. 'Sorry I'm late. Filip, darling, thanks for sending the car.'

The talking resumes as the music starts, and Aksel slides Sophie's chair in, dipping his head low and whispering something in her ear. She laughs, and Lois glances back to Filip, still standing, staring at his wife.

It is only then that he walks towards her, bending his head. Lois wonders if he's going for the cheek, from the angle; but Sophie turns her head up to him and kisses him on the mouth. Sliding her hand up behind his head, she holds the kiss for a second longer than a quick greeting.

Filip's stance, neck bent, means the back of his head is ripe for attack – if this were a war.

Their lips part and eyes around the table turn away, not wishing to be caught peeking. They make an impressive couple. As Sophie's mouth turns upwards to Filip, Lois imagines a few around the table may wonder how it might feel to be on the receiving end. She thinks of it, briefly, herself.

Sophie's hand slides round to Filip's cheek, slipping down his arm and squeezing his hand. She turns back to the table and Filip stands, flaming red, as though this were his first kiss at a disco, and not a greeting one may give a wife.

18

FILIP

Sophie is dazzling. He has drunk far too much and his gaze darts from Marieke to Sophie, but neither will catch his eye. Both laugh with their neighbour and avoid each other.

He hasn't managed to catch Marieke since this afternoon. Each time he's approached her, something's got in the way. He needs to apologise. He should never have taken the call from Sophie when Marieke was in the room. The only consolation is that he's sure she didn't hear. They never had got to the bottom of what she had wanted to talk about.

And he wants to talk to her – Marieke is his best friend at the moment. Tonight, he needs that ease, that emotional support.

Sophie sits next to Richard, a good thirty years older than her. Filip himself has ten years on Sophie, which often seems a lot. Seems a world away from her at times.

Richard is telling her something; his hands sweep wide in description. People become animated around Sophie. He thinks of those first few nights on honeymoon, when the air was still warm at 2 a.m. and Sophie had listened intently as he explained his ideas for the next deal, feeling like the world was opening out at his feet.

'She's very beautiful, your wife.' He can't remember the name of the woman to his right and panics for a moment.

She sees his expression, speaks warmly, saying, 'I'm Olivia, Liv. I'm Maarten's wife. You were talking to him earlier.'

'Of course! Yes, yes she is.' He looks back to her, thinking she is too beautiful – untouchable. Why did he ever think he could be enough for her?

He looks at Marieke. She makes him feel he is enough; her friendship asks nothing of him. But now even she won't look at him. He must have really upset her; it weighs upon him. Is he doomed to let down every woman he knows?

He just wants to be enough. He wants to talk to Marieke. Tears prick his lids quickly and he looks down, embarrassed.

Liv speaks, deliberately not noticing, and he is grateful. 'My daughters love her. She was in the film set in Amsterdam?'

'*Beneath a Sky*,' he says, and smiles. She had sung in that one. He still falls in love with her anew every time she sings. He had gone to the opening and sat beside her, falling in love with the voice coming from the screen; those eyes brown, the smile that opens up a whole world. She had been next to him, miles away.

'She was brilliant in that! We all loved it. It's so rare that romantic films these days feel innocent enough to take a ten-year-old to. She really looks amazing. I can't believe she's just got off the train and managed to put herself together. I couldn't look like that after getting ready in the car.'

'Ah, well, we have a secret. We've both done it before turning up for premieres. We travel with the clothes,' – he nods to the dress – 'then we take a room at the St Pancras Hotel. She has people to do her hair and make-up. Or if we fly, we have use of the lounges. We're lucky.'

'Where's the dress from?' Liv whispers, leaning in.

Filip looks again. 'I'm not sure. I think Prada, maybe?' He shrugs. 'I see the labels. I hear the conversations she has with her stylist.'

'Well, something I'll never get into then,' says Liv, finishing another glass of wine. 'But then again, I doubt my abs would hold up on display from the side like Sophie's. Not sure two spin sessions a week pulls it together enough for public viewing.'

Filip begins to enjoy himself. Liv's easy to talk to. And she's funny. He turns his attention from the two women in the room he should be speaking to, and laughs along with Liv.

He takes a bite of the food on his plate and gestures at Maarten, who is talking to Lois. 'I guess Maarten can't really relax much tonight?'

Shaking her head, she says, 'I don't know. It's work for him, but not for me. Wine?' She lifts the bottle and grins, pouring them both a glass. 'This is a night off for me, from watching box sets on the TV and remembering to make packed lunches for the next day. It's probably run of the mill for you.'

He thinks of his huge office at home, where sport plays

on a big screen while he clears his emails for the night. He thinks of falling asleep on the sofa, watching TV, listening for Sophie to come back from living her own life out in the city.

He shakes his head. 'No, this is still a big night for me too. You've heard we're talking to the press tomorrow, ahead of the announcement? It's taken a while to get the deal together. Ebba and Lois have worked hard.'

As he says this, he remembers his questions for tomorrow's meeting: he'll need to be sharp. The evidence is beginning to mount that the two deals are not equal. He'd had an email from Ruben, who is gathering more intel, that suggests the initial rumour is true.

Aksel is taking what is his: again.

He'd mentioned to Lois he'd wanted to go over a few things. He wanted to see Lois's expression. Ebba is so composed. There would be nothing – no tell. Lois, to his satisfaction, had looked confused, which implied that the rumours might not be true. Or maybe that she wasn't privy to them. In which case, the secrets run deep. Deeper than he'd like.

Somehow the main course is finished and dessert is coming out.

'Some music?' Aksel says, standing.

Looking up, Filip sees the string quartet have taken a break. The room is very hot now and he leans back, fanning himself with the napkin.

His head is throbbing.

Aksel walks across the room. What the fuck is he doing?

'If I play…' he says.

He gestures to Sophie with a mock bow, offering out his arm.

'Of course you fucking play,' mutters Filip, and Liv, to his right, drinking wine, chokes on a mouthful, spraying tiny droplets over her plate. He likes her even more.

'If I play,' Aksel says again, ignoring Filip, 'then maybe we could ask Sophie to sing? She could be persuaded?'

Sophie looks up, smiling, but she seems surprised. Filip feels nervous again. Glancing at Marieke, he sees her stand, roll her eyes.

He wishes she would catch his eye. He's making a mess of all of this. He still wants to apologise for earlier. He doesn't know quite what to do. Maybe he should just go to his room and leave everyone to it? He's so drunk, staying will benefit no one.

'If you like,' Sophie says, smiling and rising.

As she takes Aksel's arm, he leans in and whispers something to her. Sophie flushes a deep pink, up from the neck, and laughs. Aksel leans in again, placing his free hand over hers, which rests on his arm.

Klootzak! Kankerlijer! Filip thinks. His fists close tight and his nails bite into his skin.

He thinks of standing in the bathroom, last week, trying yet another product to see if it would help with Sophie. To see if he could last the distance. The contrast of that, with Aksel's effortless *male*ness. He's like a dog, spraying everywhere.

Filip curses himself. He couldn't spray everywhere even if he tried. Failing, always failing. There's no treatment, no pill that has worked. He shrinks further and further.

Yet here, Aksel slinks across the room like he's warming up for the tango. Almost pirouetting her round to the room, facing the table.

God she is beautiful, Filip thinks again. For the millionth time. With all eyes forward, he allows himself a moment to appreciate his wife. She walks tall, with an easy grace. She sits on the edge of the piano stool, her back to Aksel, half at an angle, so she looks at the table while he faces the piano.

'If it doesn't sound too good, it's because Lois told me it hasn't been tuned for a while. Nothing to do with the pianist.' Aksel winks and the room laughs.

They look like a fucking couple, Filip thinks, leaning back against his chair. *They look like a fucking golden couple.*

'Unless, of course, Filip, you wish to play for your wife?' Aksel pauses for a second.

But of course he can't play. Aksel waits until the room has registered Filip's lack, before beginning.

As Filip had expected, the notes fall from his fingers quickly and are accomplished. He leans to Sophie and whispers something one more time and she nods, smiling broadly. That smile. Those eyes.

'Oh, this is the theme from *Beneath a Sky*!' Liv says.

She's right. Filip lets himself stare at Sophie, knowing what is coming, pleased he hasn't left the room. Pleased she is his wife, even if it is not for much longer. He's suffused with pride. He is so very proud of her.

A tear falls from his eye, and Liv places her hand over his, squeezing quickly.

When she sings, he is lost. The music is soft, with only the piano to accompany her. She sings effortlessly and, for a few minutes, the sting leaves the air.

Filip even feels warm towards Aksel, following the melody, not competing with her voice.

When she finishes, there is a moment of quiet and then everyone stands, applauding loudly.

'Brava,' Ebba shouts.

Filip sees Richard smile at Sarah, Liv at Maarten, Lois at Ebba; and Aksel whispers something to Sophie, who instead of leaning back to him, turns and catches Filip's eye.

He claps louder, knowing a few tears are falling, knowing he is drunk. But that song and that voice. And she's looking just at him.

'You must love her very much,' Liv says.

He doesn't even need to think. 'I do. I love her very much indeed,' he replies, smiling at Sophie, desperate to hold her, to tell her he is sorry for everything. But he knows he is too much of a coward.

Too late, he notices that Marieke, coming back into the room, hears his words. She stops still, staring at him with apparent disgust. His mouth falls half open as she turns on her heel and leaves the room.

19

MAARTEN

Maarten can't see Marieke.

Has something happened?

He thinks of the letters, of the threats. Looking to the door, the PC hasn't come in, or called him.

Excusing himself from Lois, he makes his way across the room. The applause from the table is loud and there are shouts for an encore. More champagne appears in answer to Aksel calling for a toast to Sophie. The room swims with heat, with energy.

Marieke is standing in the doorway, not clapping, but holding the wall with one hand. Her chin is lifted, and he recognises a look in her eyes but can't quite place it: scorn?

'OK?' he asks quietly. 'Has something happened? Are there more threats?' Lois is clapping nearby and he sees her look, her face a question mark. He tries to answer in a smile, calming concern.

In an unexpected move, which feels both familiar and also so horribly like a statement of intimacy that he was attempting to avoid, Marieke takes his hand and leads him from the room.

Glancing at Liv, who raises her eyebrows, he mouths 'Back in a sec'; he knows this is a step too far and, as soon as he is able, he slips his hand from Marieke's and steps beside her, walking down the corridor.

In her other hand, Marieke carries her wine glass, and she comes to an abrupt halt then veers to the right, ducking into a smaller room with a sofa and a low coffee table.

Books line the walls, and there is a fire burning in a huge stone fireplace at the front of the room. There is a more muted feel to the furnishings. The sofas are darker, the rugs traditional. Candles are lit, even in here, and Marieke sinks down into the deep plush of the green velvet sofa, indicating he should do the same.

She takes a long drink of wine, gazing at the fire, slightly past Maarten.

She is very close. Her face is drawn.

'Has something happened?' he asks again, thinking he should be checking outside. She places her hand on his knee, to steady herself, and sits up.

'No. Nothing like that. I am just exhausted, Maart. I'm exhausted; I'm exhausted with the fighting – trying to tackle a business community who won't listen. And even tonight. We've got a fucking film star rocking up in a dress that cost thousands, who spends her life demanding first-class seats while there are children in the DRC digging out cobalt so she can fly and stare at her phone.'

He sits quietly. She drinks more wine. 'You know the shirt you're wearing will be made by someone paid less than a dollar a day? In a factory that could catch fire at any moment? The average cheap garment bought on the UK high street is worn seven times. Seven times. That's it! I want the world to be different. If not for us, then for our kids.'

She lies back into the cushions of the deep sofa, kicks off her shoes and puts her feet up on the coffee table. Her wine glass is empty.

'Is that booze over there?' she asks, gesturing to a side table where crystal decanters sit, filled and ready.

He nods, pouring her a drink in the heavy glass, the liquid, like peat, sloshing and swirling. It chimes when he puts it down on the table. She drains half.

'This is what's bothering you tonight?' he asks. He's surprised. She might be tired of a fight, but he doubts she'd let it interfere with an evening off.

She laughs, looking at him. 'You know me, Maart; what do you think?'

Smiling, he sits back too, crosses one leg over the other. He tells himself that his brief is her safety. It would be unprofessional not to listen to what she has to say.

'I think there's something else going on. But you don't have to tell me what it's about.'

She sips at the drink. 'You're not having one?'

'No, on duty.'

'Ever the policeman,' she says, pulling a face.

Not *ever*, he thinks. Is Marieke also thinking about the last night they saw each other? He can't face bringing it up. Shame still burns.

'Well, I like your wife. She's clever. And funny. You married well. Strange how things turn out.'

He nods. 'I got lucky,' he says. 'Thanks for…'

She waves her hand. 'History. It's all history.' She shrugs. 'Aren't you going to ask about me?'

'I think,' he says, lifting his feet on to the table, matching her, leaning back. 'I think you're about to tell me.'

There is a pattering of rain on the window. It's light, but it adds a soporific feel to an already heavy room. The fire dances upwards in the grate; Maarten looks at the clock on the wall. It's almost 10.30 p.m. and dessert had been waiting to be served. He can hear singing from the dining room and he realises Sophie must be doing an encore.

'What should we do,' Marieke says, staring at her glass, swilling the peat-brown liquid, 'about men who are such absolute shits?'

20

LOIS

Sophie's second song is just ending as the tray appears at Lois's side. One of the serving staff hired for the evening proffers it to her: a letter.

'This was found on the doormat. It's not addressed.'

'Do I need to look at it now?' Lois asks. The guests are slowly sitting. Spirits and coffee are being poured.

'I'm sorry, miss, it's just we were briefed by Mr Bari that any letters that arrived should be taken straight to DCI Jansen, but we can't find him. I'm sorry, I just thought...' The girl – she can't be much more than sixteen – looks confused and Lois is cross with herself; her tone had been sharper than she'd meant it to be. She's tired.

'No, I'm sorry. You've done exactly the right thing. Thank you.'

Lois lifts the letter and the girl disappears. Everyone is eating and Maarten isn't there. She looks round the table for Marieke, but she's missing too.

She taps the envelope lightly in her palm. It's not addressed to anyone – probably just a dropped envelope, maybe a receipt, a catering bill. There's no point leaving everyone and causing a scene, so she lifts it to open, hesitating.

Deciding quickly, she runs her finger along the seal and slides out the thin letter inside.

Seeing the paper, even just folded, with its thick black marker pen glaring through the folds, she knows immediately she's made the wrong call.

21

IQBAL

The dessert – luckily intended to be served cold, it had sat around for so long – has disappeared. The music has stopped, but the chatter has resumed with a vibrancy coloured with alcohol. Few are touching the coffee.

Iqbal had seen Lois yawn before she'd left the room, and he suppresses one himself.

He sits next to Richard. 'Tell me more about your visit to Dhaka,' he says, and Richard, who has clearly been drinking wine, his teeth purple, tells him of a business trip out there.

'It was my first time. I was in one of the good hotels before that roof fell down – horrific business. And you said you still lived there then? You lived in Savar, where lots of the factories are based?'

Iqbal nods, not saying all the words that could never come close to describing how he'd felt back then, how he'd been living.

'I read up on the history a bit when I was there. Let me tell you, Bangladesh has a turbulent history, and had a rough deal from the West. I read an article about the three million Bengalis who died of starvation during the Second World War. Bloody hell!'

Iqbal nods.

'Christ, Iqbal.' He shakes his head. 'Did you know the rivers behind the factories run coloured, depending on the dye in the fabrics that week? Red, blue... Leaking in and poisoning the water? It's a crime, what industry does!'

Iqbal drinks from his water glass, nodding. Richard carries on, telling him as though he doesn't know. Hasn't lived it.

'What kind of business were you there for?' Iqbal pushes.

Richard's face clouds with confusion, his brow wrinkling with the effort of remembering details. 'I was there for a—'

He stops, turning left as Sarah laughs. His grey hair is thinning on top; tiny lines deepen across his brow. Sarah is laughing as Aksel lifts a bottle, refilling her glass.

Richard watches them, quickly tense.

'That man is all over the women in this room,' he says, then seems to remember where he is, shakes his head. 'Sorry, I've had too much to drink.'

'Did you like it? Dhaka?' Iqbal asks. But Richard is watching Aksel talk to his wife.

Marieke and the police officer have disappeared somewhere.

Filip is barely holding himself upright. He leans on the officer's wife, occasionally looking at Sophie like she's standing on a stage a million miles away.

The clock reads almost 11.30 p.m. and, at some point, this night must end.

Aksel clicks his fingers in Iqbal's direction and, without looking at him, calls for more champagne.

Iqbal deliberately does not see.

Ebba walks towards Aksel, speaking quietly, and he shakes his head, holds up five fingers. Ebba colours pink, sits to talk to Sophie.

Iqbal checks his email to see if Obaidur has responded yet. He asked him for more details – what did the man look like?

But nothing yet.

Richard, Filip or Aksel. One of these men has placed Archipelago in danger. But which one?

22

Lois

Sliding her chair back, Lois smiles at the table in case anyone sees her leave; she doesn't want to cause alarm.

Filip and Liv are giggling like children; Filip has raised a spoon to his face and is attempting to hang it off his nose. Sarah and Richard have moved around to sit next to each other, and Richard is leaning over to kiss his wife. Sarah looks like a teenager.

Iqbal had been speaking with Richard only five minutes ago. Where is he?

Ebba doesn't look too happy. She'd been eating and glancing at Aksel every few minutes for the past half an hour. She'd mouthed '11.30' at him.

Where are they going? Why? Ebba nods to him again. They're off somewhere together in a minute and Lois's stomach is in knots.

She exits the room and, after asking a couple of servers, heads to the snug to find Maarten.

Knocking before she enters – because it's that kind of night – she finds Maarten and Marieke on the low sofa, laughing, and Marieke holds a whisky tumbler in her hand.

'Sorry to interrupt.'

'Please, come and sit down,' Marieke says, lifting her bare feet from the coffee table. 'I'm sorry, I've made myself more at home in your house than should be deemed polite.'

Maarten has sat up straighter and Lois sees his eyes focus on the letter in her hand. He raises his eyebrows.

Nodding, she hands it to him, without saying a word, and then sinks into the armchair on the other side of the table, near the bookcase with her books on gaming and Ebba's on gardening.

No one speaks. The heavy darkness of the night has crept in, creeps still. Marieke takes a slug of whisky and shakes her shoulders back, like she's bracing herself for impact.

Maarten puts on gloves from his pocket and opens the letter. He reads it silently, then stands, pulling out his phone.

'Stay here, both of you.'

'What does it say?' Marieke asks.

But Maarten is heading towards the door. He pulls it open, then pauses, and seems to change his mind. Looking back, he shakes his head.

'Here. If you're sure you want to read it.' He holds the letter in view of Marieke, who doesn't touch it. Lois can't pull her eyes from the paper, both wanting to know, and not wanting to know.

The door closes behind him, and Marieke leans back, resting her head on the sofa.

Lois lifts the glass from her fingers and takes it for a refill.

'You need another one of these,' she says.

The clock chimes in the hallway. A log on the fire collapses. Noise from the dining room rumbles.

Neither speaks. They wait.

23

FILIP

There is coffee on the table and Filip drinks it like it's water: hot and black. It scalds his tongue and he prays for some clarity to arrive, in this stifling room, where all he can do is stare at Sophie and think of Marieke.

'Are you OK?' Liv asks.

His plate is empty and he tries to remember what dessert had been. There's a creamy taste on his tongue and a burst of acid reflux takes over.

'Yes. I'm just too drunk. Far too drunk.' Part of him is grateful. He's sick of making decisions. He's too drunk to talk to either woman right now. As a delaying tactic, it's gold.

'Want me to help you find your room?' Liv asks.

Drinking more coffee, he nods. 'I think my room is a good idea. But I can get there on my own. Would you mind...' He burps, and Liv bites her lip, like she's trying to hold in a laugh.

But it escapes anyway, and he smiles. 'I'm pleased you're finding it funny.'

'Do you know how long it is since I've been this pissed?' she says, lifting the Amaretto that sits next to her coffee. 'About a thousand years. I'll feel like absolute shit tomorrow, but I'm loving tonight. I've just been to ask your wife for a selfie. Look.' She thrusts out the phone and there's a photo of Sophie staring back at him, smiling. He looks across the table. She's talking to Aksel. Again.

'I thought, why not? When else am I going to meet a film star? My girls will go bananas!'

'Want one with me?' he offers, the acid in his mouth making him feel nauseous.

'Hell yes!' she says, and they lean their heads together, grinning.

Filip is aware he can only really see through one eye. His head spins. He peers at the phone, not really making anything out.

'I think I'll leave now,' he says, aiming for some elegance, rising and steadying himself on the table.

'Let me at least tell Sophie,' Liv says, calling, 'Sophie! Filip's off to bed!'

Filip watches Aksel laugh into his plate at this and he feels strangely protective of Liv, who had sounded like his mum, calling a friend over to play.

But Aksel rises, crossing to Ebba. They both leave, and Filip feels exhausted with relief.

'He's a mean one, that one,' he says to Liv, trying to whisper. 'You ignore him. You and Maarten must come and stay in my apartment in Rotterdam! Come soon and bring your kids. Come and be my guests.'

Feeling wildly generous and warm-spirited, Filip hugs

Liv and an arm appears to his right, which he takes without really looking.

'Goodnight, Liv. It's been such a pleasure!'

It's only after a few steps that he sees it's Sophie who is helping him out of the room.

'Why are you helping me?' he asks, wondering which of the three doors he sees they should walk though.

'Filip, why wouldn't I help you?'

They move through the door frame, which he only bangs into once, and he feels proud of himself for not falling. He looks at her, carefully.

'But you were talking to Aksel. I don't mind, you know, if you want to go back to him.' As warm as his feelings were for Liv, his generosity of spirit suddenly knows no bounds for Sophie. He grabs hold of her arm, leaning into her. His whisper intimate, soft.

'I know you're not really attracted to me, Soph,' he says, 'not really.'

She goes to speak and he raises a hand. 'No, stop, let me say it. I'm not sure I've ever been this drunk, and if I'm going to say it, I may as well say it now.'

Beginning again, he tries to look into her eyes. Her beautiful eyes. 'You have such beautiful eyes,' he says. 'I know you married me for my money. I get it. I'll never be enough. Not really. But it's OK. I've accepted it. You can leave me. I won't make a fight. Will you leave me for your agent?' He frowns, thinking of this. 'I wouldn't like that. Not him. Or even Aksel – not him either.' He leans in, confiding. 'Lois thinks there's something going on between him and Ebba. And I think Aksel's ripping me off.

So not Aksel. I hope he doesn't hurt Ebba. You know their father's business collapsed? There was some history there, with Aksel and their father.' He mulls, tilting to the left, thinking about the connections.

Sophie squeezes his hand, opens her mouth to speak, but he continues. 'Not Aksel, but someone young. Someone beautiful. Like you. Someone who sings like you. You know, when you sing, my heart explodes.' He waves a hand in the air, slowly drawing an arc, thinking of the beauty of her voice. 'It explodes like a dying star, into millions of pieces.'

The hallway is quite dark, lit with candles that line the passageway. He looks at the imaginary star he's drawn with his hand, still thinking of the poetry of the image.

Sophie has tears on her face.

Serving staff scuttle past, heads down.

'Oh no, don't cry!' he says. 'I was trying to be kind.'

'Filip,' she says, and he pats her on the cheek, thinking that she really is the most beautiful thing he has ever seen. Her cheeks are wet.

'Let's get some air,' she says.

She leads him towards the heavy doors that open on to the garden, where the moon has come out, casting Halloween shadows.

The hall clock chimes twelve.

24

MAARTEN

'Did you see anyone here? Anyone?'

The serving staff are assembled in the kitchen. It's gone midnight and they're due to head home soon. They stand, all the range from sullen to terrified. The lights are bright in here and he squints under the glare.

'No one's going anywhere until I get to the bottom of this, and I'm asking you all first,' he says, staring hard. 'Someone must have seen something.' He casts his eye around. He looks for a tell.

One of the women at the front of the group runs her hands down her white apron. Her hair is twisted up into a topknot and she cocks her head at Maarten.

'You accusing us then?' she asks.

'Not accusing. But this letter has appeared on the doorstep and it's clearly been delivered by hand. Most of the guests have been in the other room for the evening. You've all been out here. I'm asking you if you've seen anything. The front door is watched by a PC. The French doors have been open in the dining room, but I think we'd have noticed if a stranger had come in. There are no signs of breaking and entering. This letter has been left on the mat by someone in here. By someone in the house.'

Six pairs of eyes stare back at him.

'I want to reiterate—' His eyes are hurting now. He realises how tired he is from the flashes of light behind his eyelids when he blinks. 'I want to reiterate the serious nature of the investigation. The serious consequences to any failure to comply with our questions. Did anyone, anyone at all, see anything?'

The six pairs of eyes look back; most look nervous. The staff range from very young to older than him. Not so obvious in their uniforms.

One looks younger than the rest. A young girl, who can't be more than seventeen. He remembers passing her in the hallway earlier. She has red hair and she kicks one heel against the other foot, fidgety. Her eyes, when he looks at her, look away, look down.

'What's your name?' he asks her, trying to sound gentle, approachable.

'Alison.' She speaks to the toes of her shoes.

'Alison, can you come next door and talk to me?'

Leaving the room, her head drops, her shoulders sag. Her walk has guilt written all over it.

They move to a study. Compared to the other rooms in the house, it's tiny, but it's actually the size of his lounge, fitting a three-seater sofa, a coffee table and one large window, open to the gardens, which are black in the dark. The female PC nods as she enters from her position in the garden.

They sit. Alison's knees cling together, her hands clasp tightly. Her cheeks are flushed; a pale-pink scarf is tied in her hair. She's all the shades of ochre.

'Alison,' he says, 'could you tell me what you know?'

The wind in the trees rustles up against the glass panes behind her head. She flinches. Laughter can be heard coming from the dining room. The front door bangs.

Her head bows slightly lower, like she is offering up a prayer.

He says nothing. He can sit out the longest of silences.

The branches tap again, fingers of the night. Alison jumps, turning quickly, eyes darting round the room.

Still Maarten says nothing.

'I didn't mean to cause any trouble!' Her voice is quick, high-pitched.

Maarten nods.

'I didn't. I mean, anyone would have done it, wouldn't they? For the money.'

Raising his eyebrows, Maarten tips his head to one side, offering up an agreement of sorts.

'They're so pissed in there, all them rich people. They won't miss it!' Even higher now, the tone of Alison's voice becomes thinner, like it's climbing in altitude and thinning in oxygen.

'I didn't mean to!' And she bursts into tears, her head falling to her knees. Maarten pulls a tissue from the box on the coffee table, passing it to her.

'Can you tell me about it?' he asks gently. 'Go from the start.'

Through tears and snot, the girl tells her story in bursts.

'I was on my break. I got my coat, so I could go outside…'
Big sniff, big blow. 'Anyway, while I was outside, having a
fag, I felt an envelope in my pocket. It was thick and I just
knew it had money inside. Like notes, you know.' Another
sniff. Maarten passes another tissue.

'So, I pulled it out and, on the front, they'd written: £500
for anyone who can pass on a letter. Someone had stuffed it
in my pocket.' This time a big gulp of air, sucked through an
open mouth. 'So, I opened this envelope, and there it was,
five hundred pounds. In fifties. They're red, you know? I've
never seen one, have I?' She shrugs her shoulders and she's
looking at Maarten now, calmer. 'Anyway, at the back of the
notes was another envelope. And a note. It said to leave the
envelope on the mat. And that was it.'

She leans and takes another tissue. She's not quite
enjoying herself, but she's settled into the story.

'I thought, what harm can it do? That's more money
than I'll see in a while. So, I did. I left it on the mat and
then I carried on.'

'What time was this?' Maarten asks, thinking that
whomever had chosen Alison had known exactly what
they were doing.

'Don't know. I don't wear a watch really, I just use my
phone. But we're not allowed to carry our phones at work.
We have to leave them in our bags.'

Nodding slowly, Maarten considers this. 'What time
was your break?'

'Ten o'clock, innit. I had a fag outside,' she answers,
her eyes a little brighter, but still scared. 'Will I get into
trouble?'

'You've been very helpful. I'll need a full statement,' Maarten says. 'Do you have the original envelope?'

She nods, smiling at him now. 'I know where it is. I was going to get rid of it later so I stuffed it in my bag.'

'And the money?' The words hang for a second; her face clouds over. He feels sorry for her. She's right. It is such a big sum.

'All of it?'

As he nods to the PC to sit and take Alison's statement, Maarten catches a flash of something in the trees.

Is there movement outside? Something is stirring tonight. There are secrets at work in Ostle House. Either someone has breached its walls, or someone already inside is making trouble.

Hours stretch ahead of him. This night is not done with him yet.

25

LOIS

'Marieke, how are you?'

Lois brings hot chocolate into the snug, where Marieke is waiting to be told she can go to bed. A PC stands in the corner of the room and he nods to Lois as she passes.

'Tired, mainly. I'm a bit sick of being told on Twitter to shut up, that they'll kill me in my sleep. That I'm a whore! And these letters say they're watching me. It's not a day out; it's not a minor downside to my job.' She sounds angry, weary, but Lois sees shadows and shade: she looks scared.

'When did it all start?' Lois asks, sitting next to Marieke, passing her a blanket from the sofa.

'The letters? A few months ago. I'm used to threats warning me off. It's part of life in the public eye. I've been pushing this legislation for years. But the letters? They first arrived to my office, in the post, from a central letter box in Rotterdam. The next from Paris. Then a few arrived at my home. One from the US, the UK... Nothing too detailed. One suggested I take a holiday; one that I think carefully about my actions. They're short. Never explicit – a menace rather than a clear threat. But my team are taking them seriously. And now tonight, here. With no postmark. Delivered by hand. That's the worst part. This girl who laid it on the mat – she has no idea how it makes you feel. So vulnerable!' Marieke shakes her head and Lois takes her hand.

'Well, we've got protection.'

'You know, it's not that I'm scared – I really don't think anything will happen. I think if it was going to happen, it would have happened by now. It's the feeling of being watched. It's been widely publicised that I'm here this weekend. So, I get it. But who goes to the lengths of finding out the members of staff and getting one of them to sneak the letter in?'

Lois nods. 'Is that what happened? I haven't heard.'

'Well, I assume so.' Marieke drinks the hot chocolate. The wind has picked up outside and it rushes in bursts up to the house, whining.

'No, you're right. How stupid, but when I saw it, I worried it was one of the guests!' Lois shivers. 'How ridiculous.'

Shaking her head gently, looking into the mug, which swirls with the sweet dark liquid, Marieke says, 'It's not ridiculous. You never know what people have to lose. We eat and drink together, but it could be one of us. One of us round that table might want me stopped, very badly. If my legislation goes through, the cost implications could be huge. This deal is a great start, and paves the way for others. However, for those with other investments, it would be far less profitable if they had to pay everyone fairly. It could easily be someone round the table.'

Marieke stands and looks outside. 'One of the letters mentioned my daughter. You have no idea how vulnerable it makes me feel. It's the surest way to get to me. Worrying about her has been the closest I've come to stopping.'

'I didn't know you had a daughter. How old is she?' Lois asks.

'She's just had her twentieth birthday. I try to keep her private. Keep her out of the public eye.' Marieke sags, sitting back down.

'Oh, Marieke. Can her father help?'

'Her father is an old boyfriend. He has nothing to do with her. Never has.'

There's a startled yelp behind them. Lois turns. 'Oh, Liv! I didn't see you there. Do you want to come in?'

Liv shakes her head. She looks pale.

'I was… I was looking for…' she starts, but tails away. She's looking at Marieke.

'Maarten's in the other room. I can take you?' Lois rises.

But Liv shakes her head, taking a step backwards. 'I'll find him. On my own.'

Marieke looks after her, her features settling into a different expression. Some discomfort. 'That was…'

'That's Liv. Maarten's wife,' Lois says, reaching for her drink. Her head is starting to ache. 'She's lovely, don't worry. She won't mention your daughter to anyone, if you're worried about it.'

'Do you think she heard it all?' Marieke asks, her voice soft. She bites her lip.

'She'll be discreet,' Lois says, wondering at the colour Marieke has turned. She tries to reassure her. Something has just happened, and it's slipped by quickly; Lois replays the last few minutes in her head. 'Here, let me get you another drink.'

26

MAARTEN

It's almost 2 a.m. – it's officially Saturday – and it's not that the letter looks any different to the others. He sits in Lois's study downstairs, reading the letter again, which he has laid down gently, awaiting fingerprint dusting:

SLUTS LIKE YOU ALWAYS GET WHAT THEY DESERVE.
I KNOW WHERE YOU SLEEP TONIGHT.
THINK A BIG HOUSE CAN PROTECT YOU?
LOOK OVER YOUR SHOULDER.
THERE I AM.
WATCHING YOU.

Short and vicious. In thick black block English capitals.

Next to it he's laid out the envelope that contained the money. Next to that is the money itself. The PC stands guard.

'There are more officers coming soon. It seems like it's come from the house, so as long as no one is allowed to leave, I don't see any point in pursuing anything further tonight. This looks similar to the rest of the letters. I'll get the other officers to station themselves outside Ms Visser's door and at the exits to the house. We're watching for anyone unaccounted for. Anyone off the list. If anyone already in the house asks to step outside, then obviously let them, but no one leaves the grounds – no cars. Let's get some statements in the morning.'

The sounds from the dining room are raucous now.

He repeats, 'No one is to leave the grounds, so garden only – we can't stop people stepping out to smoke, but no one gets in a car; no new people are to be admitted to the house. I want the evidence fingerprinted then bagged. We'll leave it at Alison Hampshire's statement tonight, while it's fresh. Everyone else is tired, or drunk.' He thinks of the dining room, of the champagne. He'd phoned it in to the super and she'd been anxious about disrupting the guests. Her message had been unequivocal: *Be discreet, Maarten.*

'Can you take the fingerprints of all the staff tonight? As long as all the guests remain, we can do them in the morning.'

Tired, he thinks of his coffee, undrunk in the dining room.

'Not quite ready for home yet,' he says. But it's past midnight, it's the thirty-first. Candles flicker on the wall, and the goblins are getting ready.

Halloween has begun with a trick.

27

LOIS

Lois steps into the kitchen, which is quiet now. The staff are in another room with the officers. There's a flicker outside. Someone is there.

Partly curiosity, partly just to be outside, needing air, she steps through the doors.

The night has a bite to it.

The warmth from earlier has disappeared, and she shivers – but that could be fear. The fairy lights surrounding the house are behind her as she makes her way down the lawn, past the trees. Her hands shake as she steps into the black of night: the moon is behind a cloud and she spins at the crack of a twig, the hoot of an owl.

This letter is vicious. Much like the rest. Is whoever posted the latest one waiting outside? Is there more to come?

The leaves crunch underfoot as she passes under the final trees, which head down towards the Roman amphitheatre. A crunch sounds, further away – an animal? Lois clamps her arms to her sides for extra warmth, for extra protection.

Who did she see? Are they still there?

She takes the steps down to the theatre surrounds. Usually the gate is bolted, but they'd had permission this weekend to leave it open for the guests. The moon reappears; it's high now, and the shadows black.

'Hello?' she calls.

What is she doing? She's come out so far, alone, and a threatening letter has been delivered in her home tonight. What on earth is she thinking? Sweat slides down her back as she shivers, and she breathes quickly, her chest tight.

There's a shout behind her, and the sound of running feet, behind the stones. The amphitheatre is huge. Grass, low stone walls, all massing into a circle, looking down on the old stage. In the dark, nothing is clear. Is there someone behind the wall?

She runs up the side of the grass to get a better view, feet slipping on the damp. Over in the far corner, by the hedge that follows the perimeter, she is sure she can hear sounds of crying. It looks as if someone is lying on the ground, under a tree. Is it more than one person? Maybe a couple?

She can't think why anyone from the house would have come down here. It can't be Ebba – not with all the rooms in their house. Perhaps someone has broken through the hedge to the theatre: teenagers with alcohol and cigarettes, or a rough sleeper?

Lois finds she can't move – the black of the night is overpowering. The letter flashes up in her mind: *Watching you*.

The moon passes back behind a cloud. The dark of the sky shades her view. The sound of crying faint on the wind.

28

MAARTEN

Exhausted, Maarten pushes open the door to the snug.
Marieke is there on her own. The velvet curtains are open,
and the windows reflect the room.

A figure moves in the trees, catching his eye. It's black
outside, but the fairy lights cast mini haloes in the garden.
It's only a flicker, but he was right – someone is out there.

'Stay here,' he says to Marieke. 'Back in a minute.'

'Maart, I have to tell you something…'

'Tell me in a minute. I think there's someone on the
lawn, heading down towards the trees, the amphitheatre.'

'What? Be careful, Maart,' she says, and she half rises
as he turns the key in the French doors that lead down to
the lawn.

'It's probably nothing. Just teenagers scaling the hedges
into the garden, daring each other. They probably heard a
film star was here. It will just be messing around. I'll check.'

He leaves her on the sofa, to the fire, with the whisky.
He doesn't think it's kids messing around. This evening is
too spiked.

The doors open on to the grass and his shoes sink as he steps outside. The cold of the air is a shock after the heat of the room, and his first thought is Liv – how hard tonight might have been for her. Or not. Is he making too much of it? His past, which he feels is secret and close. Maybe it would melt into the air if he spoke the words aloud?

Work, he thinks, *can be hard*. And he thinks again of the drunk vomiting over him last night, how much he'd stunk, how tired he'd been. Exhaustion had settled in his bones like decay.

And tonight, facing a threat, facing his past.

That laugh. He hears it so far back in his mind. Seeing that man in Marieke's apartment when he turned up with that stupid bunch of flowers. She'd been remorseful, but there had been pity on her face. And the laugh of the other man, derisive, full of scorn. Marieke had run after him when he fled her apartment. But he hadn't stopped, couldn't stop.

Even once he had driven away, his face had burnt with the shame, the embarrassment. When a call had come through from work...

He'd lied when he filed the report. Marieke had known and said nothing.

If he'd only behaved differently, would he still be in Rotterdam? Instead of here, chasing the demons of others?

Speeding up, his feet pad on the grass and he jogs under the trees. The rain has started. It's wet against his face, like a mist, and his glasses are quickly speckled with water, which blurs with the fairy lights from the trees. He catches sight of the figure again, up ahead. He sees the Roman amphitheatre. There's movement on the steps. He runs.

There's definitely someone there.

He weaves through the trees. The bark catches his arm and he ducks from a low branch. Down the steps now, he can see a solo figure by the stage.

Leaves fall behind him and he pushes his back up against a thick trunk and looks out.

His breath is loud to his ears – he hopes whoever it is can't hear him – and he sees an arm; the limb is bare, catching traces of light.

He takes the central steps down two at a time, moving towards the figure.

Is it a woman?

Stepping quietly, he inches forward. He's still quite high up, where families spread their picnic blankets in the summer.

Whoever it is has stopped by the remains of the stage. The figure stands still, looking as though it's waiting for someone. Is it Lois? Is she meeting someone out here?

And there are sounds nearby. He glances left. There is movement on the ground, beneath the trees, by the hedge. Someone else is out here too.

'Hello?' he calls. 'Police. Is everything OK?' He keeps his voice low so as not to alert whoever is standing near the stage.

From under the trees comes the sound of crying, and now the sound of someone being sick. He glances back to the figure ahead. His glasses are wet again and it's hard to see, but he's sure it's a woman. These two people are too far apart to be here together. What's going on? Is the letter writer here? Have they hurt someone? Is that why there's crying?

He takes a step forward.

'Hello!' he calls.

As a cloud uncovers the moon, Maarten sees the woman up by the stage; it really looks like Lois, and he glances left, towards the sound of crying. He'd thought there was only one other person, but he can make out at least two figures beneath the tree, bent, kneeling in the grass. Is someone injured?

What's going on in the dark?

Stepping carefully down to the next level of grass, he tries to make his way to the sound of crying – his senses alert for a weapon, some danger. His heart races.

Perhaps it is just teenagers?

There's movement behind him, sudden. Footsteps. He goes to turn, about to spin, to see where the noise comes from. The click of a twig is so close; if he reached his arm out backwards...

The pain in his head is sharp and his eyes roll beneath his lids. Lights flash; he can feel himself begin to topple. He has been felled.

Reaching out, his fingernails catch a splinter on the bark, and he opens his mouth to call, but he can't make a sound.

He feels himself begin to fall. Then feels nothing at all.

29

Lois

Lois sees the tail end of the blow. Standing on the stage, she has full view of a figure falling to the ground. Maarten. And above him, standing, arm holding a stick...

No, it can't be. She blinks. Surely not? For a second, Lois does nothing. The stick falls. The sound of feet, running away.

'Help!'

The shout into the night is full of fright, and Lois's heart beats quickly, pounding, rising in her chest. This time, she runs towards it, a woman's voice.

'Help!'

It sounds like Marieke.

A man's voice had called out *hello*, and there had been sounds of crying from underneath a tree, over near the hedge. And Marieke has received the letter tonight. What's going on?

Despite the chill in the air and no coat, she is sweat drenched, panicking; a stone snags on her dress, pulls at her.

'Help!' The shout again. It sounds like Marieke.

Please no, Lois thinks, *please nothing happen to Marieke, not here.*

'Marieke?' she calls back. Lois runs upwards, tripping over the uneven ground.

'Lois? Is that you? Come quickly. I followed Maarten down here. But he's unconscious! I can't wake him!'

Chasing the voice, Lois finds Marieke up near the steps. She kneels on the grass, bent over what looks like a body.

'Lois, it's Maarten! Oh my God.'

Lois can see the long body of the DCI sprawled out on the grass. Her hands are shaking. What is going on? Had it really been…

Maarten is face down and curled, as though he'd been reaching out for something before he fell. His right arm is flung outwards from his body; his other arm flat to the floor by his side.

'Maarten!' Marieke screams again, the quiet of the night heightening her call, her fear.

Lois kneels and, putting her fingers to his neck, quickly feels a pulse. At her touch, he stirs. His hands, flat on the wet grass, sink into the ground and he pushes himself up, soaked and soundless, until he pulls out his phone and speaks. 'Liv…'

'Oh, thank God,' Marieke says, sitting back on her heels. She covers her face with her hands. 'Oh, thank God. I thought…'

What had happened? Lois is confused. She'd seen someone in the trees. It's so dark. She can't trust her eyes tonight. Her mind is full of demons, of questions.

Teenagers have been found out here before, smoking,

drinking. And it's Halloween. That's what it must have been. Maybe one of them was taking drugs, and saw Maarten?

Marieke is crying. The tears, missing about her own threat, begin for Maarten. They soak into the night. He sits up and she reaches for him, taking his hand.

'I thought you were dead,' she says. 'I thought you were dead and it would be my fault.'

'Maart!' The call comes from up towards the house. Lois sees Liv running, flat out, in bare feet. She must have kicked off her heels. She's followed by the PC, beginning to overtake her. They scramble down the steps.

'Maart!'

'We're here,' Lois says, shouting out in the dark, wishing she had her phone for a torch.

She doesn't know what to do. Maarten checks the back of his head with his hand, but no blood appears, and he rises with an authority that radiates quickly. He'd been polite at dinner, respectful. Now he's angry. She shivers in the flimsy light.

Aksel has appeared from nowhere and Lois hears Ebba say, 'Christ, what now?' from behind her.

There had been someone in the amphitheatre, Lois thinks. *Someone over behind the stage, under a tree, much further away from the steps. Why?*

Looking round the stone ruins, there's no sign of anything now. What's going on?

Filip and Sophie approach. Filip has thrown up and vomit stains his shirt. He can't walk without leaning on Sophie's arm, and his face is wet with tears. Something has happened between them. Sophie is pale, washed out.

Lois climbs a step higher, scanning the ground, so she misses what happens next. Coming in at the end, Lois hears Liv say, her voice angry and hurt, '...*my* husband.'

Marieke says, 'Sorry, I'm so sorry. I didn't mean...' Usually so composed, intimidating, Marieke is still crying.

And then Aksel whistles, long and low. Lois looks at him quickly. His profile is shaded under the black sky. She's sure she hears him say to someone, 'It's you. I thought I recognised you. Well, well.'

But she can't work out to whom or to what he's referring. The group is tight, slowly loosening, as Liv starts crying. She reaches up to touch Maarten's face. He takes her hand and speaks to the PC. 'Check the grounds. Someone attacked me.'

What is going on?

What is happening in their home?

NOW

30

FILIP

The smell of the helicopter crash floods his nostrils, sharp and familiar. Richard's seat has been thrown part out of the broken door, leaning out of the main body of the helicopter; a stone of a theatre step protrudes where Richard's seat had been. The seat is upended. Curls of polyester leak from it, and metal protrudes, like a blade.

Filip's arm is bleeding, and the dull pain is distant. He's wary as he approaches, shouting, 'Richard!'

He is face down, his body hanging off the seat. *Shit*.

'Richard, can you hear me? Richard, it's Filip, I'm going to release your seat belt. Richard, can you tell me if it hurts?' he shouts again, trying to rouse him as he speaks, quickly fumbling with the seat belt catch, which is hot beneath his fingers. The smell of fuel intensifies.

Released, Richard's body slumps unsupported. Filip knows his neck might be broken, his back...

But the leaking, curling of smoke is even stronger now. Flames dance in his peripheral vision like firecrackers.

The sound of running feet comes fast from behind. Someone is shouting, 'Step back, sir! Step back!'

There are screams loud from the lawn. Sirens. The smoke, like a curtain, cuts him off from the safety of higher ground.

His head spins.

He picks up Richard, carrying him, feeling his body limp. Arms rush and lift them both. A watch lies on the ground, bloodied, its face shattered.

Filip's mind is dense with fumes and thoughts of the crash. Had Aksel seen something? Is that why he'd stood up? Had someone tampered with the helicopter?

None of them had taken Marieke's death threats seriously. What had they been thinking?

Hands pull him, helping him away from the helicopter and the fuel, dense in the air, like its own oxygen.

Richard is in his arms, and there is a tremendous heat surge from behind him. He is thrown forward, lifted.

The bang is loud as he lands on the soft earth, debris spraying in front of him. His head spins and he knows he will pass out. The flames are dancing now, climbing higher, and the fire is overwhelming.

He can't remember if everyone got out.

BEFORE

SATURDAY MORNING, HOURS EARLIER

31

Lois

Lois leans out of the window, sucking in the morning air. It's laced with mist; the damp is cool, relieving the burn on her cheek, the ache in her head. The fields lie flat and empty. It's not even 8 a.m. but nausea had woken her. She's not actually thrown up, but her stomach is ready to overturn at any moment.

They'd got to bed so late last night. Most of the guests had known nothing of the letter. The attack on Maarten had deflated the party atmosphere. There had been a general consensus that it must have been teenagers messing around in the amphitheatre. He was OK. It wasn't a serious attack – at least, it was an attack without serious consequences. But she is determined to put it behind her. Today she would focus on launching the game. Her beautiful game. She's never been prouder of anything. The visuals, the sound! Closing her eyes, she imagines the reactions later, after they take the helicopter to the VR studio. They will be stunned. There's no way they can't be. The interaction with other players, the detail...

This game will be huge. As will the subject – with the game based on the next big studio release, the audience will be massive.

Lois feels the adrenaline overwhelm her. Dizzy, she can feel tears at the back of her throat. Some moments in life feel too big. Too unreal. In a few hours, with the confidential press conference ahead of Monday's announcement, every dream she has ever had will be realised.

And as for last night? She shakes her head. Lois had decided the sounds of crying and vomiting under the trees must have come from Filip and Sophie. He'd been red from tears and covered in sick. Sophie had looked raw, too. There's some tension there.

But the figure she had followed down the steps…

She had no idea who that had been. In the end, they'd all been out there. It had been impossible to tell who'd appeared after the attack, or before.

Once inside, she'd sat with Marieke; Aksel had sat with Liv. Maarten had brought in more officers and the grounds had been checked, but there had been nothing.

And yet, Lois knows that Ebba had started the teenager whispers, worried that people may leave, that the deal might be affected. Nothing is clear.

Maarten had been attacked at their home and something is rotten about this weekend.

This morning she'd taken another test. The blue line is clearer than yesterday. Staring at the trees that fringe the huge lawn, she counts in her head the weeks since her last period.

She'd been at a conference, listed as a speaker, so

there it was, in black and white. That was almost nine weeks ago.

Then it had been easy. Working the rest out. She'd been with Helen for a while, and the only other person she'd been with was the fling the day after Helen had broken up with her. Rebound sex. He'd been sexy. Sexy sex. No hint he'd cared, but it had been cathartic. At least, it had felt like it then. Now, regret stirs with the acids in her stomach.

Leaving the windows open, she sits on her bed, pulling her legs up and wrapping her arms around them. He'd not been kind so much as practised. He'd taken his time. She shivers as she thinks of it. He'd been a treat to herself. Like ice cream on a hot day. You know it's not good for you.

She'd seen him on the beach that morning and, initially, she'd hoped he wouldn't come over.

The previous day, her presentation had gone down well and then Helen had dumped her. She was on a high and a low, spiralling. But he'd come over, and she hadn't even bothered getting up from the lounger.

He'd ordered drinks for them, *to celebrate*, he said. He'd told her how impressed he'd been with her presentation, and she'd seen it in his eyes, the glimmer of interest that hadn't been there before.

After a cocktail, heady with success from the speech – not her comfort zone at all – she began drinking in his flattery, his praise, which was precise and careful in its detail. It hadn't taken too long. She'd known about two hours ahead of the actual event. She'd agreed with herself she was allowed a holiday fling.

And also, with the sun on her legs, with the cocktail

in her blood and with the presentation behind her, she was due a release. The exchange with Helen had been exhausting the night before. They'd both known. She'd cried. Both had pretended it had meant something.

It had been a cliché almost, their flirtation on the beach. Like seduction by numbers. Tracing her foot with his finger, suggesting lunch at the hotel. Then a pre-lunch drink on his balcony, so he could grab a shirt. She'd almost laughed at how much of a cliché it had been.

He'd asked room service to send up champagne and canapés. She'd only been wearing a bikini and her beach throw, and he'd never bothered putting on the shirt.

It was not the usual kind of thing she did. He wasn't the usual kind of man she was attracted to. But it had felt like grown-up sex.

She was normally drawn to ideas, to a characteristic, a quality that seemed unique. She liked difference in her partners: artists, gamers.

It had been everything she'd expected, and she'd allowed herself to enjoy it all. He'd done everything right. He'd played her out in full, taking his time.

She'd stayed the whole afternoon. In fact, she'd only slipped away after he'd run her a bath and ordered room service, which they ate, cross-legged on the bed, wearing barely anything at all.

The death knell had come when the quiet arrived, and she'd clammed up, her shyness returning. He already looked bored. The sex over – raw and satisfying – once his flattery had run its course, he didn't bother saying anything at all.

Borrowing a T-shirt from him, she'd made her way down the thick-carpeted corridor to her room. And that had been that. She pulls the T-shirt round her now. To warm the baby.

Now, there's magic. There is a spark of life in her belly that will kick and flair, if she keeps her fingers crossed. How much she'll need to tell everyone else…

There are months to think of that. He is not who she'd have chosen. She's not sure she wants to tell him. He doesn't seem the type to care.

She's always wanted to have children, in a kind of arbitrary way, at some point that seems just ahead of her, but never quite arrives. Now it's real, she wants this baby. But how will she cope? She's never been good on her own.

Lois thinks of her parents. How they would have celebrated.

She has time. It's their secret right now. Hers, and this cluster of cells that cling and feed off her, in her very first act of motherhood.

They just both need to survive this weekend. To avoid the poison that eats into their celebration, seeps into her calm.

32

MAARTEN

Liv is still asleep when he leaves. He'd left a mug of tea by her bed, but it will be cold when she wakes. He hates leaving her after the row. They very rarely row. But she'd been so drunk; he convinced himself there hadn't been any point in telling her the whole truth, not then.

Trust is solid, until it's not. And jealousy can spread like a virus.

Luckily, he thinks, she'd been so very drunk, it had been over quickly. She'd fallen asleep in the car on the way home after the hospital had checked his head, and she'd woken at the house with her contact lenses dry and a raging thirst.

'I'm sorry,' he'd said, and he had been. He still is.

'What were you doing out there with her in the first place, Maart?'

'I wasn't outside *with* her...'

But she'd not been listening. She'd been tired. And raw.

'And you know what else I heard?' She'd not finished; she'd looked away. Mute.

'I'm sorry,' he'd said again. He's not really sorry for

anything last night. He was doing his job. But he is sorry that he still hasn't really told her everything. It was all long before her, but it's leaching into the present now.

'Marieke has...' She paused. 'No. I'm too drunk. Let's not do this now. We'll talk in the morning.' Maarten could hear anger in her voice. Had Aksel said something? But what could he say? What did he know?

There's traffic up ahead and he curses. Adrika is meeting him at the house; Sunny is heading to the station. He's asked Sunny to bring in the six members of catering staff that had been working last night. They'd taken Alison's statement, but it will be useful to speak to her again today, see if anything else has occurred.

He'd told Lois to keep the house closed until the serving staff were cleared. The house guests were the only ones on site.

He can't shake the feeling that it's one of the guests. No fingerprints were on the letter itself, other than his and Lois's. It had been the same for each letter – no prints. The super had been clear: *No reason to hoist the red flag with any urgency. It could just be another letter with no real consequences. Remember the level of investment in the local area, Maarten. We cannot play this wrong, or jump in too soon.*

And why had he gone outside? He'd seen someone standing on the grass, but whoever it was had been knocked clean out of his head. He touches his bruise. Tender.

'Morning. How's the head?' Adrika is waiting for him.

He shrugs. 'So-so.'

'Do you want me to go back and take statements from the staff once I'm done?' Adrika asks, as they climb the steps.

'Yes, just have a quick look round here first. Get the lie of the land.'

Iqbal and Ebba open the door.

'Most of the guests are asleep,' Iqbal says.

'We can wait,' Maarten says.

'Please, Maarten. Please don't cause too much of a fuss, unless it's absolutely necessary?' Ebba asks, her face tight, her hand on his arm. 'We're due to speak to the press just before lunch, and Marieke has been receiving these threats for a while. Marieke doesn't want the deal delayed any more than we do. We're showing we can abide by the new code of conduct she wants adopting. If we delay announcing the deal, then the letters have worked. We need to stand firm...'

It is a tiny speech, but delivered clearly, and it is much of what Marieke had said the previous evening. And what the super had said on the phone.

'Even if it seems it came from inside the house, ma'am?' he'd asked.

'Conclusively, then maybe, but we don't know that. All it would take would be a bribe and the package could have been sent to any member of the catering crew. And have we ruled out the drivers of the cars?'

She was right. They needed to go through all those steps first.

'Ebba, as I've said, no one is to leave and no one to

be admitted to the house – the press conference is on the lawn. But no, we're going to leave statements until after the press briefing. To be honest, they will be in no fit state to remember what happened last night for a while anyway.' He thinks of Filip. 'Let them have breakfast first.'

They walk around the back of the house to speak to the uniforms.

'Nothing, sir.'

Adrika scans the garden. 'It's beautiful. And that's the helicopter they're leaving in later?' She nods down to the garden where the lawn lies open, flat, and sitting in the centre is a sleek black helicopter. It's almost like a large toy.

'Yes, apparently it's a hybrid. Brought in for the weekend. They're flying to these games after lunch, after the press briefing. Then back to the house to celebrate with a Halloween dinner.'

'Has it been checked?' Adrika asks.

Nodding, Maarten walks towards it. 'Yes, it was done first thing. We're keeping an eye on it. Everywhere is checked.'

'They're vicious, aren't they?' Adrika says, as they walk down the October lawn, the ends of the trees holding their red leaves like fistfuls of ribbon. 'The letters. Calling her a whore, a slut. The creepiness of her being watched. The personal detail.'

Nodding, Maarten turns back to the house, its stone looking secure, impenetrable. 'Yes,' he says. 'It's what they convey – the spite behind them. That's the unnerving thing. I don't know what I am expecting, but it's bad.'

'Do you really think it was kids last night? Your head?'

He looks up. The sky is clear. 'No. I don't know. I saw someone walking down, so I followed them. It can't have been teenagers, I don't think – when the gates are locked, the lawn can't be accessed from outside. Not without some difficulty.' He touches his head. 'But when I got to the amphitheatre, I heard someone else crying under a tree. That could – I suppose – have been a teenager up to no good. I started to move towards the lone figure, but then I remember nothing. I don't know what happened. Maybe I fell? Maybe I tripped and banged my head? The blow wasn't hard enough to do anything other than knock me down. I don't know…'

He's sure he was hit. But it had been so dark.

The air smells of a bonfire somewhere, five days early. Fireworks will start soon, once the witches and the ghouls are safely tucked back in the drawers.

'I'll have a word with the PCs and then head back to the station,' Adrika says.

Nodding, Maarten looks up at the house. 'Good idea. Let's start the interviews at five. They should have finished the games by then.'

'No one seems particularly concerned. That in itself seems strange,' Adrika says.

'I think they're all focused on the deal. From what I can gather, there's a lot of money involved for most of them. Myopic money – all you can see.' He shrugs.

'Call if you need anything.' She heads up.

Maarten watches Adrika walk away. A sound makes him jump, and he turns to see Aksel running at speed up the lawn.

'Maarten,' he says slowly, breathing heavily, leaning his arms on his knees and bending to rest. His sportswear is slick and expensive. He wears a large watch, which he checks as he stands.

'Aksel, how are you?'

Upright, Aksel's breath floods from his mouth like smoke, and he doesn't answer immediately, looking at Maarten long and hard.

'How's the head?' he says.

'So-so,' Maarten says, thinking that it is still tender, but he stops his hand from rising instinctively to touch it.

'Any idea what hit you?' Aksel asks.

Shaking his head, Maarten says, 'No idea. Maybe it was some teenagers, messing around in the amphitheatre. We checked the area and nothing seemed amiss.'

'So not one of us, then?' Aksel asks.

Maarten feels cold; it creeps into his bones quickly, making him shiver. He's been out in the garden for a while now and the temperature has dropped today. It's thinking of last night, he reasons, wanting to head back inside, but Aksel seems on the point of something, so he stands quietly, waiting for whatever it is.

It doesn't take him long.

'Last night, with you injured, and Marieke looking after you... It made me think of something from years ago.'

Looking at him, Maarten knows now why the cold is suddenly so pressing. He knows now why he shivers. He says nothing.

'Marieke and you. I remember. There was a night, years ago. Over twenty years ago. It was late. I'd been at

Marieke's. You knocked on the door. You were carrying flowers.'

Unmoving, Maarten feels the cold clutch harder. Stone cold.

'Wasn't that the same night one of your own died? It was all over the press. I looked it up this morning. Your name was in there.'

Maarten can't speak.

'I was thinking about it. How close it was to Marieke's. Can't have taken you long to get there. Funny,' Aksel says. Then he smiles, like a shark. 'Anyway, I'm getting cold after my run. Time for a hot shower, I think. Good to have you on board this weekend. Always a relief to have someone around who'll keep an eye out for me. When they know it's good for them. See you later?'

There's no backward glance. No look at what he'd left behind.

So, it had been Aksel.

That man in Marieke's apartment. That night. It had been Aksel. Aksel knows.

Aksel knows *all* the details.

The world, as Maarten knew it only a day ago, spins on its axis. Knocked off, speeds up.

Now he joins the rest of them. Those whose colour fires up in Aksel's presence. Those who hate him. Have reason to fear him. Maarten is no longer impartial.

33

FILIP

Filip's mouth is paper dry and his head aches. Like someone's built a road straight through it and the traffic is at rush hour.

Pausing outside of Marieke's door, he raises his hand to knock. It opens, and Aksel steps out, smiling at the sight of Filip. 'Filip! Morning, how's the head?'

Caught out, Filip stumbles out a reply. 'Sorry, I thought... Marieke?'

'Yes, this is her room. I'll leave you to it. Shall I come and get you in about fifteen minutes? We need to head downstairs.'

The door open, Filip sees Marieke walk slowly over to the coffee machine, fill a cup.

'Ah, Filip.' She doesn't look at him, lifting her cup, staring out of the window over the green grass and the marine-blue sky.

He steps into the room. He's just left Sophie, asleep, hair spread on the pillow, and he knows that something important happened last night. Something had fixed itself between them, he just can't remember what. They'd had sex. Real sex. Not sex where he feels she's taunting him. Not sex where he fails, and he flees. But real sex. Sex that had meant something. And he'd done it right, all the way to the finish. For the first time in almost a year.

Something had fixed itself between them, and he feels like he can walk tall. He feels like he has shed a skin. Despite his hangover, he feels new. He can't remember anything else. Something happened, and he dares to hope.

Quietly, so as not to disturb her as she is silent, not looking at him, he says, 'Marieke, I came to apologise. To say…' He stalls.

She lifts her head, raises one eyebrow and shakes her hair back. 'To say what?'

'Well, yesterday. The phone call. I shouldn't have taken it when you were there. It wasn't very respectful.'

'Oh, Filip. No, no it wasn't.' She turns to stare out of the window, and he thinks he's never seen her back so ramrod straight.

'I am sorry, Marieke, I—'

She stops him, holding up her hand. 'What do you think you've been doing, these last few months?' Marieke cocks her head to one side, slowly turns to face him.

'Sorry?' His head pounds and he feels left behind. 'Doing?'

'Filip, you've been confiding in me. About everything. We've had late-night dinners. You've been telling me over and over that you're going to leave your wife. You've told me I'm your best friend.'

'Yes.' He's still confused. 'Well, you have been. I've been so grateful. Marieke,' – he steps forward and reaches for her hand – 'you've been a lifesaver...'

She pulls her hand back, flipping him away. 'Stop, Filip. Stop. What kind of message do you think you've been giving me?'

'What do you mean?'

'I'm the first one you call. I'm the one you've taken out for dinners. I'm the one you've bought late-night drinks for. I'm the one! You've made me feel like *I'm the one*, Filip. That's what all this has felt like. And now – I saw you look at her last night. She's the one. *She's* the one, Filip. Then where does that leave me?'

'But I never said...?' He shakes his head.

Like a flash of flame, her arm lifts, darts, and she throws her glass across the room. It shatters hard, and she leans in, screams at him, in his face. 'You never said? You never said? You told me in a thousand ways! What is this? *Kak!* You never said? You couldn't have been clearer, Filip!'

Her hands shake. She takes a breath.

He watches her, stunned. The idea rocks him. But the situation rearranges itself with her words; he looks at it again. At his actions.

How naïve he has been. How disrespectful. Christ, if Sophie had known...

'Look at your texts,' she says. 'Look at how many you send me. And tell me, have you never compared me to your wife and, in your head, picked me?'

Stung, he thinks of looking at them both last night. That

Sophie was the more beautiful, but that Marieke made him feel he was enough. And that had been all he had wanted. He can feel himself flush red, hot.

She nods, her eyes full of scorn. 'You have. You have leaned on me. You have mentally picked me. And *don't* say I'm wrong, but if you had managed to leave your wife, it would be because you thought you could possibly come to me.'

His mouth falls open slightly. She arches an eyebrow, watching him read the truth.

And the truth is prickly and uncomfortable. He thinks of yesterday, of the whisky in his room. Had he been on the verge of saying something? Had she? Fuck, she had read him before even he himself had known.

'And then you take a call from your wife, you take a *phone sex* call, when I'm in the room. I think we all know where we stand now.'

'Marieke! I'm…'

'Time to leave, Filip.' She turns away from him. 'Time for you to go. Enough.'

There's no point in saying anything else. He hadn't thought about it in those terms. It had never been physically sexual. He'd never thought of it as any kind of betrayal of Sophie. It had never occurred to him. He can't read people. He can't read himself.

He worries quickly about how it could seem, being in her room. He doesn't want to be a predator.

'Marieke, I never meant any of this. I'm so sorry.' And he backs out, stuttering. She doesn't even turn.

The door slams behind him.

'Filip? Heading down for the meeting? You called it, didn't you? Come on, we'll be late,' Aksel calls from the end of the corridor.

Feeling shell-shocked, smaller than he has for a while, coated in shame like someone has dressed him in goose fat and feathers, he listens to Aksel talk of the countryside, of the runs here.

The numbness creeps back. Who is he to be happy? So capable of hurting others.

Pushing the door, the office is quiet as he enters, and they're all sitting round. Ebba rises and greets him. 'Morning, Filip. Did you get some breakfast?'

He nods, sitting down at the table with Aksel, and Lois looks up, smiles. The prototype is on the table, and he picks it up, knowing he is pleased with what he sees. The design is sleek. It's made of recycled plastic and the materials don't feel flimsy in his hands. It feels expensive but just undercuts the leading competitor; the quality of the experience is unmatched. And of course, the games – those brilliant games. Lois is so observant. No one notices details like her. These games are alive with all the senses. She misses nothing from life.

His head is still swimming with a hangover and with thoughts of Marieke. How must she have felt yesterday? Knowing everything she knew, and seeing him answer Sophie's call?

He forces himself to focus on the VR set. Just holding it, he can feel himself wanting to smile, but even in here he feels branded. He's such a fool, now, even with work. They must be laughing at him. Ruben had been clear:

Aksel is reportedly getting the better deal. And work is his safe space. Here he doesn't go wrong. Here he can read situations like crystal.

'You look tired this morning,' Aksel says, shaking his head, raising his eyebrows. 'Do you want to start? You had some concerns?'

The other faces wait for him politely. His mind is playing tricks.

Nodding, Filip finds and holds on to the feeling he had, of being part of something promising and exciting. He needs to stop his troubled brain leaking into the day.

Lois pours him a coffee, nodding at the controller on the table. 'It's good, isn't it,' Lois says. 'I'm so pleased with how it's looking. I always worry that when it enters mass production the quality might slip, but if anything, it feels better.'

'Quality slippage? With our products?' Ebba says, in mock horror. 'What is this of which you speak?'

They laugh, and Ebba smiles at Filip, encouraging him again. 'You had a few questions? What a good idea to go over the details one more time before we speak to the press.'

Filip nods, glancing at the clock. It's 10 a.m. and the confidential press briefing is set for 11 a.m.

'I've heard...' – and he laughs, to indicate how unreasonable it would be – 'that Aksel has been given a much better deal than me.'

They all laugh, but there is tension around the table.

Aksel starts. 'Filip, I'm sure, like me, you're aware of the basics of the deal. We're all signed off on the PR statement.

We're both paying fifty million GBP for our shares. Then we have separate distribution agreements?'

'Yes.' Filip taps his pencil on the table. He takes his time.

'But I've heard...' – he lingers over the words, smiling – 'heard rumours that the distribution rights are different. In effect, I've heard that Aksel is being paid forty per cent more than me for the distribution. Because of this, over the next four years, Aksel will effectively get a large chunk of the shares for free. And if that is the case, then I'm not sure I'm ready to announce at all.'

He lets it sink in. No one says anything, and he looks to Lois for support. Not that he needs it, but he trusts her. And he knows instinctively she will be on his side if this is the case.

And he's not wrong. 'Ebba, you're more over the details than me, but I know that isn't the case. I'm sure we can reassure Filip.'

Watching her, he sees that Ebba's colour has altered a fraction. What is it – does she hesitate before replying? He doesn't look at Aksel at all. Whatever the situation is, he won't let anything slip. And nor would Filip, if the situation were reversed. But if Archipelago is messing him around, he won't hesitate.

'Look, Filip, if you're nervous, then let's arrange another meeting to go over the distribution deal at a later date. I think we can all agree we've worked long and hard to get where we are?' She looks round the room.

Filip nods.

'And I think I can say that we're all on board with what we're doing here – we like the product, we like the franchise deal that we're signed up to?' She speaks the last line easily, lightly. No one is reluctant to get started on the launch of the new game, timing with the release of the next film. Their franchise contract is very generous.

Filip mulls.

'If we delay the confidential press announcement, we don't want to cause jitters about our ability to fulfil the demand.' She closes on a strong point and Filip can feel himself sway. She's not wrong. Loss of confidence can kill a deal faster than anything.

'So, we go ahead? And I promise to go over the distribution with you later?' Ebba glances at him, but also round the table. 'Lois? You're happy? We'll get the lawyers back in, go over the distribution contract and iron out any issues. We've kept the deals closed, and I don't think this is the place to open everything up – we simply don't have time. But I promise you, we can look at that side again? Next week?'

Lois nods, and so does Filip.

'I'll have Ruben set something up in the next few days?' he says.

'Absolutely.' Ebba smiles.

There's a knock on the door. 'That will be my reminder. Maarten Jansen is here with a few questions.' Ebba rises, looking round the room. 'I'll have to go,' she says. 'I think we're all set? I'll let the press know to expect us as planned.'

She exits.

'Good decision,' Aksel says, and it is this, and the tiniest smile at the corner of his mouth, that reawakens the hangover in Filip, the crushing weight of his sense of a need to fight. Fight against the apathy and acquiescence that is draining everything he used to be. He sees Aksel again, with his arm around Sophie. He's never known if she slept with him on their honeymoon. If she had, it would kill him. Aksel has already robbed him of his self-esteem, his confidence with Sophie. Months of failed sex, embarrassment, shame. Months of it. And he's been close to throwing it all away. It's eaten into him. He can't roll over on this too.

'No,' he says, standing up. 'I do want to think about it. I'm not speaking to the press just yet. I'll speak to Ruben. Give me a couple of hours.'

'Oh, for fuck's sake,' Aksel says. 'This is the big league now, Filip. There's an international spotlight on this.'

But Filip leaves the room. His hands are shaking.

'Filip!' It's Lois. She runs after him in the hall. 'You do whatever you need to do, I'm not going to pressure you. Look, I have something to show you. It's not about the deal,' she says. 'Do you have five minutes?'

Nodding, the weight of the morning crushes his brain.

She opens the heavy front door and steps out into the damp, and the freshness of the morning is a physical relief; wetness clinging to the air like it's pulling on an autumn coat.

The mist sits low over the trees as they head towards a clump of willows, whose arms fall and curve to the ground like they're shielding their young. Standing next to them,

Lois gives him a headset device, to cover his eyes and his ears. It's sleek, padded. It's lighter than he was expecting.

'Try it,' she says.

'What, here?' He glances around but her excitement is infectious.

'Yes, try it. Put it on as normal. It's fully charged. The graphics are all programmed into the headset – you can take it outside. And here, these gloves too; they have panels in the fingertips. Then you control the panels like this.' She points at the raised keys. 'Look, you can feel the different buttons, they've shapes. It's for inside or outside. It's a new mindfulness programme. You don't *need* to do it outside, but I like feeling the grass under my feet. It's better—'

He's picking the headset, feeling the buttons, and he slips it over his head.

And the world changes. He feels the stress ebbing away. This is what he loves. This is a product he believes in.

The screen opens up and he chooses his location. He picks a mountaintop, and birds fly above him, the sound sliding with them. He turns his head up to see them, and they're heading towards the horizon. The sun flashes, and he has to duck his head slightly, blinking. Changing locations, he's in a rainforest. He walks forward, hands outstretched. There's a waterfall ahead and, as he reaches out, there's a light spray on his fingers.

'But how?' he asks.

'Do you like it? It's built on the same principles as the superhero game, but I've moved the sound and touch qualities across to encourage mindfulness. You can be anywhere, in your own room. We can market it as aiding mental health. It will help those who feel isolated. We all want the games, but we also just want to feel as though we're outside, somewhere else. You really feel it, don't you?'

Filip nods. He switches to a beach, and the sound of the waves laps ahead of him.

'Lois, this is something else. And we will bring this out soon, once the game is launched?'

'Yes. We'll need to agree it. We're all shareholders now, but I want to run a demonstration soon. Iqbal's been working really hard with me – we've worked round the clock recently.'

And Filip feels his indecision wavering again. 'I feel like I own the world in here.'

'Yes, it's a way to really reach out in nature, from the most urban of rooms. And you can join friends here. Even those from other countries. Face-to-face connection is important, and now we can do it side by side.'

He's lost at sea, he thinks, watching the waves lap before him. He needs anchoring.

34

MAARTEN

Maarten's head throbs. Marieke goes to reach out, but seems to think better of it and instead asks, 'Does it hurt?'

'It's fine,' he says.

She looks tired today. He feels exhausted. Wrung out. The garden is colder. October seems to realise it's drawing to a close, paling, stepping out of the way for November's chill. He plunges his hands in his coat pockets, digging for warmth.

'What do you think? Really? I've asked Ebba to cancel today. If it were up to me, we'd shut the day down. Someone has found a way into the house, via the staff.' He pauses, not wanting to scare her. 'Or maybe, even the guests themselves. Don't discount it, Marieke. Someone is here to maybe hurt you. It could be closer than you think – they could be closer.'

He thinks of the guests round the table. Of the tension in the air. He thinks he doesn't want Marieke to be hurt. Not just because he's protecting her and it's on his watch: she meant something to him once and that still counts.

Lifting her head, she stares at the sky. Clouds skit quickly across the pale blue.

There must be wind up high, Maarten thinks. They will need to think about the helicopter ride later. But he can't control the skies. He's pushing against his boss, Ebba, and even Marieke. He wants it all shut down, because it doesn't feel right. It feels dangerous.

'I think we should just go ahead,' Marieke says, still looking upwards. 'I hear what you're saying. It could be close to home. But there's a lot at stake here. Archipelago have made a big public statement reducing their slavery footprint and trying to pay a living wage, all the way down the chain. You know how much that costs? And yet they're thriving and won the franchise by standing up for those values. They're proving it's possible and beneficial. I'm trying my best to make the world follow suit.'

Her eyes, brown and serious, are steady. 'This is important to me, Maarten.'

She kicks a pile of leaves. The trees wave in the breeze; more leaves fall, brown, orange and twisting in their descent. 'It's important.'

With a last look at the helicopter, they head to the house. Maarten's feet land heavily on the grass. He drinks in the crisp air. The heat from yesterday has fallen away.

Lois's laugh sounds clearly across the garden. She and Filip stand in a cluster of trees up ahead.

Maarten and Marieke make their way towards Aksel, sitting outside the huge French doors at the table that overlooks the garden. Coffee and croissants are laid out, and Ebba steadies herself, with a tray of cakes and biscuits.

'Let me help you.' Aksel rises, taking the tray from Ebba.

Maarten pulls out a chair, waiting for Aksel to say something. Will he say anything? Surely he wouldn't have mentioned it earlier, if he wasn't planning something?

Sophie appears at the door, leaning against the frame for a second.

'Coffee?' Ebba asks, filling cups.

'Hello. How lovely you could join us this morning!' Sarah greets Maarten with kisses on each cheek, and he shakes hands with Richard. They both pull up a chair at the table. Maarten tries to smile. A weight of responsibility sits between his shoulder blades, cutting.

'We've just walked down to the Roman theatre. It's beautiful,' Sarah says, her arm looped through Richard's. 'If you get a chance, you should visit. It's like an amphitheatre, but it's actually the only Roman theatre in Britain – it has a stage, which I think is the difference. We've seen a few things there, over the years.' She aims this last part at Marieke, and they all settle into their chairs, the iron feet scraping against the stone terrace. Maarten sees Filip wincing at the sound as he climbs the steps with Lois.

'Tea? Coffee?' Ebba calls. 'We have something stronger for anyone who wishes. Lois is bringing cocktails out in a little bit. Not everyone had a chance for breakfast, so croissants are here too.'

The breeze gusts Lois and Filip up the last steps and Sophie pulls a thick cardigan round her shoulders, offering her cheek to Filip as he pulls out a chair beside her.

Like miasma, the previous evening hangs as everyone

assembles around the table. Filip's eyes don't quite meet the group. His face, blank.

Maarten takes a croissant, trying not to look at him too hard. Filip had been the angriest last night when he'd spoken to him, but Aksel is clearly playing his own game. He'd been over-courteous to Sophie, who today looks pale, hugged by knitwear, her hair loose and long.

The croissant melts as he chews and he takes another. He's had no breakfast, and drinking the coffee makes his stomach rumble.

'Looking forward to the games later,' Aksel says, looking at Lois. But Filip stares at him, frowning. Sophie watches Filip. Lois tries to catch Ebba's eye, but she is talking to Sarah. Richard drinks coffee, staring at the helicopter, looking nervous. 'Have you flown in it often?' he asks no one in particular.

Leaning back in the wrought-iron chair, its green cushion soft against his back, Maarten scans the guests. They speak of the weather, of the helicopter sitting much further down the lawn. It looks like a huge drone. Again, he feels caught out of time. Like he's in the setting for a play. Did one of them send the letter? Did one of them hit him? What secrets do they all know? How do they all fit together?

Someone round this table, he thinks, is playing tricks to get what they want. Someone is unbalancing the scales.

He has to unravel it all quickly. Before it's too late.

35

Lois

'We have Halloween treats!' Lois sees Marieke, in casual trousers and boots, coming out of the house with armfuls of something.

'What's this?' Aksel says. He wears a roll-neck jumper and Tom Ford sunglasses, black, and he looks like he could be fresh off the slopes, tanned, relaxed.

Marieke had disappeared upstairs for a sweater and she returns, cashmere snuggled up against her skin, and slips a Halloween mask on her face. 'I've a few, here.' She hands them out. 'I thought we could make a photo – an informal shot before we do the press conference later.'

Sophie takes one, laughing, and pulls a witch's mask over her face. 'Give me a kiss, Filip,' she says, pressing the mask up against his cheek.

There's something different about them, Lois thinks. Last night he had been jumpy; Sophie's fingers – they'd shaken as she'd arrived; and there had been his blush when he'd dropped the lie that she had been ill. Now they seem relaxed, open.

You never know, Lois thinks, *you never know what's happening between people*. Maybe even they don't. She watches Filip reach for Sophie's fingers, then almost as he's about to hold them, he pulls his hand away.

Filip hadn't agreed to release his signature, and she hasn't told Ebba yet. She needs to find a time to do it before they leave in the helicopter.

Ebba is talking to Aksel. They stand slightly apart from the group; his mask is green like a goblin, and her hair stands out blonder still against the black of his clothes.

They really look good together, Lois thinks again. She wonders how she will cope with it, if she loses Ebba to him.

'You want one?' Marieke says, her voice soft at Lois's elbow.

'What about this?' She pulls out a Venetian-style clown mask, which covers the surrounds of her eyes. 'What do you think?'

'Stunning,' Marieke says, leaning in. 'Here, a photo.'

Lois smiles and Marieke whispers quietly, 'Are you feeling OK, Lois? I heard you being sick this morning.'

Stricken, Lois nods. 'I think I must have drunk too much last night,' she says, looking at her toes, glancing at Ebba and Aksel, looking at her fingernails.

'It's OK, I will say nothing,' Marieke says. 'But you can talk to me, if you wish. I suffered terribly, all the way through. They say ginger helps, but sometimes nothing helps. It's a blessing, but not for everyone?'

The urge to come out with all of it is strong. Lois manages to smile. Marieke isn't usually so kind to her. Lois's eyes are wet, she bites her lip. 'A blessing – yes, exactly that. But so soon. Too soon! I'm so happy, but…'

'Say no more. Tell me when you're ready, if you want to. I raised my child on my own. I never regret any of it. I just don't talk about her – avoid the trolls, to keep her safe.'

Biting her lip, Lois shakes her head. 'I know it's too early to trust in anything, but if we make it to the twelve weeks, I'm definitely going through with it – my body, it's different even now.' Closing her eyes, Lois thinks of how fate unwinds. That one afternoon.

'Well then,' Marieke pats her arm, 'you are already fighting.'

Cakes with Halloween faces are passed round. Iqbal winks at Lois as he brings the tray.

'Is it Iqbal? The father?' Marieke asks.

'No,' Lois splutters, cake crumbs spraying from her mouth. 'No, Iqbal is like a brother! But he knows. He's the only one.'

Marieke presses her hand on Lois's arm.

'I can't tell Ebba. Not yet.'

'The father?' Marieke's question is quiet.

'I… I don't know what to say. He was a one-off. A treat. A restorative present to myself. God, does that make me sound terrible?' Lois rolls her eyes.

'Can you get in touch with him? If you want to?'

Lois nods.

'Well then. You have time.'

'Is the father involved with your daughter?' Lois is curious.

Smiling, Marieke says quietly, glancing quickly to the left, 'I've never been married. And no, the father isn't involved. I'm not sure the father even knows she exists. We've done well, the two of us. There's nothing wrong with the number, Lois. Don't forget that. Numbers don't come into it when you love your child. Two is big enough.'

'More cake?' Maarten has appeared and passes round a tray. 'I'm the catering assistant for the morning. Now that I've banned the serving staff from coming in until we've completed the checks and statements.'

He towers over Lois, and she thinks how good it is to have two tall men in her company. She's often as tall as most of them in every room, and there's something about height – you don't realise it until you find yourself smaller. You can hide more. She feels more hidden. It's not an unpleasant feeling.

'Did you bake these yourself, Maart?' Marieke asks, and Maarten laughs.

'I'm very good with rice,' he says, 'and I can baste meat, choose cheese. Not ever been one for cake.'

'Nothing's changed there then,' Marieke says. 'How's the zabaglione coming along?'

'Marieke Visser!'

Lois is surprised to see Maarten laugh hard as he pronounces her name, and she looks from one to the other.

'Do you two know each other? From before this weekend?'

Marieke nods. 'Maarten was a member of my staff, a million moons ago when I worked for the Rotterdam police force, at the central politiebureau. Anyway,' she winks at Maarten, 'one night we had a team dinner. Only it was almost Christmas, and we gave a course to different members of the team. Maarten pulled the ticket for dessert.' She pauses, smiling at Maarten, passing the narrative.

'Not my finest hour,' he says. 'Marieke invited us all to her flat – we all lived in tiny rented boxes. We turned up at this huge, luxurious flat, and I decided to make my dessert there. I picked zabaglione.' He rolls his eyes. 'I thought I was being clever.'

'What he didn't realise,' Marieke continues, 'is that when it says "whisk eggs", it really means with an electric mixer. He went in to hand-whisk some egg yolks, thinking it would only take five minutes, then you mix it with some sugar, some cognac…'

'…Cognac! It's not like I was being cheap!' Maarten says, laughing.

Richard and Sarah join them. Everyone is laughing. Even, Lois thinks, if they don't get the whole story. It's that kind of laughter.

'So off he trots, after some fantastic course of duck…' begins Marieke.

'…We decided no turkey for us,' Maarten says. 'And there had been at least two courses before that. I thought I had it made. Zabaglione is more a drink and dessert. How hard can it be?'

'And after twenty minutes, I go into the kitchen, and there he is: red-faced, bent over a bowl of split egg yolks and sugar. He's practically crying into the food.'

'I'd had a fair bit to drink!'

'So, I gave him my electric mixer and the cornflour. If

you mix in a spoonful of cornflour, it helps prevent the mixture from splitting.'

She offers the last bit to Lois, who knows she's standing looking confused. She can make a number of things in the kitchen, but they're all basic, and most involve pasta.

'So, what happened? Did it work?' Sarah asks, fully involved. And Aksel and Ebba have turned their way too. Ebba is smiling, even though she doesn't know the joke, and Lois winks at her.

'I go back in the other room. I pour wine, I tell everyone to be kind. And then...' Pausing for effect, Marieke takes a deep breath and Maarten rolls his eyes, comically, up to the grey-blue sky and back again. 'And then we all hear this scream.'

'It was not a scream!' Maarten says.

'It kind of was, Maart,' Marieke waves her hand at him, looking at her audience, 'but we can call it a cry of desperation if you like. Anyway, I rush in, and there he is. He's plugged in the mixer, shoved it in the shallow bowl he was using, and turned it on. Everywhere. The eggs are everywhere. He was cooking for twelve of us. That's a lot of eggs.'

Hanging his head in shame, even now, Maarten sounds contrite. 'Sorry, Marieke. I'm still sorry.'

'My light fittings,' she says, 'my artwork, my tiles, the grouting – that's the word in English? Everywhere. And while it missed most of his clothes, it was in his hair, all through his hair. Raw egg and cognac.'

The group laugh, pleased to be laughing, delighted that the story is genuinely funny, and Maarten is pink.

Through her laughter, Lois reads his face, reads the whole story.

Interesting, she thinks. *I never would have thought it.*

Aksel stands on the outskirts of the group, drinking. His face is blank, but he looks dangerous. He always looks dangerous.

Lois feels a flash of fear for all of them.

36

Maarten

'It's time for the drinks,' Lois says to Maarten. 'I'll go and bring them out.'

'Let me help. I'm serious. I'm the one who has sent all your staff away.'

Smiling at Marieke, he heads inside. The rest of that night is vivid to him. He'd stayed behind to help clear up. The kitchen had been covered with egg; the floor had been hard. She'd washed his hair in the shower. He'd been so young. That's when it had begun. Their relationship had only lasted three months, but it had been intense, real. And the end had been abrupt. Her running after him in the dark, the night soaked through. And now Aksel could use this knowledge to end his career.

He looks at Aksel, whose gaze must feel his. They make eye contact. Aksel lifts his chin a little, a gesture of... something. Maarten doesn't know what. His entire future sits in another man's hands.

* * *

The kitchen is quiet as they enter, and cocktail glasses sit ready. Names of all the guests have been hand-painted on the glasses, with Halloween faces, the glass paint catching the light of the sun, dappling the walls.

Maarten looks through the huge window, down across the lawn. The helicopter waits on the flat grass.

Pumpkins line the granite worktops, some missing their faces, some with eyes peering through the orange pulp; eyelash strands of pale flesh fall in the gaps that haven't been finished. The smell is sweet.

'Please don't tell me you'll have to finish these on your own?' Maarten looks at them in dread.

'Iqbal and I will. We've done most of the work. We've decided to stay here and get ready. The staff will be back for dinner, hopefully, and after last night it will be good to have some quiet in the house. A few stolen hours before they all return.' Lois nods to Iqbal as he enters.

'Quiet will be good,' Iqbal says.

Lois pours from a heavy glass bottle, the green almost opaque. 'We're out. I'll go to the library and get another.'

Iqbal lifts the first tray of cocktail glasses. 'It's an important weekend for Archipelago. But Lois wouldn't want to risk Marieke's safety. We're not missing the staff too much.'

'Not just Lois who's concerned?' Maarten asks causally.

'Well, of course, Ebba as well!' Iqbal laughs. 'But Ebba is the one driving the company. Lois is excited about it, but Ebba is the one promoting it, pushing it. Lois is the creator. I suppose she's shy about forcing it on people.'

Ebba enters the kitchen, her voice arriving a beat ahead

of her feet, carrying a green bottle. 'Come to help!' she calls, tapping in on the stone floor, sweeping up another tray of drinks. 'Iqbal, thank you, and you too, Maarten. I've sent Lois out. She's looking a bit tired.' Lifting the tray, she looks out of the window. 'Thank God the weather is holding,' she says, half to herself, and then directs her gaze at Maarten. 'And thanks for making sure nothing else will go wrong.' Her brow creases. 'I have no idea what could have happened with the note. I do hope that whichever member of staff brought the letter into the house in the first place confesses quickly. It will be much better for Marieke to be able to dismiss the worry.'

Nodding, Maarten thinks that it will be much easier for everyone else too. He lifts the last tray of drinks to follow Ebba. Iqbal steadies a jug of cocktails on his tray.

'Let's go.' Ebba leads the way. 'I've asked Aksel to lead a toast. Maarten, you must join us!'

Almost at the open doors, Maarten's phone rings, and he puts the tray down. 'Adrika?'

'Nothing yet. The checks have all come back clear. There's nothing on any of the files. The catering company have offered to send in workers that are booked on a different job, and swap the staff, so that if there is anything pre-planned, it will shake things up. I think it's a good idea, sir. What do you reckon? We're almost done with the statements.'

'Yes, do that. But ask them to work on a minimum staff and make sure you run the checks on them too. Also, meet them. Can they turn it round in three hours?'

'They said that's fine. They have a wedding just up the

road and it's just a question of swapping the staff and briefing them. I've already started checks to make it easier. I think we could be ready to bring everyone back in around four hours?'

'Good, that's a relief. The super will be pleased.' Maarten thinks that the party will not quite have returned then. And catering have agreed to prepare off site. It should go smoothly.

Looking outside, Ebba is chatting to the group. Maarten thanks Adrika, picks up the tray.

A twist in the air, the smell of rain, but the sun is winning.

'A toast,' Aksel is saying, 'to the real star of the show. The tech. We have a brilliant game about to launch on a new platform. Archipelago have secured the rights to the next big studio superhero gaming merchandise, and *KnowLimits* is already taking over the teen market. The parents' choice for safety, the teens' for the games. And all of this in the name of humanity. People Before Profits! I feel like I'm saving the world today!'

Everyone laughs. The drinks are handed out and as Aksel lifts his glass, the base of the stem breaks, falling to the floor and shattering. Ebba holds up her hands. 'Hang on, toastmaster!'

In the process of handing Marieke's drink to her, she instead passes it to Aksel, saying to Marieke, 'I'll give you another. He's in full flow so let's not stop him.'

There is laughter, and Ebba lifts the last drink from the tray for Marieke as Aksel raises the glass again. 'To Archipelago, and its brave new world!'

They drink. Maarten smiles, holding his glass. He's on

duty, and he notices Lois holds hers still too.

Chatter breaks out and a pilot appears, coming up the steps, led by Iqbal.

'Almost take-off time, ladies and gentlemen! I'm here to give you a quick briefing.'

'Another photo!' Marieke calls. 'We need one with the pilot as well. Quick!'

The group assembles.

'I'll take it,' offers Maarten, holding out his hand to Marieke for her phone.

'On three, we say Archipelago,' Marieke says.

Maarten lifts the phone, looking at the screen. They're all in, although the pilot is slightly out on the left. The nine of them, and the pilot, ready for take-off, as the deal is ready to fly.

Filip and Sophie walk to the side, near Maarten, as everyone claps once the photo is done. 'I'm not coming,' she says to him and Filip sounds confused as he replies, 'But why? Have I upset you? I'm sorry, I was drunk last night and I had the meeting this morning.'

Maarten tries not to look at them, listening.

'No, Filip, it's not that. I just can't quite face it. Come back to me later? I'm going for a run. Come and find me when you return. Before dinner.'

She steps closer to him, and Maarten turns away, embarrassed at being within earshot.

The pilot is finishing her briefing: 'The most dangerous part is take-off and landing. I just ask you all to stay sitting down and strapped in, like you would on a plane. This will keep you safe and keep the helicopter balanced.'

'You want to join?' Lois asks Maarten. 'There's room on board.'

'No!' Maarten says. 'But thank you. The staff will be back soon. I think you're all good for the afternoon. I'll head back to Liv and I'll swing by once your press conference is all done, and we'll do the statements then.'

Thinking of heading back to Liv, Maarten feels relief. He can relax at home. He can explain it all. It will be good to have told the full story. Cathartic, if not without its shame.

37

FILIP

Sophie brushes his fingers and Filip grabs them, squeezing them lightly. It feels like he's announcing his affection to everyone, despite the briefness of touch. He feels, not sees, Marieke watching him. Exposed and in the wrong. He has promised and let them both down.

He can't speak to Marieke in front of Sophie. She is back, has come back to him. Whatever has happened, has happened. There has been a shift. He doesn't want to parade it in front of Marieke.

For some reason this morning, he can hold Sophie's hand. He can smile at her.

Last night is a blur. He's not really sure what happened. He remembers crying to Liv at dinner. God, the shame. His toes curl when he thinks of it, his stomach sinking in horror.

He remembers Sophie's voice. She had sung and he'd been more a fan than a husband. But then it's always been like that. Maybe that's the problem. He can't bridge the distance to the stage – he feels caught in a crowd. Marrying her had only made the gap wider.

Something had happened last night.

He remembers the air cold and the sky dark. He can remember looking upwards: stars, heavens, galaxies. He remembers looking at it all and feeling like a dot in such vastness. But strangely, it hadn't hurt. Not like it normally did. He thinks again of the ledge. Of hanging, a second from leaving it all behind. Today that scares him. Seems untenable.

He'd definitely been outside. But with Sophie? He thinks so. It's all a blur. Or rather, it's stuck like mud. His mind is thick and stupid – he can't dig out whatever is buried there.

What remains is the feeling that something *good* happened. He feels steadier than he has in months. The deal is complicated; he doesn't know what to do about it, but in himself he feels calmer. Like a see-saw tipping the scales and plummeting down the other side. The load had slid. Emotional confusion had transferred itself to work, and in himself, he feels… calm.

Sophie is standing close to him. Her fingers curl round his thumb, lightly. Her perfume is like musk; he can smell the shampoo in her hair. The sun is pale; steel and sapphire – shafts of light fall, like drapes. The coffee in his other hand is hot and steam drifts upwards, vanishing into the air.

Lois is talking to Marieke. Their heads bend close. Others drift into their groups and the talk turns to laughter.

Marieke will not meet his eyes and in many ways he is grateful, because he doesn't know what to say. Even if he had not intended it, he had indicated a future that he won't deliver. He had used her – leaned on her. And now she is an onlooker to him discovering the love he thought he had lost.

If Sophie is coming back to him, his world has righted itself. He has been lost to her from the start. It's time to begin again.

In fact, he thinks, with a clarity that feels new and real, he is the one causing her the pain. Sophie was open this morning, soft. He'd woken and she'd been in his arms. There had been no anger – nothing to fight against. Maybe he should talk to her about his problems, rather than leaving her each time? If he could speak to her, confront it?

Something had happened last night. Something good. Something truthful. He just wishes he knew what it had been.

'OK?' Sophie asks, stepping closer still; her breath carries honey, strawberries, tea. 'You'll come and find me when you're back? I'll be pleased to see you.'

He nods.

Something good.

38

Lois

'Ebba, I'm not going to come,' Lois whispers. 'Iqbal and I need to get going on the decorations for later.'

'No problem. You look exhausted,' Ebba says. 'We'll be back for the private press conference. I think it's 6 p.m. now. Is that enough time?'

Lois thinks. 'I'll rearrange for around 7 p.m.?'

'Christ, that's late!' Ebba is edgy. Lois knows she hates any changes. It's been planned for so long.

'Maybe, but Filip's still not released his signatures. Did Iqbal not tell you?' Lois tries to remember if she'd asked him to. Her brain is working more slowly at the moment. 'Filip refused. He wants to think about it. He's asked to do it later today.'

'Oh my God, Lois, this is a disaster!' Ebba pales, paper-white.

'No, I knew you'd think that! It's OK – I took him outside, showed him the new mindfulness VR stuff. Blew his mind – I knew it would. I told him it was top secret – for his eyes only. Really – I'm sure he's a safe bet. He just wants to have his moment. I checked again and the investment figures are the same. I don't really know what he's angry about. If they're both paying the same for the shares, what can his beef be? It's a great deal.'

Ebba leans back against the iron table, her hand reaching for Lois's arm. 'I think I'm going to faint. These fucking men. He was fine with the deal until he worried Aksel has a different one. Can't they just stick with what they've agreed? It's all about winning with them. They care about little else.'

'Honestly, Ebba. It's OK, I really think he'll be ready to speak to the press. Let's delay the conference until 7 p.m. You go ahead with this afternoon, I'll stay here with Iqbal. The new staff will arrive at some point. After the press conference, we'll be ready to eat and celebrate.'

'I think I'm going to be sick,' Ebba says. 'I can't...'

'I've got this, Ebbs. Really, the tech has got him. We just need to promise him the deal is fair. But the deal *is* fair, so that part's easy.'

Ebba sways before her, and Lois holds her arm firmly. 'Go on. Head down now. I'll go and get the decorations ready for the party. We will celebrate later. He won't say no, Ebbs. I know it. I can tell.'

She tries to smile at her sister. Sometimes she forgets that she's the elder; she's so used to taking her lead from Ebba. But she can feel the excitement from Filip earlier. It's still sharp. She knows they're on to something big.

Aksel steps up, offers Ebba his arm. 'Let's go!' he says.

A wave of premonition sweeps Lois, but she writes it off as nausea. She wants to shout to Ebba, call her back.

Later, Lois will think that this is the last image she has. All of them standing there, Aksel leading the charge.

If she had shouted, told them all to stop – would they? Could she have stopped it all?

39

FILIP

Filip tightens his seat belt. It's not the helicopter that frightens him – he likes flying – it's the fact that he doesn't know what to do next.

For the first time in a while, he's flailing. When it comes to work, he always knows. Like black and white, he sees things clearly – except now. This indecision is uncharted territory. He feels almost squeamish.

His instinct is usually spot on, and it's telling him to step right back.

The problem is he *wants* to do this. For a change, it's not just a question of money. He loves the product, is excited about it. Loves the concept – he wants to embrace the deal. Yet he feels sticky with it; the corners are darker, grime in places there shouldn't be.

Aksel, a couple of people behind him climbing in, pauses as he heads down to his seat, up close to the pilot. He looks thoughtful, places his hand on Filip's shoulder.

'Let's chat later. I know you have some concerns. I think

it's time to show you the paperwork. I think we can work through this.'

Thrown, Filip leans back, his head up against the cushioned headrest.

'Really?' Can it be that simple?

'Look, Filip. We both want this to go through. You've heard my distribution situation might be different to yours. Why don't we sit down and thrash it out? I don't know your details and you don't know mine. Come on. There's a future with this company, we both know it. If you're not happy with my end, and you're not ready to proceed, then let's sort it out. We're both men who make things happen. Let's make it happen.'

Nodding, Filip's mind is popping, like bubbles on plastic wrapping. Each tiny stress that he had entered the weekend with seems to be bursting. If the distribution can be sorted, and they're on an equal footing, then everything they've worked so hard for over the past couple of years...

The contract is good, the forecast is excellent, the investment is sound. Of this he is sure. Facts and figures are his comfort zone.

'OK, Aksel, if you're ready to properly sit down, then so am I.'

Aksel extends his hand, and Filip takes it. He catches Ebba's eye and smiles at her. It's what they all want – success for Archipelago.

Aksel moves up and takes his seat. He touches Ebba on the arm. Filip looks away. He doesn't want to pry.

The seats run the two sides of the helicopter. Richard is towards the rear, near the door. Aksel and Ebba are up towards the pilot, opposite each other. There are a few empty spaces, meaning they all have a fair bit of room.

Marieke sits diagonally opposite Filip, locking in her seat belt without looking forward: the only pocket of air still trapped in his head, bubbling around.

'Everyone ready?' the pilot calls.

The blades are turning, and Sarah looks white. She closes her eyes; Richard leans and puts his hand on hers.

'Not too late to back out?' Richard says. 'I can ask the pilot to let you out? You could just take the car.'

Sarah shakes her head, lips pressed tight and blanched.

'We'll be fine!' Filip shouts, over the swish of the blades, cutting through the air. The six of them are well spaced in their two sets of threes. The seats are thick black leather, soft, new smelling. The buckles are bright, shiny with fresh polish.

'The way of the future!' the pilot calls. 'And we're off!'

Filip watches the ground lower beneath them, having the sensation of barely moving at all. Then his stomach lifts, and he sinks back against the seat, enjoying the release of rising.

He sees the tops of the trees fall beneath them; the Roman city lies sprawling out, as they rise to join the clouds in their tumbling and scattering. Richard's hand is tight on Sarah's, whose face is pushed back, head pressed into the rear of the seat. She looks green, staring at the ground, her eyes opening and closing slowly.

'Hold on!' Ebba calls, laughing. 'This helicopter is one of a kind!'

'Archipelago takes flight!' Aksel calls.

Flying is as close as Filip gets to feeling free. It's not so much exhilarating as relaxing, and his shoulders settle back; he watches out of the window, thinking of the figures Ruben had sent him, the bare-faced lies he was told that morning. He had been angry, but he never does anything when he's angry. Decisions are about rational action. Everything can wait.

A shout comes from up ahead.

It's not clear what's happening, but Sarah screams. He looks to her first. But she's looking to the pilot. She shouts, 'What's wrong?' and he realises her fear is coming from the noises at the front of the helicopter.

A shout again. Craning his neck, he sees it's Ebba shouting. The noise of the helicopter is loud, but he listens, and he can make out part of it: *seat belt*.

And this all begins to make sense, as, despite the take-off, Aksel has stood up. He falls to the side, bent over.

'Put your seat belt back on!' Ebba screams again.

Aksel stands, wobbling. He clutches his chest and his stomach, bending double and lurching forward. He grabs Ebba, opposite, and she looks terrified.

'I...' He doesn't finish.

'Sit down! You'll throw the weight off!' Richard is shouting again.

Now Marieke has joined in the call: 'Sit down, sit down!'

Sarah is crying.

But Aksel howls, bestial.

Something is going badly wrong.

Marieke, opposite Filip, pales, and looks at him with eyes wide and full of fear. He hasn't known how to speak to her since last night, unsure of what is happening, terrified of her wrath. But he leans forward and takes her hand, which she grips tightly. 'What's happening?' she asks, her nails biting tight into his skin.

The sound of the wind rushes outside, like a train.

'It's OK,' he says, and then he looks back to Aksel, who is now bent double, one hand on the side of the helicopter, the other grasping the back of the pilot's seat in front of him.

It isn't going to be OK, he thinks.

Aksel pushes himself off the back of the pilot's seat, and as he turns, he stumbles forward. Time slows, the whirling of the blades slow, and Filip loosens his seat belt so that he can rise to reach Aksel. The helicopter veers slightly as Aksel catches the head of the pilot.

Taking off is the most dangerous part of the journey.

'Fil...' His name is twisted, spat out and dry, and Aksel leans into him, arms embracing him like a lover. Filip smells his breath, smells the adrenaline, smells his fear. Aksel is many shades of pale, light of breath. He pants in puffs, danger signals.

'It was never, meant...' Aksel says, and then speaks in Norwegian; Filip understands most of the words, but they're broken and wrenched out.

'What is it? What is it, Aksel? You've got to sit down! Land the helicopter! Land it now!' Filip shouts to the pilot.

They are caught between heaven and earth; screams and shouts from all around.

'Oh my God! We're going to crash! Oh my God!' Sarah is screaming.

Pushing off, Aksel stands in the middle of the two rows of seats, then falls backwards, managing one step; he collapses hard against the pilot, whose head crashes forward, on to the controls.

'Please, land…' Aksel grabs the controls, wrestling with the pilot as the helicopter swings like a cradle in the sky.

'Aksel!' Ebba screams.

Sarah is crying; Marieke is moaning. Filip feels locked down. His life spins out before him. What has he been thinking? Why has he kept himself so small?

The lurch is sudden, dropping down to the right. There are screams from all around, the sound full of engine noise, of fear; Filip can feel the pilot fighting gravity. They jerk upwards again.

Now Ebba has undone her seat belt and she steps forward towards Aksel, pulling at his waist; she pulls him off the pilot and he falls back down on his seat. His head tips on to the floor in a roll.

But it's too late.

Filip shouts, 'Buckle up!' They are going down.

They're not high enough to have room for error. They're off balance. They're going down.

The pilot is fighting. Fighting with everything she has.

They lurch again, this time downwards to the left, and Ebba falls backwards, landing heavily on the floor. Filip undoes his seat belt and rises, reaching and holding the seat opposite, managing to grab Ebba's shoulder. He heaves her up, pushes her in the direction of her seat. 'Do your belt up!' he shouts. 'We're going down!'

Marieke grabs her seat belt. Her eyes catch Filip's, wide with fear, bright with tears.

His words summon another scream from Sarah, still crying. Richard, white as a sheet, holds her hand and pushes himself back into his seat. He's next to the sliding door, and he turns his face away from it.

Filip manages to push himself backwards and his fingers are quick on the buckle.

His military service training kicks in; he issues commands to those nearest him, holding Marieke's hand, and thinking of Sophie, luminous in his head.

'Brace! Brace!' he shouts. 'We're going down! Once we land, we need to get clear of the helicopter. Undo your seat belt and get out. The fuel will be dangerous. Hold steady. Here we go!'

The lurching is more violent this time, like a roller coaster. Aksel's body slides down, slipping backwards, landing on the floor.

There's no chance of reprieve, the damage is done. The pilot wrestles with the controls, and while the helicopter levels briefly, Filip can feel the momentum has gone. They're spinning.

Down. Plummeting, falling as heavy as stone.

Marieke screams, still grasping the seat belt with knuckles white like snow. The helicopter spins. It picks up pace and the pilot shouts loudly, the rasp of her voice like gunfire through the rushing air, competing with the whir of blades. The slow-motion quality to the falling is like a movie now, with seconds inching slowly. The blades seem to wind down; their spinning and tipping takes hold of the helicopter. It turns in the air, pushing Filip back into his seat. Air rushes in, cold and hard. Opening his mouth is difficult, breathing impossible.

There's a shuddering. A great rattling, and his bones shake. *We'll be shaken apart*, he thinks, and he closes his eyes.

The rotor's gone. Leaning out and looking down, he starts shouting how far he thinks they are from the ground.

'Thirty metres!' His shout enters the cacophony and he has no idea if the pilot can hear but he carries on. 'Twenty metres!'

They're close enough to survive, even land, if the pilot can hold it. The spinning flings him further to the back of the seat. His eyes close again and he forces them open. *Stay alert, stay alert.*

As they fall to the earth, he catches a glimpse of the others in the edge of his vision. Fingers grip tightly to anything they can touch. Mouths offer prayers.

'Brace, brace, brace!' he shouts.

The noise of the falling is so loud he thinks they must have crashed into the ground, and he opens his eyes just as the black of the helicopter meets the earth.

40

LOIS

The explosion lights in a flash. Screams around her are loud, as vivid as the flames; like a mini sun, the fire forces her to turn her head, colours bright and sharp. They bite like hot metal.

'Ebba,' she cries, standing and running towards the fire. It has been the two of them against the world for so long. She cannot lose her sister. 'Ebba!' she screams. The heat beats her back.

She sees Iqbal, making his way slowly, bent, with Ebba on his arm. Both of them walking towards her, dark against the bright flames.

'Ebba!'

Sirens are loud behind her.

She sinks to the ground, holding her sister, who is conscious but shaking. Hugging her, trying to calm her, dropping tears as she says her name over and over, 'Ebba, you're OK. Ebba, Ebba...'

So many people running now. So much smoke.

Lois strokes Ebba's brow. She sits cross-legged on the

high seats of the amphitheatre. Ebba stirs beneath her hands and she cradles her head. The fire before her makes the surrounds shimmer, unsettles every horizon.

'Did Aksel get out?' Ebba asks, her lids opening slightly.

'I think so,' Lois answers, desperate to reassure her. 'And Filip, and I saw him carry Richard. I haven't seen Sarah. But Iqbal brought out Marieke.'

'I went for Aksel and started to pull. He was unconscious…' Ebba's voice is weak.

'Shhh, it's OK, I'm sure I've seen him,' Lois says, thinking that she had seen Filip dragging him out earlier. What she does see, but can't say, her heart rising towards her mouth, is that Filip is bent over a mound of a body nearby. The helicopter is burning on the stage, but higher up, Filip is giving someone mouth-to-mouth. Whoever it is, she doesn't know.

What has happened? How can it have come to this?

Filip is pumping the chest now.

The smoke on the lawn is thick and obscures her view; Lois turns her head away. Anxiety tight. She can't see if the body is male or female. She looks back quickly, not knowing what to do. Filip is bending repeatedly over the body.

Lois glances to her left, where Marieke lies. Iqbal had brought her first, and Lois had checked her breathing and laid her in the recovery position. She is unconscious but her pulse is strong and Lois couldn't see any serious bleeding beyond scratches.

Ebba has not lost full consciousness, but drifts between disorientation and lucidity, sleepy and jumpy.

She opens her eyes again now. 'Filip? Is he OK? It's all my fault. If only…'

'He's with the others. He's helping them.' Lois looks again, but doesn't want to say that Filip is now banging with his fist on the chest. The ribs must be breaking beneath those hands. There are two others helping now. They're not stopping. But it's been a few minutes.

Watching with growing horror, she tries to even out her tone, to reassure. 'Ebba, you organised an outing, you couldn't know the helicopter would crash. This is not your fault.'

The fire is getting stronger.

There's another figure lying on the grass, at the edge of the Roman theatre, but it's impossible to make anyone out. Whoever it is lies in the recovery position too.

A few metres away, Iqbal half carries, half helps someone up the steps, walking up to the house.

Lois scans the scene. Blood and fire.

Looking back at Filip, it isn't good. He's back to giving mouth-to-mouth. Someone else takes over on Aksel's chest. Filip sits back on his heels. His jacket is off, his T-shirt ripped. The black smoke creeps towards him and his face, already dark, marks a silhouette against the greying grass. He rests, but his stance sinks into sadness, and, with a stab, Lois realises that whoever it is, whoever they are working on, is already dead.

A wind chases the smoke away. Looking back to the body, Lois stares in horror.

She's got no doubt. It's Aksel.

Aksel is dead.

PART TWO

41

LOIS

Broken, Lois watches the fire climb.

Fire crews have arrived, running towards the amphitheatre. The main entrance is via a lane accessed from the main ring road round St Albans, leading to a big estate further up. The red engines hurtle down, all lights and noise.

The ambulance crews enter via their drive and have started to arrive on the lawn. The walking wounded sit; like a MASH unit, paramedics are beginning to assess and attend.

'Can you tell me how many were on the helicopter? I need to check. I didn't see everyone get on.'

Lois looks up into the face of DCI Jansen. He'd been here earlier. He mustn't have left. Or maybe he came back? He's smudged with smoke, sweat glistens black.

'I think six?' she says, forcing herself to concentrate. 'The pilot, Ebba, Marieke, Richard, Sarah, Filip, Aksel… Not Sophie, she's on the lawn somewhere, she didn't go up.' Lois rubs her brow. 'And I didn't go – catering, and I thought I should look after Sophie, after last night.'

'That's seven, not six. Are they all out?'

She looks around, desperate to see. With the smoke, it's impossible to tell who is who. 'Yes, I think so. I haven't seen Richard or Sarah?'

She stands, searching. Ebba sits, her head bent over her knees. Lois stands close to her, letting her sister lean on her legs.

The other figure lying on the lawn is still impossible to make out. Is it Richard?

A few metres away, Iqbal half carries, half helps someone up the steps, walking up to the house, and looking again, it's clear it's Sarah.

'There were seven,' she hears Jansen saying to someone. 'Seven on board. We think they're all out.'

'Ebba.' She takes her sister's hand. 'What happened?'

'Christ, Lois. I feel sick. The shock of it. The falling. I thought it was all over. For a second, I thought I'd be pleased. Just to have everything stop. You know. But God, I wanted to live.' She closes her eyes. 'I thought of Dad.'

Holding her hand, Lois lifts her fingers lightly.

'Did something happen?' she asks. 'On board?'

Ebba turns her face away. 'I don't really remember. I'm so tired, Lois.'

'Pilot's unconscious!' someone in a uniform shouts, and Lois watches a stretcher go past.

'Miss, can I check you?' The face of a young man, a boy, looking barely out of school, kneels before Lois. He moves his hand towards her face; she touches her cheek.

'I wasn't on board,' she says. 'I must be covered in smoke.'

'There's some blood,' he says.

'It won't be mine. Please, there are other people to see.' If anyone is kind to her, she will start crying and she's not sure she would stop.

His partner is already sitting with Ebba and Lois makes space for them, standing up and looking round.

'Marieke,' she says, as softly as she can manage, as softly as she can be heard, against the background noise. She walks towards her as Marieke watches the helicopter burn. She's wrapped in some kind of foil. The kind they put on you after a marathon.

'Oh, Lois,' Marieke says, her eyes red and her face hollowed out, aged. 'Oh, what I have I done?'

42

Maarten

Cordons are going up. They're only just beginning to get a handle on the scene. There are ambulances arriving, even now. The air is acrid with black smoke, biting the back of his throat. Emergency crews flood the scene.

'Maart? It's all over WhatsApp! Tell me you're OK!' Liv answers, her voice strained over the phone.

'I'm fine. I wasn't on board. I just wanted to let you know. I love you, Liv.' There is so much he wants to say, but it can wait. There's noise everywhere.

Adrika runs towards him. Shock stamps itself on her face.

'Oh my God!' Adrika says. 'Are you OK?'

'I helped – I wasn't on board.'

'What happened?' she asks, looking round.

He shakes his head. 'I don't know. I was here, halfway down the drive, when I heard it. It was loud.' He thinks of the smoke, visible in the rear-view mirror. 'But Marieke was on board. It's probably just a crash, but we have to question if this is to do with the letters.' He shakes his head. What had they been thinking, allowing this to go ahead?

'This was on our watch, Adrika. The super will be livid.'

'SOCO are on their way, sir. I just spoke to the Control Centre.'

'The Roman theatre will be the incident scene, as soon as we're able. We need interviews when those who were on board are up to it. There are crews waiting to assess the helicopter, once the fire is out. *Kak*, after the letter last night, the threats! The helicopter was checked earlier, but was it tampered with in some way? Was this just an accident? Adrika, we need to get this right. Can you get Sunny to help with the interviews?'

Maarten sees Filip on the lawn. Sophie sits with him.

'I'll make a start over there,' he says to Adrika. 'Let me know how you get on.'

'Filip?' Maarten says, as gently as he can manage. 'Are you OK?'

'I don't know what happened. What happened?' Filip's voice is hoarse.

Maarten shakes his head, sits down. 'We'll find out. What happened on board?'

'I don't know. I think Aksel was ill? I don't know.'

Maarten raises his eyebrows. 'He was ill? He was fine before.'

Filip shakes his head, his eyes dark like soot, his face smeared as much with confusion as with blood.

'He stood up, on board. I think he knocked the pilot off balance. We're just lucky she brought it down as cleanly as she did. Other than that, I don't know. I just don't know.'

'Why did he stand?'

Filip closes his eyes, tries to visualise it all. It flashes back with frightening clarity. 'He clutched his stomach and his chest. Maybe a heart attack? Maybe food poisoning?'

'He was so healthy.' Maarten looks across the lawn. 'And we all ate the same things…' Maarten thinks of the bowl of croissants on the table. 'Did he say anything? As well as standing up, did he say something?'

Filip frowns. 'He did. I've been trying to remember. It was loud, stuff was going on. I think he said, "*It was never meant…*" and then a few words in Norwegian, no sentences.'

'Everyone's out? And Aksel. Is he…' Maarten doesn't finish, and waits for Filip. There's a pause.

Filip nods. But he is pale. 'They're out. But Aksel's dead.'

43

IQBAL

Handing out water, Iqbal is tense. The fire is getting to him. The pennies are back in his mouth, and he will need to get inside soon, get to his room. It's all come back. The fire, the chaos. The suspicion.

Marieke's words remind him of when Obaidur was rocking back and forth under the desk in the fire; when he'd pulled him out, almost wrenching both their arms, he'd been saying something over and over.

'It's my fault. What have I done?'

And he hears it again. Guilt that somehow it could have been averted. Marieke is muttering, taking the water from him with barely a glance. Ebba, Filip, shells of themselves. He'd helped Sarah up the lawn. Richard had been in one of the first ambulances, but there are more coming, and so far, only the unconscious have been taken.

'I could have stopped this!' Sarah was weeping. 'I knew Richard wasn't happy with the weekend, with Aksel. Why did we ever put ourselves close to a man like that?' She'd sobbed on his arm. 'Thank you, Iqbal, thank you. He always liked you.' Fresh sobbing.

He'd taken out her phone. 'Call your daughters,' he'd said. 'Call them.' But her phone had been smashed, so he'd looked their house number up for her on the office records, then lent her his mobile to speak to them.

The bright day is dark with smoke. His longing for Rajita is a physical pain. This weekend is stirring up all the ghosts. The flames bring back his panic; he had searched for Rajita, he had searched and searched. He searches still. The fire has never left him. It had scorched more than his body.

Sarah returns his phone and he thumbs back to the messages from Obaidur. After no contact with him for so many years, Iqbal is still getting over the shock of being in touch with him again. Obaidur replied to tell Iqbal more about his meeting with the man. He never gave his name, just said he was a researcher for a new tech company. He looked official – ID, business card. He paid Obaidur five hundred dollars for an idea he'd had. Obaidur was proud, grateful to sell on his invention. Iqbal must word his reply sensitively, so as not to alarm his friend. But he shakes with rage, even now. A paltry sum. Exploitation. Theft. A criminal act. And if Obaidur saw this man pictured in an article about Archipelago, then it must be one of the men here today.

Iqbal has a sudden thought and flicks back to the group photo taken earlier on his phone. He sends it off to Obaidur. *Which one is the researcher?*

He wonders what he will do when he gets the response.

Lois approaches. 'Iqbal, you look terrible. Don't stay out

here – the smoke… We're fine. Don't put yourself through it. I can't believe it crashed. I just can't believe it.'

It's bad for her too, he can see it on her face.

Fire, the smell of burning. The screaming. It never leaves you. Not really.

44

MAARTEN

'The doctor's ready.'

Maarten takes a long last look at Richard through the glass. He's connected to machines. Sarah sits by his bed, sobbing. She hasn't changed and her clothes are dirty, torn.

Adrika waits for him, standing quietly. She speaks again. 'The consultant is ready. Come on.'

Tired, grey, the consultant says, 'Aksel Larsen was pronounced dead on arrival.' There's noise and shouting from the corridor. 'I'm sorry, it's a busy evening.'

'What was the cause of death?' Maarten asks.

'Well, you'll have to wait for the post-mortem. I can't tell you that. Whatever the reason, you're going to have to wait for more investigation. I'm not wrong, he was in a helicopter crash, wasn't he?'

Maarten nods.

'Well then. It could be any number of things. I'm surprised so many have survived. They've been lucky.'

'He...' Maarten is about to say that he'd heard Aksel had stood up on the ascent, but it's not a symptom of anything, so he changes tack, tries professional courtesy.

'There may have been some level of foul play. There have been some letters.'

'Threats against him?' The consultant nods to someone who passes, and hands him a form.

'No. Not him, but someone else on the flight.'

The consultant shrugs; his eyes look dry, red-rimmed. Maarten wants to feel annoyed with the lack of additional offers of help, but it's getting late, and he has no idea how long this doctor has been on for.

'I wish I could give you a magic bullet answer,' he's saying. 'From my point of view, it looks like a non-urgent post-mortem. There's no obvious cause of death. How was he before the flight?'

'Fine,' Maarten says, thinking of Aksel's more than fine appearance, his speech. He'd outlined the anti-slave-trade policies, been poetic about the new game.

'Well, you know protocol. There's clear trauma to the body, in line with a crash. But nothing apparent apart from that. I had a look at him quickly. You'll have to wait for the pathologist at the hospital. You're welcome to request a Home Office post-mortem. You know that will be much faster.'

A bell rings somewhere, and a group of people walk past them. Maarten squeezes into the side of the corridor.

'Look, if we weren't so busy...'

'It's OK. Thanks for your help,' Maarten says. 'I appreciate it.'

'As well as the helicopter crash, we've had two RTAs arrive in the last hour. One clearly drink-driving. We're stretched to the limit.'

'I'll get going with the HO pathologist. Hope the rest of the night is easier.'

Maarten watches him disappear down the corridor and then lifts his phone, speaking to Adrika, as he taps at the screen. 'We're going to need to move quickly. And hope the super is on our side. Come on.'

Stepping outside, Maarten leans his head back against the wall of the hospital. A few smokers are dotted around.

Adrika takes a deep breath. 'I hate the hospital smell.' She shakes her head, shivers. Dusk has taken over. 'How come it's nearly five already?' she says.

Maarten looks at the darkening sky. There is so much to do. His head is crammed.

'So…?' Adrika says, pulling out her notebook. She checks they're far enough away from the smokers.

'Well, we've heard he stood up on take-off, took off his belt. No one behaves like that unless something's wrong. Apparently, he said, "*It was never meant…*" but I can't see yet if it's important.' Maarten thinks of all the threads.

'So, what made him stand?'

'Well, it could be anything. A heart attack? He was fine before. Adrika, the man gave a speech and practically skipped on to the flight. Something happened in that last half an hour.'

'What are you thinking?' Adrika asks.

'I have no idea. It's a helicopter crash, so there's no real sign of anything. However, with so many threats to Marieke in the last month – we can't ignore an incident like this with her on board.' Someone walks by, and Maarten pauses, waits until they're out of earshot. The cold is setting in.

'Maybe Aksel's taken a dart, been shot with something through the glass that was supposed to hit Marieke? Maybe someone did tamper with the controls last minute,' he says.

'I suppose he could have simply had a heart attack?' Adrika says. 'Or maybe he was poisoned?'

Maarten nods, thinking they feel far from the truth. 'It's possible the helicopter itself was shot with something and Aksel stood up to warn everyone.'

Adrika writes and Maarten wonders what else is playing out here. Something is tapping away.

'Whatever it is, we can't act on it until we've got confirmation. We're going to need to get permission to search wider than the crash site. The Roman theatre's our incident scene. The house is different. We'll need permission or a warrant to search it.'

'Think we'll get permission quickly?' Adrika asks.

'No idea. But with one guest in a coma, it's going to be difficult. If this does prove to be more than a heart attack, we need to be ready. It will be tricky – the super will not want anyone upset. This is still a high-profile event.' Maarten thinks of the press who were waiting in town somewhere. They had delayed the confidential press briefing but many had come up from London. They will sniff out a story. With Archipelago, a film star and a high-profile politician involved, there's no way this will stay out of the press for long.

'We need to get a warrant, but to do that, we're going to need some evidence, maybe toxicology, fast. If there is something in his blood, then we can move forward. You know the cost involved in an HO pathologist, at this point in the weekend.'

Adrika nods. 'Think the super will agree the additional spend?'

Maarten breathes in the damp air of Halloween, laced with the cigarette smoke and traffic. 'I hope so. Let's head back to the crime scene. I need to finish up there. If there's anything of interest, I want a look. And can you phone ahead, let them know we're coming? Get ready. It's going to be a long night.'

45

IQBAL

Iqbal presses his nose up against the glass of his window, overlooking the crash site. One floodlight remains. It is quiet now.

The panic attack has calmed. Lois had pressed a packet of jelly babies into his hand. One sits in his mouth, on his tongue. But he doesn't have the energy to chew.

Lois has gone to the hospital with Ebba, and he'd asked her to let him know how Richard was. *Surrounded by machines*, she'd said, when she called him.

Had it been Richard who had tricked Obaidur? He'd been in Dhaka by his own admission, at the right time, which means he'd been there for the fire.

Richard would have been able to see the chaos. If he'd had the opportunity to speak to Obaidur, and Obaidur had told him about his idea...

Richard had been an early investor, so it would make sense. Someone at that point would have had the chance to influence the company, to enable them to make the products that had the edge over their competitors. They would have had the chance to rip off Obaidur and make a multi-million-pound steal.

The thought creeps like salt working its way into a wound, that maybe Lois knew too.

He had protected her this weekend. His hands still feel the weight. He had acted on instinct, thinking only of her and not of the consequences.

What had he done?

His hands shake and he puts a fistful of sweets in his mouth. He can't remember the last time he ate. He needs to investigate, he needs his wits about him. While they're all at the hospital.

'Obaidur, Rajita,' he whispers, the names falling from his lips like prayers. He closes his eyes, reaching for Rajita in his memory, asking her for help, for strength.

Shivering, despite the heat of the house, he stumbles across his room. He has some time, at least, before anyone else comes back. He burns with the need to find out who it was that stole Obaidur's idea. Who it was that has put the whole company in danger. But he can't be caught. His hands shake as he rummages for the torch.

The house is empty. It stands, hoarding its secrets.

And Lois. She'd been out there, in the garden. Had she been meeting *him*? Obaidur's 'researcher'? His instinct had been to protect her. But he needs to know. Is she involved?

Not daring to put the light on, Iqbal creeps along the corridor. His feet are bare and the wooden floorboards are warm and solid beneath his toes. The dark is frightening, even though he's chosen it. It presses, it threatens.

He turns on the torch; shadows flicker, shape-shifters.

There's a noise downstairs. The front door bangs.

Sweat, like a fever, consumes him, and he shakes as he tries to open the door. He catches his thumb; the skin breaks.

There is another door bang, not the front door this time, but somewhere else downstairs.

Running, as quietly as he can, he crosses Lois's room. Hating himself, he finds her laptop and opens it. He knows her password. He skims straight to her email, then her personal inbox. The problem is, he has no idea what it is he's looking for.

Something creaks on the stairs. It's like a footfall, but a slow one. Measured.

He hesitates, breathing in a heavily perfumed breath. The house is stuffed with fresh flowers for the weekend and the heat intensifies the scent.

Still nothing.

Then one, in her drafts folder. To Aksel, but unsent. Entitled: *Our secret.*

Holding his breath, he goes to click on it. His finger trembles. His darkest fear is that Lois has known all along. Then everything he has believed in is a lie. He skims the first line:

This isn't an easy email to write. I feel guilty about keeping this secret. But it's not just me who is involved now.

There is another noise outside; his heart leaps and pounds.

Dizzy with the fear of being discovered, he slams the laptop lid down and makes his way to the door. Opening it a fraction, he sees a bobbing light much further down the corridor. It goes round the corner and he has seconds to cover the ground to his room.

Someone else doesn't want to be discovered.

He pulls the door open quickly; the corridor is still in darkness. He closes it behind him, gently, softly – his breathing loud in the dark.

Someone else is here, creeping.

Another door bangs, further down the west wing, and he almost yelps, biting his tongue to stop the noise, tasting blood.

Were Aksel and Lois in it together? Had Aksel been threatening her? Now Aksel is dead. And she hadn't got on the helicopter...

No, not Lois. Surely not? But he of all people should know that in the right circumstances, gentle people are capable of violent acts.

He sits hard on his bed; tiredness sweeps him.

He waits for sleep. Would it erase the bitter taste in his mouth?

What is the secret between Lois and Aksel?

It's impossible. The room is dark, silent. The ticking of the clock is soft. Sleep will not come.

His thoughts turn to Rajita. Could she be in England? Trafficked? Kept hidden in fear and silence beneath the hum of the daily pattern of UK life? So many are, in nail salons, houses, farms, restaurants...

Please, let them find Rajita.

He still wakes at night and reaches for her. Wakes with the smell of her skin, just out of reach. He has a photo of their wedding by his bed, and he lifts it now, holds it.

The wind picks up outside. It will be light soon. The smell of the flames yesterday has stolen his sleep; stolen his peace of mind.

His fingers tremble.

Lois had offered him a job when it had been clear Rajita had vanished. She'd stayed with him for weeks. He'd searched everywhere, tried everyone he could speak to. But then the other factory collapsed and there was no work anywhere. He was struggling to survive; he ran out of leads. One day he couldn't pay for food.

When he'd asked about the products, Lois had explained in detail, and she'd made them magical. She'd taught him the rudiments of coding and it had been wizardry speak. Maths come alive. He'd made a suggestion about something and they'd worked long and hard, solving a number of problems with the first game with which Archipelago had achieved success.

Lois had paid him for his work, and he'd searched again. There was no sign of Rajita anywhere. Whichever route she had followed to find work as a maid, she'd been swallowed up. He wasn't sure she was even in the country any more. Obaidur was nowhere. They'd both vanished.

In the end, when it was clear Rajita wasn't coming back, that she was no longer in Dhaka, he'd accepted the job. He couldn't search for her if he starved.

Archipelago had paid him well, and now this deal

activates his employee share scheme, which makes him wealthy. It's finally time to go home.

Lying down, he closes his eyes to the crackle of fire, the smell of smoke. Everywhere, with eyes shut tight, he sees the flames. Trembling for what happened; trembling because he plans to return to Bangladesh.

Dhaka, for all the bad memories, is his home. It's where he first met Rajita, the only place that smells of his childhood.

He will return. And he will find his wife.

46

MAARTEN

'What have we got?' Maarten asks.

Adrika sits next to him on the perimeter of the amphitheatre. Night-time has settled in, but the floodlights set up are bright. The remains of the crash are vivid under the dark sky.

The wreckage, smoky and black, sits mainly on the old stage. It has been picked over by the team. Parts have already been taken away, and they are beginning the clear-up exercise. It's almost 10.30 p.m.

'No sign of any malfunction with the helicopter itself, not yet anyway. No sign of any engine blow-out; they don't think we're looking for an explosive device.' Adrika stretches out her arms, bending them back, and fights a yawn.

She continues, 'We can't rule out someone tampering with the controls, but it's highly unlikely. Everything was checked over first thing this morning. The pilot is still out cold, but we know it happened very quickly.'

'And the other statements?' Maarten asks, wanting

clearer answers than those he has already. Filip's account had made no sense.

'That for some reason, on take-off, Aksel stood, fell against other passengers, and tried to wrestle with the controls. They never recovered.'

An officer waves and shouts, 'All done, sir.'

Maarten nods his thanks.

Adrika continues. Rain begins falling, starting as a mist. They both stand as she speaks. 'No hint of anything unusual so far. Could just be a straight heart attack, sir.'

'I know. It just doesn't... Well, it doesn't feel right.' Maarten thinks of the anger at dinner on Friday. There was so much anger in the room. 'And Marieke receiving the threatening letter, it certainly feels as though the helicopter crashing so soon afterwards, with Marieke on board – well – it feels more than a coincidence. But no other attempts have been made on her life. Why here? Why now? Why like this? It's not as though the tone of the letter has changed – it didn't read as though something had changed. There was no real increase in threat. What's changed?'

'Well, until we get the full forensics back on the helicopter, and the pathologist's report, we're just speculating,' Adrika says, tilting her head as she speaks.

The floodlights on the lawn are bright, and Maarten squints; the contrast of the surrounding darkness seems blacker. He swigs water. His throat is still raw from breathing all the smoke. Adrika's right. There is nothing obvious that could have caused Aksel to behave so chaotically. From his brief acquaintance, he would describe Aksel as anything other than chaotic.

Maarten says, half to himself, 'We can't ask him.'

For the first time with the death of another, Maarten feels something like relief. As Aksel dies, so does the threat to his future.

Since Aksel had looked at him, told him he had recognised him, Maarten has been coiled inside. The knowledge of what he had done had been heavy enough; but the idea of Aksel telling others – the force finding out. He thinks of the faces of the super, of Adrika and Sunny. He's worked so hard to establish himself, to earn respect.

The idea of one night, one mistake, one man, undoing all his work of the last twenty years – it's been crippling.

Now, with Aksel dead, he can lay it all to rest. He will never get over the guilt, but now he will not feel he might have to walk away from his job.

The private relief, sudden and forceful, hits him, and his hands tremble.

The wet rain hides the tears that prick at his eyes, make his voice thick, choke his throat. He waits for control to return. Pleased with the darkness, the wetness.

'I've managed to get a pathologist on standby. He could be with the body in under two hours. It's a bit of a miracle. So hopefully the blood tests will tell us something. Once we hear from the super, we can go ahead. No word as yet.'

Maarten nods. He thinks of Aksel's eyes, glassy, unseeing. He thinks of the drinks before the flight. Aksel had had a couple, but he certainly hadn't had enough to cause him to act so senselessly.

'Is everyone still at the hospital?' He thinks of the need

for questions, and he wants this finished before the press get hold of it.

'I think so. Most seem to have come away relatively unscathed, except Richard Arkwright. He's in a coma, still hasn't come round. They don't know.'

Watching the teams work, pulling a tarpaulin over a patch of grass, a huge truck arrives to take the wreckage away. Maarten hopes there isn't too much damage to the old ruins.

It's still the thirty-first of October; at least an hour left. Maarten thinks of children in the city, with their Halloween buckets and ghost costumes, and he thinks of the blood spilt on the grass.

'There's a lot I don't know. How do all these people fit together? We need to get under the skin of this group,' he says. 'You know what I heard mentioned a lot last night? Bangladesh. I can't tell you why it's important, but it is. I know Iqbal Bari is from there originally. I heard Iqbal asking Richard Arkwright about his time there. And earlier, Lois was telling me about their visit. Something happened there. Iqbal, Richard, Lois, Ebba... Can you find out, in the interviews? Find out what went on.'

Adrika nods.

Maarten repeats an earlier statement. It still rankles. 'This was on our watch, Adrika.'

The floor they work on at the station is quiet. It's gone 11 p.m. but Sunny, Adrika and Maarten look at the board.

'What have we got so far?' Maarten says. 'Let's run

through it.' He's tired and his head hurts. Adrika has got biscuits from somewhere and he's on his sixth.

Sunny stands. 'Guests for the weekend include Marieke Visser; Filip Schmidt and Sophie Atwood; Sarah and Richard Arkwright; Aksel Larsen. The hosts are Ebba and Lois Munch, and Iqbal Bari.' Their names are all up there, with photos. 'And you and Liv were at dinner too. So, shall I add you both?'

Maarten nods. 'Go ahead. That's eleven for dinner.'

'Yes. During the dinner, a letter to Marieke, telling her she would *get what she deserves*, I paraphrase a bit, is found on the doormat of the house. Eleven p.m.?'

Maarten nods again.

'A member of the catering staff, Alison Hampshire, finds the envelope in her pocket, with money, and then leaves it on the mat. Initially we were thinking that the catering staff must have brought the letter in with them, but after extensive interviewing, we feel confident that the letter was left in the pocket after the dinner began. Alison keeps her cigarettes there, and she'd had one earlier, without seeing the packet.'

'And you're sure the rest of the staff are telling the truth?' Adrika asks.

'As sure as I can be. The PC on duty checked all their bags on entry. It would be hard for them to have got anything in. The guests' luggage wasn't checked. It was felt unnecessary.'

'Our first mistake,' Maarten says, thinking of the super's reluctance to unsettle the VIP guests.

'So, one of the guests is our letter writer?' Adrika says.

She takes the last bourbon biscuit and Maarten inwardly curses. He's starving and there are only custard creams left.

'And Marieke was on the helicopter. No evidence yet, but it's a bit of a coincidence that the helicopter came down with her on it.'

'Who wasn't on the helicopter?' Adrika asks.

'Sophie Atwood, Lois Munch and Iqbal Bari.'

'Well, let's assume that if you were going to try to bring down a helicopter, you'd not get on it. Is there any reason we can see that one of those three could be the letter writer? And we also need to think about who might want to bring down the whole helicopter. Is more than one person here the intended victim?'

'There's no obvious motive for the death of Marieke or indeed for anyone to bring an end to this deal. They all benefit from the transaction. Having Marieke stay away from the Archipelago expansion would be less helpful to its success. Her support has been huge. She's been promoting their ethos for months.' Adrika dips a biscuit in a mug of tea.

Maarten blows air from his mouth, thinking. 'We need results on Aksel. It could still be just a heart attack. Just a coincidence.'

Adrika smiles. 'You don't think that at all.'

'No.' He shakes his head. 'No, I don't.'

'Is there any reason for any of them to try to kill Aksel Larsen?' Sunny asks.

'I'd say there are a few individuals who had varied reasons to wish harm to Aksel,' Maarten says, thinking of how Aksel's death has made him breathe easier. 'Filip Schmidt clearly hated him. Aksel was all over Filip's wife – he was doing it deliberately, clear provocation. And Filip mentioned something to do with their agreements with Archipelago; he implied that Aksel was getting better terms, and they were trying to rip him off.'

'What about the others?' Adrika asks.

Maarten thinks back to Richard's anger. 'Richard Arkwright hated him too. I don't know why. It came off him in waves. Did you get anything from his wife?'

Sunny nods. 'She was a bit evasive. She's obviously upset about her husband. I got the impression there was something she was holding back about Aksel when I asked how he and Richard were getting on.'

'Hmm...' Maarten thinks. 'Make a point of following that up? As for the others, there was tension. Lois was unsettled about something. Marieke mentioned thinking men were "shits" – I assumed she was referring to the letter writer, but I can't be sure.'

'And your attack, sir,' Adrika prompts.

He nods, touching his head. 'Yes, someone clunked me over the head. I'd seen a figure running down to the amphitheatre and I followed it out. I think it was Lois Munch I was following. Can you speak to her? She looked like she was meeting someone. I have no idea who, or even if it was suspicious, but someone hit me, and I'd be surprised if it wasn't to stop me following her. Though why, I have no idea. And someone else was out there, under a tree, crying...' He thinks of the tears and the vomit. 'I think that was Filip Schmidt. There was tension between him and Sophie Atwood for most of the evening. He barely spoke to her.'

'Fun night,' Sunny says.

'Yes, cracking.' Maarten smiles wryly. 'I'm starving. Can we get some takeaway in?' He really does hate custard creams.

Sitting in his office, Maarten looks over the statements Sunny had taken from the catering staff. One stands out:

> I think the blonde one was having a bit of a thing with the handsome one. I saw them earlier on in the kitchen. She came out all flushed, like he'd been… Well, you know. Tell you what I did see, was that dark-haired woman talking to Filip Schmidt. Really angry, almost passionate like. Something going on there, if you ask me.

Maarten pauses over this last statement. Ebba and Aksel? Filip and Marieke? That hadn't occurred to him. That might change a few things.

47

LOIS

The kitchen is empty. A few coffee cups sit, pumpkins, the knives. All like before, except now the world has shaken around her like a snow globe.

Lois hasn't eaten anything for hours. They'd been due to have lunch after the helicopter had left. The cocktails on the lawn had been handed out, but she hadn't touched hers. A cup of tea? The calories from the milk had long since burned off. She is running on nothing.

She takes another bite of a stale croissant sitting on the table.

A scrape of a chair makes her stir. Sarah slips in next to her and, for a moment, they say nothing.

'How is he?' Lois asks, leaning to hug Sarah, pulling her in close; feeling overall a sense of guilt that they had organised the weekend. They could have cancelled. They could have asked Marieke not to come.

Sarah is stiff in her arms. Sitting slowly, Lois sees the lines under her eyes, the redness. In the kitchen lights, her ragged tear marks are still clear.

'He's still unconscious. They don't know why. Nothing. His neck is... They think his neck is OK.' She cries, her shoulders sagging low, and her back curves forward and down, her head too heavy.

'My daughters made me come and get changed, have a shower. I said I'd eat, but I can't eat. I'll lie to them. If I eat, I'll throw up.'

Lois is quiet, watching her unravel, certain she must blame them, blame Archipelago.

'Anyway, I'm pleased you're here. Lois, I don't know what to do.' Sarah cries fresh tears.

'What, Sarah? I'll do anything to help.' Lois puts her hand on the older woman's. Sarah, who is usually so practical, is fraying at the seams.

'You remember I said Richard had been upset with Aksel? But I didn't know what it was? What the problem was?'

Lois nods, thinking of walking into the dinner only the night before, her arm linked with Sarah's.

'There's something I've found.' She sounds tired, but she also sounds scared. She opens her handbag and pulls out a letter, creased at the edges. Laying it on the table, she slides it to Lois with her three middle fingers. It's still in its envelope, with Richard's name clearly printed on the front.

They both look at it. Sarah rubs her temples with two fingers from each hand.

'I knew he'd received something. Richard brushed it off the other day, but I heard him curse Aksel after the post arrived, and he stuffed something in his pocket. To be honest, I didn't think much about it.' Her eyes are sore, and she rubs them. 'But he'd hidden it. I just found it in his suitcase, slid between his clothes, inside a book. I was looking for some clean clothes for him...' She shakes her head, and starts to cry again. 'I knew he was angry before the weekend, cross with Aksel. Though I didn't realise who Aksel was until Friday. Now that I've met him, I'm still surprised.' Her sobs are loud. 'Lois, he hid it from me! I can't even read it! What has he done? What has Richard done?'

'It's OK, Sarah.' Lois can't think of anything to say.

'I was interviewed at the hospital – I didn't mention this. I didn't really think about it, but now I've found the letter, I have to show them. Lois, I daren't even read it! Why would he have hidden something from me? What will I do, if it suggests...'

Lois looks at the letter. So many letters. This one is differently addressed. This is formal, free of the thick black marker pen from last night.

'Lois, what do I do? Like I said, I haven't even read it. It's the last thing I want to do right now. What shall we do? I can't face talking to the police. And if there is something behind it...' She shakes her head. Tears fall through her fingers to the kitchen table, splashing. Liquid grief.

Lois feels sick.

'You just need to focus on him getting well. I'll take care of this,' she says. 'He'll be OK, Sarah. This is Richard we're talking about. He'll pull through.' But she knows this is just something people say. She has no idea. And neither does Sarah.

★★★

'I haven't read it,' Lois tells Maarten over the phone. 'But he'd hidden it from his wife, and she's convinced it's something to do with Aksel. It looks as though he's written Richard a letter.'

'I'll have it collected now,' Maarten says.

Lois can feel the desire to lie down on the floor take hold. What else can this weekend throw out?

48

MAARTEN

'Richard Arkwright was being blackmailed by Aksel Larsen. Listen.' Maarten reads:

> I have evidence that you have avoided paying tax on the death duties on the inheritance you received after the death of your parents. You will of course be aware this is a crime. I will have no choice but to report you…

'Shit. What would he have to gain by revealing that?' Sunny asks.

'Aksel Larsen is asking for the shares. Cut price,' Maarten says, reading down.

Adrika shakes her head. 'But if Aksel Larsen owned Arkwright's shares, then…'

'…then Larsen would have become the majority shareholder. Lois and Ebba were lucky Richard held back. They would have lost control of their company. But this gives Richard Arkwright a clear motive, if Larsen was killed.' Maarten leans back in his chair.

'Sir, we need to get the house shut down as soon as possible. What else is in there?' Sunny shakes his hair back from his head. His face is pale with exhaustion.

Maarten nods. 'Yes, but we've no authority yet. This letter was sitting there. You're right, what else is in that house? Where are we with the post-mortem and the toxicology?'

'Apparently the toxicology results will take ten days to come back. We still can't hold…'

Maarten doesn't listen to the rest of it. He calls the super; she answers quickly.

'Maarten, I know you're going to…'

'Look, ma'am. I know you don't want to push this. But I'm convinced we're looking at a suspicious death. And until we get some evidence, I can't get the search warrant for Ostle House. And the Munchs will not give permission to search the property.'

There is a sigh, tired and fraught, down the phone. 'I've just had Ebba Munch on the phone.'

'Ebba?' Maarten is surprised.

'Yes, and what she says makes sense. She can't authorise a search on behalf of all her guests: one still hasn't woken up, and his family are stretched to the limit. The wife was on the helicopter. She just wants to give everyone a chance to get the medical attention they need before she pushes them for an answer to a search. Maarten, he died in a helicopter crash. I'm not saying you're wrong, but the evidence isn't there, not yet. And if we go in too hard on this, then the press will be horrendous. This deal is important to us, as much as it will be to Rotterdam and Bergen. Archipelago are investing in the local community, and with such high-profile guests, we have to be careful. We'll be hauled over the coals if we don't do this by the book.'

'But ma'am, a high-profile figure is now dead, and we need to be seen to be doing all we can,' Maarten says. There're only so many times he can be told no and ask again.

'Yes, but I'm not sure that involves placing a number of other high-profile figures under duress to search their property. You're going to need evidence and a warrant. We need this to be all above board. I'm not risking relations by doing anything other than taking every necessary step.'

'Can you authorise the spend on the HO pathologist?'

The sigh returns, deep and reluctant. 'Yes, I've read your report. I think there's enough evidence to warrant the early exam. I've sent word to the forensic lab to fast-track the tests. You do not move until you get toxicology back, Maarten. You do nothing. If I hear that you've…'

'Yes, ma'am.'

The line goes quiet, and Maarten's brain flies through the coming hours.

'Adrika, can you get the application written? We'll need to send Sunny with the Bible to the magistrate's house for the search warrant, as soon as we hear back from the forensic lab.' Maarten's head stabs. The pain from the whack he'd received has dulled, but the bruise is tender and as he rubs his head, he winces. 'I think whatever killed Aksel also brought that helicopter down. Our primary suspects must be those who didn't get on board. We've got hours to get what we need out of that house, before someone gets rid of it first.'

49

FILIP

The kitchen is hot. Lois has made tea and toast. Filip has lost all track of time. It must have crossed midnight at some point. The cars have been bringing them back from the hospital, slowly. The three of them sit, faded and gaunt.

'I've had better days,' Ebba says. 'But all in all, you bloody well saved all of our lives. Thank Christ you were there. Honestly, Filip. I've never seen anything like it. You became like Superman. A proper fucking modern-day hero.' She bursts into tears.

'Well,' he says, 'I bet Superman could manage a better cup of coffee. I've just given you something that tastes like soil. I'll make some more. I hate tea.'

Still crying, she manages a laugh, and wipes snot and tears away with both her hands. 'I'm a mess. Honestly. You're a fucking superhero and I'm a total mess.'

'Oh, I don't know,' Lois says. 'You looked worse an hour ago.'

'We made an effort for Halloween?' Filip says, laughing too. The knots that are wound tight in his stomach need unclenching, and the three of them clutch mugs and their laughter becomes hysterical.

'And to think,' Ebba says, 'I was worried my witch costume wouldn't be sexy enough for the party we were supposed to have.'

'How about this?' Filip says, lifting back his jacket and showing them the bandage that dresses his shoulder wound, red seeping through. 'Blood-soaked enough for trick or treats?'

'Think the little kids might cry? I could carry a pumpkin, offset the dried blood?' Ebba gestures to the cuts on her head. 'Christ,' she says again.

She holds Filip's hand, squeezing it tight. 'I'm not kidding, Filip, thank you. I was only just working out what the hell had happened when you carried Marieke out. Seconds later and you and Richard would have been in the explosion. If you'd not been in there, pulling us all out, making us act, we might have just sat there waiting to be saved. I owe you my life.'

Filip shakes his head. How could he have ever thought Ebba intimidating? What has he been thinking of these past few months? This life is not to be taken for granted. These people are not his enemies. They're alive, which is what counts. Most of them.

He will call Ruben. He will call him tonight and tell him to release the signatures. He believes in the product. It's time to stop worrying.

Lois checks her phone. 'Richard hasn't regained consciousness yet.'

'Oh God, do they think he will?' Ebba asks.

Lois shrugs. 'He's breathing on his own, his back is OK. He's just not awake.'

Ebba closes her eyes. 'Fuck.'

'Poor Sarah,' Filip says. He thinks of her laughing last night. There'd been something, though – Aksel had offered Richard his hand at some point before dinner and Richard hadn't taken it. There is so much from last night he doesn't remember. His brain had been alcohol soaked. *Kak*, he'd even arrived drunk.

Yesterday, he'd been swamped with a sense of nothingness, of numbness. Of thinking that life held nothing for him.

And now, his blood rages round his veins as though his life has been given back to him, anew.

Aksel's mouth had already been cold when he'd leaned in. Two rescue breaths, then he'd begun on his chest. He'd felt the ribs breaking beneath his hands as he'd pummelled. He'd known from that first touch that Aksel had already been dead. He hadn't given up. The rhythmic presses, the pressure. His shoulders still ache.

He'd stopped when the paramedics had arrived and taken over.

But the taste of his mouth – he was giving the last kiss to a dead man.

Aksel was dead before the crash, he's convinced of it. He's heard discussion, the police, the doctors... Aksel had died in an unfortunate crash, and how sad. But it just doesn't feel right to Filip. Those lips. They'd been so cold. He wouldn't have been surprised if he'd died before the helicopter hit the ground.

'What happened to Aksel? Does anyone know?' Ebba speaks, her eyes still closed. 'Was there something wrong with the helicopter? I wondered if he'd stood up to tell us?' She pulls her legs up on the chair and circles her arms around them. Her face is covered in tiny pieces of tape, pulling together cuts, preventing scars.

'He stood up?' Lois says. 'I heard you say it before. He stood up when the helicopter was taking off?'

'I think a heart attack,' Ebba says. 'It looked like a heart attack.'

There's silence for a few seconds. Filip thinks of the screaming on board. He'd never seen anyone have a heart attack, but it didn't look how he'd imagined a heart attack would look. 'Maybe food poisoning? He clutched his stomach. Maybe a poison?'

'No.' Ebba shakes her head. 'It looked like a heart attack. And if it was food poisoning then we would all have had it.'

Filip nods. He thinks of Aksel. He'd clutched at Filip, and Filip had been unable to do anything. He wished he could remember clearly what Aksel had said. Something uneasy is circling. Something dark.

'Unless... Well, you know there was another letter delivered last night? To the house? To Marieke?' Ebba speaks slowly.

Filip wants to speak, to say something, but he's not sure what it is. There's something he knows about the letters, and it's stuck in his brain.

Lois's mouth falls open. 'You mean it might have happened on purpose? That it might have been someone's plan? God, Ebba. You just need to leave it to the police.'

Filip shakes his head. This idea that the sender of the letters had something to do with the helicopter feels wrong, but he doesn't know why. He opens his mouth to speak, but nothing comes out.

'I...' Ebba starts to say something, but Lois stops her.

'Ebbs.' Lois's voice is gentle. 'The police will work it all out. We don't know anything yet.'

'No, Lois. If someone has tried to kill Marieke, and Aksel has died instead, we need to face it. The sooner we find out who has been sending those letters, the better. It could be anyone!'

Filip's filled with a dread that he can taste, viscous, like a glue, stuck to his tongue. What does he know about the letters? He needs to remember. His heart beats quickly. He needs to remember. Soon.

50

Lois

Lois makes her way to the kitchen, filling a glass with water and drinking it straight down, then filling another.

There must be answers to the questions, bright in her head.

Had she really seen Iqbal hit Maarten last night? She still can't quite believe it. She'd been out in the amphitheatre, standing by the steps, following a shadow in the dark, and there'd been a sound.

Swirling, she'd seen Maarten. She called out to him, but then there'd been a flash of movement in the pale light and Maarten had fallen.

The shock of it had made her stand for a second, stunned. Petrified. None of it makes any sense. Why would Iqbal hit Maarten?

The water is cold and she needs more. The smoke has made its way down into her belly and she wants it washed clean.

This idea that Ebba had mentioned. That what happened this afternoon might not be just an accident...

If Iqbal had committed that act, then what else had he done?

She can't believe it. Ebba had almost died.

The glass clinks in the dark as it makes contact with the hard white of the ceramic sink.

She waits until the silence of the kitchen is so intense she can almost hear the blink of the clock on the oven, and then she steps over the flagstones towards the stairs.

The dark of her room is heady and hot. Opening the window, she leans out and drinks in the night air. The cold is a relief.

Lois realises she needs to get some sort of plan ready. Their future, the company, which she had confidently left to Ebba, is now hanging, dangling from a cliff face.

Ebba has thrown everything behind Archipelago. For all her polished performance the last few months, Lois has seen her taking sleeping pills, seen her sitting in her office until late at night. She's been drinking real coffee, which she never does. Her nails are bitten, beneath the shiny professional job.

And after what happened to their father, the business drive lies in Ebba, like an inherited bone. Lois thinks the stress lies there too. If the deal collapses – their future, their house, everything they've worked for along with it – will Ebba collapse?

She forces herself to confront the awful truth. Aksel is dead. A great sadness wells up in her, but she focuses on the details. Where does that leave Archipelago? Does that mean his signature means nothing? No, although Aksel is the owner, his signature commits his company. The agreements with his company are binding. She'll need to make sure it's not railroaded. So much rests on this.

She will ask Filip for his help. She doesn't know the differences in the distribution deal, but she will ask Filip to release his signature and promise him that she will make it fair. She can do this.

But she needs to get to the bottom of this quickly. Before the delay becomes public and the other parties find out. Before Ebba is hit with the full weight of it. She needs to find a way out for Ebba. If the deal dies, she doesn't want to lose Ebba, too.

Lying back, she tries to imagine actually killing someone. Could she?

She thinks of the baby growing inside her. Already, she thinks she could kill to save her baby.

So does that mean it could have been Iqbal? Can anyone kill, given the right motive: jealousy, power, love...?

She looks at the clock. It's 3 a.m.; she has until 7 a.m. Monday morning, before the stock market opens in Norway, the Netherlands and later here. She has twenty-seven hours. To stop it all falling apart.

There is a knock on her door.

'Hello?' she says, opening it a fraction, angry that she's afraid to open the door in her own home.

'Lois? It's Marieke. Can I come in for a bit? I went to my room, but it's difficult to settle. Just for five minutes, can we talk normally? Like nothing extraordinary happened this weekend?'

'Of course.' Lois opens the door and walks back to the bed. 'It's been unreal. I read that letter. If I were you, I'd be frightened. Can I get you a drink? A hot chocolate?'

But Marieke is still standing by the door, her mouth open. 'Lois. That top.'

Lois glances down. She's wearing the T-shirt she'd borrowed after her one-night stand at the conference. She'd never given it back. She's been wearing it to bed since the test result. She wants the baby to feel it has a mother and a father. Silly, really.

'Yes?' she says.

Marieke clutches the door. 'Oh my God, Lois. It's Aksel's shirt. It's his hockey number. Aksel is the father, isn't he? Oh, Lois.'

Clutching at the shirt, Lois stares at Marieke, scared she'll judge her.

Then the grief, like a wave, rolls up and out. She stumbles towards her, finally able to tell it all.

51

FILIP

Sleep will not come. Filip lies in bed, listening to Sophie breathe. He's convinced she's awake.

'Filip?' Sophie sits up, confirming it. 'I keep thinking about you on that helicopter. I keep thinking about the flames. About Aksel, dying.'

The clock above the fire chimes gently: 4 a.m. He puts his arm around her. Pulls her in close.

'I'm pleased you came back to me,' she says, her voice speaking into his chest. His Sophie. Although he still can't remember what they talked about after Friday's dinner, he had awoken on Saturday to feel they were united. Now it's early Sunday morning. Less than thirty-six hours, and so much has happened.

'God, Filip. What a nightmare this has all been. These last six months, this weekend.'

He holds her close.

She pulls back. Stares at him. 'You don't remember anything I told you in that amphitheatre, do you?'

He shakes his head, bites his lip. 'I'm so sorry! Please, tell me again.'

'Oh, Filip, why would I think you would, after the crash! I thought you'd died. I thought my life was over, without you.' She looks down. 'But the last months. Well, you shut me down, shut me out.' Her words sound as though they were once angry, but her voice is empty of it now; quiet in the early morning hours. It's like she's learning lines to a powerful argument – the words come from her mouth but land flatly, almost a whisper. She touches his face. There are tears in her eyes.

'I don't...' He really doesn't know what to say. All he had ever done was love her and not be enough. Whatever they had said on Friday night had fixed them. He's nervous he will undo it all.

'We went over it all. Sitting under a tree, on the wet grass.' She sinks her chin lower still, head hanging, more defeated than anyone he has seen.

'I'd tried everything, Filip. Filip. Filip.'

She says his name over and over, and each time sounds hollower than the last.

A flicker in the back of his mind. A tree had brushed his head and he'd been holding her hand. It had been dark. He'd been dizzy. His feet had been wet.

What had she said?

Clarity arrives, like a shot of ice.

She had told him who had sent the letters.

His head had ached, and he'd thrown up under a tree. She'd stroked his back. He'd said over and over how sorry he was. *Sorry, Sophie. Sorry.*

Despite the damp, he'd sat back against a tree. Everything had spun, and the night had been cold and dark.

'It was me, Filip,' she'd said. The words soft but clear in the dark. 'I guessed you were having an affair. I listened to you, watched you. How much brighter your face was after you'd seen her. How much you mentioned her, how much you checked your phone... I knew. And I had just started to feel dead about us. I tried not to care, but I cared. I just had to get her away from you. And you were seeing her all the time, over this fucking business agreement...'

'But you... But you didn't want me?' he had said. Echoes of it leave his mouth now. 'You want me?'

'When did I ever say I didn't?'

The news that she might be jealous of Marieke had been so startling, he'd lost the grain of something important in the exchange.

He'd been sick again, and then he couldn't remember a single word.

What has he caused? 'Oh my God. This is serious. We need to move quickly.' He thinks fast. 'Are there any more letters?'

'I have two more,' she says, fear in her voice. 'I thought of ripping them up, putting them in the bin... but what if they find them? They're searching for a murderer now! I had nothing to do with the helicopter. Christ...'

'Give them to me, any more you have,' he says quickly. 'The paper, the pen... Now.'

He bends, lighting the fire in the grate.

'Is that all of them?'

She hesitates. 'No. I planted one for the mat on Friday

night. I had a cigarette outside with one of the catering girls. I knew she'd do it.'

'Fuck, Sophie. The police have that letter!'

Crying now, she pulls out letters from her suitcase, wet with her tears, soggy at the edges. 'I wondered – I searched in her room, when you were all at the hospital. I didn't mean any of this. I just said stupid stuff. I called her a whore. I wanted to hurt her. I thought maybe she'd disappear from view. From you.'

Handfuls burn and hiss. And he fights a thought, *What if Sophie is responsible for it all?* But he silences this, like you tell yourself the noises in the night aren't real.

'I wore gloves, to hide fingerprints,' she says. 'I didn't mean for this to happen. I didn't mean for any of it to happen. I just wanted her to be afraid. As frightened as I was, when I thought I might lose you. Everyone wants something from me. You made me feel like I didn't need to be anyone except myself.'

'Sophie, no! I only talked to Marieke, she's been my friend – how could you think anything else?' He shakes his head. 'I've always wanted you, Sophie. Always. I didn't dare touch you because I thought you couldn't want me—? I've been consumed with self-doubt. I can't… I can't perform.'

'Oh, Filip. I just want you back. I want you to talk to me again!'

Slowly, he shuffles next to her. With a tenderness he never thought he was capable of, he strokes her cheek. 'I'll never leave you.' He curls an arm around her. She lowers her head to his shoulder, and they sit and stare at the fireplace, where the flames eat the paper.

'Even if it's not sex, you can betray me, Filip. When you talked to her, it made me feel so alone. Even when I tried my hardest to get your attention, you couldn't seem to hold it for me. You'd phone her before you'd phone me. You saved your smiles for her. She's been the one you've turned to. Not me.'

'I've let you down,' he whispers. 'Not any more. Not any more.'

52

MAARTEN

'Sir!' Adrika shouts, running into his office. He'd gone back to finish up the paperwork on the incident scene. So far there was nothing suspicious about the helicopter crash.

'We've got them!' She slows, slapping down a printout. 'The results came back – they can't identify what it is yet, they will need longer. But there's something in his blood – some toxin. They think it's plant based.'

'This is it!' Excitement lifts him off the chair, and he calls out across the open-plan floor to Sunny, who sits, white as a sheet, lack of sleep slowing him like a clock winding down, going over the interviews from earlier.

'Get your Bible, Sunny, I'm sending you out to the magistrate's house now. You should be able to get there in about thirty minutes. Adrika, can you amend the application form for the search warrant with the forensic info?'

She nods and is already moving backwards, turning to the computer.

'I'll call now. If we can get a search warrant signed within the hour, we should be able to get a team going soon.'

Lifting the phone, he thinks of the lawn, of the croissants on the table, of the cocktail glasses. 'Adrika, can you call back and find out if there was the same toxin on the cocktail glasses? The glass that Aksel drank out of could be a match with the toxin in his blood. Now I think about it, I don't think the glass he drank out of was his glass – it was Marieke's. Maybe a poison was intended for Marieke? Maybe it was given to Aksel when the glasses were switched?'

Sunny leans forward, shakes himself into action and leafs through some sheets. 'Here! In the initial statements back from the hospital. Two have mentioned it: there was some confusion with the drinks before they all got on the helicopter.'

Maarten remembers the clinking glasses in the October sun; he had swallowed the foreboding, bitter in his mouth. Those glasses had sat out there with all of them. It could have been any of them. But if there is toxin in the glass, then it must have been one of them. No outsider this time.

'Yes. Aksel spilt his drink, I think?' He fights his memory for the details, wading through, muddied and muddled. 'And the glasses were hand-painted, with names and Halloween figures. It would have been easy for any one of us to have put something in Marieke's glass.'

Aksel had given a speech...

'Yes. Aksel's broke, so Marieke gave hers to Aksel.' Sunny reads from a statement.

Maarten looks to Adrika quickly. 'So, Marieke's...'

'Yes. Hopefully the go-ahead from the super to push ahead with the forensic lab in the next twenty-four hours will do the trick, then they can test the glasses. We can't wait until Monday. They might come back with something; it's possible that if Aksel was poisoned, it could have been intended for Marieke. It looks like it could still all be about Marieke.'

All about Marieke.

Eleven for dinner. Ten on the lawn for cocktails. With one dead, one unconscious, there are seven suspects still standing, able to kill again.

This isn't finished.

53

LOIS

Tiredness, like a physical impairment, pulls at Lois's arms, slows her brain. She pauses over the tea and coffee pots, confused suddenly about which is which, and wondering if she dare ask again what they all wanted. It's only 7.30 a.m. How will she get through today?

She glances at the table. No one speaks. Luckily, Ebba has flicked the radio on. The silence is taut.

'Sleep much?' Ebba takes the coffee pot from her hand and lifts the lid. 'You look terrible. Here.'

She pulls the tea pot from Lois's hand too and Lois feels her fingers soften their hold. 'Not much. You?'

Ebba shakes her head. The kettle boiling, the mugs waiting, she puts her arms around Lois and pulls her in. Ebba's blonde hair looks paler than normal, pulled backwards, and her skin too seems washed of colour. But maybe it's Lois's eyes. The brightness of things has dimmed. The sparkle of the weekend crashed when the helicopter came down.

Unable to help it, Lois looks out over the lawn, the grass and the stone of the Roman theatre.

'I still can't believe it,' she says.

Ebba's hand remains on hers as they wait for the kettle to boil.

'Are you OK?' Lois asks.

'About Richard? I haven't heard from Sarah this morning.'

Confused, Lois frowns. 'No, Aksel! You must be upset. Ebba, I know there was something…'

Tears fill her eyes. She hadn't decided whether to tell Aksel about the baby. Now she will never be able to. She'd cried on Marieke last night. She'd started an email to him, before the weekend, in which she'd told him. But she'd never sent it. And now she never can.

The kettle whistles and Ebba turns away, reaching for the switch, but Lois sees her fingers are unsteady. Ebba's voice is muffled when she says, 'There was nothing.'

'Ebba…' Lois speaks softly, aware of a roomful of people, hollowed and shaken. 'Ebba, it's OK. You don't have to be strong through this. It's OK to say.' Lois thinks of Ebba's fragility, how she drops quickly with disappointment. Her highs, her lows. And always, the memory of their father, literally falling down with disappointment as his company slipped through his fingers.

They'd not had a clue. No warning. Out of the blue, the press had run a bad news article about their father's company. Someone had clearly leaked information about a potential issue with a product. It had been 2008, when loss of confidence could kill a company. By noon that day, the shares had fallen so steeply, their father clutched his chest and crashed to the floor; Lois hadn't even had the chance to speak to him before the stress had felled him. Ebba had called her. She'd been with him. She'd held him as she'd waited for the ambulance. What that must have done to her, Lois will never know.

'Ebba, please, speak to me.'

'I can't. Not now. Lois, it's...'

And whatever she had been going to say is lost in the clatter of a cup, as Marieke's voice comes from behind, saying, 'Sorry, my fingers.'

Lois leaves the rest of the drinks to go to Marieke, who is ghost pale. She'd lain in Lois's bed, not sleeping.

'Maarten is coming this morning,' Lois tells them all. 'The police will come back. We will have some protection, until all this has passed. We're hoping to hear news of Richard this morning.'

'Filip, what did he say to you?' Marieke asks.

No one speaks for a second, and Sophie looks confused. She looks at Marieke, and Lois wonders at her expression. Come to think of it, she doesn't remember Sophie and Marieke speaking at any point this weekend.

'What do you mean, what did he say? Who say?' she asks.

'Aksel,' Marieke says, but she looks at Filip, not at Sophie. 'When Aksel fell on you in the helicopter, I heard him say something. What was it? You know they would have been his last words. What were they?'

Filip looks round the room, and he too is tired. There are bruises and scratches on his face. His shoulder hangs limp. It's clearly been giving him some grief today. He tilts to one side, resting it.

'Nothing. He said nothing.'

'Nothing at all?' Marieke says, her eyebrows raised. 'I heard him speak. He must have said something.'

Filip shakes his head again. 'It was babble – the helicopter was loud. I honestly couldn't say.'

But Lois watches him stare down as he speaks, fiddling with the spoon next to his cup.

Marieke shakes her head and stands. 'This is all such bullshit,' she says, but her voice is quiet. She makes her way to the coffee pot, refilling the kettle and adding more coffee to the jug.

Lois waits for a minute, and when Sophie stands to go to the side, to get more milk, she slips into the chair beside Filip.

'Really?' she says quietly. 'Did you really not hear anything?'

He looks at her, as Marieke asks loudly who wants a top-up and Sophie offers to bring round milk, and leans close to her ear.

Ebba sits opposite and her phone lights up. She glances down. 'Maarten,' she says.

Filip's voice is soft. 'He said, "*It was never meant…*" and then he gasped, and then some stuff in Norwegian, but nothing. Just the odd word.'

His forehead touches hers, and his hand is tight. 'Lois, I'm scared. I don't even think it's me I'm scared for, but it's not finished. I'm sure it's not finished.'

'Coffee?' Marieke says.

Filip lifts his head and Lois's mind is racing. What does it mean? What did Aksel mean?

'Yes,' he says. 'Yes, please.'

'Milk?' Sophie asks, not waiting for an answer, pouring quickly.

Ebba stands. 'He's on his way,' she says, and the room falls silent again.

'Thank God,' Marieke says.

Lois wonders if this is it. Will this bring an end to it?

Iqbal enters. He too looks tired, drained. 'I'll help you clear,' he says to Lois.

And slowly, they all leave.

Looking back out of the window, the frost is light this morning. It's fresh, like everything's been washed clean outside.

And tomorrow they announce the deal, and still Lois has no idea what will happen. She watches Ebba leave the room, her head pale like a watery sun, and she prays that whatever the outcome is, she still has a sister by the end of tomorrow.

54

Maarten

'Maarten?' Answering the phone, Maarten's head aches. Eight a.m. Dehydration, lack of sleep. He'd slept at his desk for a few hours. It will have to do. He manages to speak, but even to him his voice is raspy, brusque. Even by his standards. It's the super.

'Yes?'

'The team is ready, Maarten. You can go in.'

On the doorsteps to the house, he reminds them of the plan. 'Adrika, Sunny? We'll stay out of the search. Use this time to take statements. I know you both spoke to most of the guests yesterday, but they will have slept, might remember more. We can't rule out someone from outside, as unlikely as we may think it, not until we have confirmation on where Aksel Larsen consumed the poison. And we can't rule out suicide or overdose. We need to find out what's been going on, but gently does it. I think we still lead with our assumption that Marieke was the intended target. Keep your ears open.'

Sunny nods, swinging his head to the side to flick his hair out of his eyes. It's a move Maarten finds intensely irritating, despite how much he likes Sunny. Why can't he just get his hair cut? He can feel his irritation increasing with exhaustion. This weekend feels like it will never end.

'Adrika,' he says, facing her. 'I want you to do the interviews together, but if you think you might get more out of Ebba or Lois, then catch them afterwards. I'm sure there are things to unpick here. Richard received that letter threatening exposure over tax evasion. He's a suspect. Marieke received violent letters, threatening physical harm. Two different types of letters, of threats. There might be others.'

'Do we know if they're from the same person?' Sunny asks, pulling out a pen and pad.

'No, they look different. Aksel's letter is formal and signed. It offers no physical threat. There might be more we don't have access to. The teams will search for anything.'

The early morning light shines pale blue over the lawns, either side of the drive. There is a morning frost, arriving with November; a low mist lies over the fields, and Maarten imagines Liv, lying warm in bed. He shivers, thinking of the warmth of the duvet and the frost by his feet. But the scene is beautiful. Behind the house, the fields lie low and flat, stretching out for miles. Trees appear above the freezing mist and they had trodden the first footsteps of the day across the gravel from the car. Such mornings are meant to be experienced. Not hidden from, in bed.

Adrika leans in and knocks on the door, stamps her feet.

Her breath comes out like smoke, and Maarten thinks of yesterday. Of the flames, and Aksel's body, lying cold on the lawn.

Banging his gloves together, Sunny says, 'Shame we couldn't have shut the house down yesterday.'

'You're right. And we still don't know for sure that it's murder. There's a chance Aksel ingested poison by accident. Or took it as a recreational drug.' Adrika shivers, digging her hands deep into the pockets of her black coat. Her brown bob gleams in the pale light. 'Nevertheless, I don't trust any of them.'

'They're here,' Maarten says, looking down the drive as the teams arrive for the search. 'We'll get the results back from the cocktail glasses soon. That will help.

'Let's get this done.'

55

IQBAL

'Lois,' Iqbal starts.

She's in the kitchen, loading the dishwasher.

'Maarten is on his way in,' she says, looking out of the window. There are huge scorch marks and ambulance tracks leading down to the amphitheatre. The grass is blackened, and against the trees waving their bare arms, the view looks stripped back. Every inch the morning after Halloween.

She checks her watch. 'He'll be here any minute. They're classifying the house as a crime scene. They will move us all to the dining room for the search. There's a small team in there now, making a space. God, Iqbal. What's happened?' She lowers her forehead on to her hand, raised up on its elbow. Slowly massaging her temples with her palm, she looks broken.

He flicks on the kettle and as the water bubbles, screaming to its boiling point, he clatters with two mugs, teabags, milk.

Pulling out a chair opposite, he sits across the wooden

table, pushing tea towards her. 'Lois,' he says again, but continuing is difficult. It's too hard to say. It makes no sense. But then again, if he's right, it makes perfect sense.

He shakes his head, leans back. He can see Ebba walking across the lawn towards the black marks scored, burnt.

'Iqbal, what is it?'

Sweat breaks out on his back, trickles down. What is he going to say?

'Go on, Iqbal. I want to hear it.'

A door bangs in the hallway.

Lois rises and slams the kitchen door shut, sitting back in her chair, waiting for him to continue.

Slow to start, nervous about speaking, he watches Lois scratch at the polish that still covers her fingernails, cracked and peeling, dulled strips of varnish, hanging and fragile.

'You're scaring me,' she says, biting the nail now.

The words burn at the back of his throat.

'Is it about Marieke?' she asks. 'Is what you're going to say about Marieke?' But he shakes his head again.

'Iqbal.' She grabs his hand, squeezing it so tight it hurts, and there is a burst of sunlight through the window, despite the breeze rattling quietly on the pane of glass. 'Tell me what it is. If it's something important, I need to know. Even,' she says, rearing her head back, steeling herself, 'even if it's something that will hurt.'

Nodding, he places his other hand on top of hers, peeling at her fingers to release the pressure, then immediately regretting it, as sometimes pain is a release in itself.

There's nowhere to begin but the beginning. 'I've had

an email from Obaidur,' he says, and her face clears and breaks into a smile.

'Oh, Iqbal! You found him! Such good news!'

'Yes,' he says. 'Yes, it is.'

The wind picks up, buffering, and the sun's brightness fades. The room seems muted in its colours, its sounds; and his words roll out smoothly, filling the edges of walls, the floorboards, the cracks everywhere.

'I need to tell you... How to start... Obaidur had ideas – back then we all did. But he was always sketching plans for how the products he made could be better.'

Lois is very still. 'Go on.'

Iqbal feels like he's started in the middle. Maybe he should start at the end. 'You know we, Archipelago, have insisted on guarantees in all the production contracts – no exploitation, minimum wage. And if anyone breaks these, the contract is broken...' No. The end doesn't make sense. He shifts to the start, where he started with it all, on Friday. 'He told me in his email that just before the fire, he'd been talking to an American journalist about factory conditions. The interview was in one of the fancy hotels. When the journalist went to the bar, a man approached him, said he'd heard mention of a product and Obaidur could earn some money. And you have to understand how low the wages are – even a hundred dollars can be four months' salary... Obaidur went with him to another bar, talked about his idea, about how to improve a product.' Iqbal shakes his head. He can imagine Obaidur's excitement. 'He'd guessed that this man was working for a company who could be interested in his idea.'

Lois listens carefully, waiting. She drinks her tea. There are noises from the corridor. They'll be interrupted soon.

'He was right. He was taken to meet a man, a researcher, and they bought the idea from him.'

Lois is nodding but looking confused. 'This is all good news, surely, for Obaidur?'

This is the hard part. He takes a deep breath.

'It was an idea about how to tighten up the first VR headsets. He was making them in the factory at the time, and he tried them out. You remember what the first ones were like – motion sickness, clumsy. Well, he came up with a simple idea: he moved the vision lens closer to the eye in a particular way – and the result was no motion sickness. Normally an idea would disappear, because there's no access to anyone to tell. But because of the journalist writing about conditions, because he got to speak to this other man...' He speaks quickly. 'I don't think he knew the real name of the man he spoke to. And they made him sign a contract, but it was written in English. They said it was a formality. Obaidur can't *read* English, so the contract is invalid. Whatever he signed away, he will legally still own the rights.'

Lois shakes her head. 'But... Well, that's what we did? Moving the lens so close to the eye was how we first broke into the market?'

'Yes.'

Lois is silent. The wind has dropped. The front doorbell sounds and Iqbal knows they will need to go and speak to the police soon.

'I sent Obaidur the photo from before the helicopter, the

group shot of us all. I asked him to let me know if the man was in it. The man who stole his idea, this "researcher". If he was, then Archipelago's success was built on this theft. Our guarantees in our contracts – we'd be built on a breach of our own guarantees.'

Lois's eyes are like polished green stones, hard, shiny. 'And did he get back to you? Who?' She clasps Iqbal's hand again, tight. 'Who was it?'

His fists clench as he speaks. 'It was Aksel. Aksel bought his idea. But when I checked the patent, it's registered to Archipelago. Do you even remember who on our team suggested it?'

'No. I don't remember exactly who, but it was in a team meeting. When I asked them later, they said it had landed in a memo on their desk as something to try. Unsigned. In the end we agreed it was a collective decision, a natural product of development.'

There's a knock on the front door.

'Did he say how much he was paid?' Lois's voice is very quiet. She hasn't dropped his gaze, but her words leave her mouth like they taste foul; she spits them out. 'Oh God, I had no idea Aksel was even in Bangladesh! I only went to see the factory conditions, when we were thinking about production. I imagined the worst, and I was right. It was why we moved production to Europe.' She paused. 'Iqbal, how do we tell Ebba? This could destroy the whole company if it gets out. The ethics clauses in the franchise contract – we'd be breaching our own contract. We'd lose millions.'

'He replied to me this morning. He was paid five hundred dollars. It was worth so much more.'

There is movement in the hall, footsteps. Voices carry even through the closed door and time presses. Lois leans forward, her voice dropping to a whisper, and he's scared – scared that her tendency to secrecy is a sign she had known all along? He can't bear to believe it, but he recalls the flash of suspicion when he saw her in the amphitheatre at midnight, sure she was there to meet the 'researcher' from Dhaka. He protected her secrets then, thinking Maarten was suspicious. Would he do it again? His fingers flex at the memory.

Iqbal shakes his head. 'He said he signed a document, but he couldn't read it. He can't read English. He was told it was a good idea, but it needed a lot of improvement. They offered him the money, and said it was up to him if he took it and wanted to sell his idea.'

Lois is ashen. Green stones staring from a white wall.

'So, he took some money, was told he was getting a good deal. And *if* it is our product – *if, if, if* – then Archipelago used fraudulent means to obtain the IP. IP theft. It would ruin us.'

Shaking his head, Iqbal says, 'What do we do?'

'Have you mentioned this to Maarten?' Lois asks.

'No,' Iqbal says. It needs to be handled carefully. Compensation with no legal battle – it seems to him the most sensible route. If they could credit Obaidur, pay him what he's owed, then it need never see court. They could easily avoid being in breach of contract on the new franchise gaming rights.

With his skin, teeth, nails and bones, he hopes Lois doesn't ask him to ignore it. To ignore Obaidur.

'Can we fly to him? Once the police are finished with this? Can we fly to him, and explain it all in full? I'll come with you. We can tell him the whole thing, and he can choose what to do next.' Lois leans and pulls him in close. He can feel her heart thudding at speed. He thinks of her hands shaking in the hospital. Those same hands pulling him in tight now.

'Iqbal, I'm so sorry. We'll fix this.'

The door rattles, and she can hear Ebba talking to a voice she doesn't recognise, and shouting from the stairs, calling everyone down. There's barking somewhere. The police must have brought dogs.

'Iqbal.' Her voice strangled, Lois pleads with him; her nails dig into his forearm, and he's surprised by the sudden panic in her tone.

The footsteps are louder now, almost at the kitchen. Lois speeds up her words, they tumble quickly, quietly. Like breath against his ear.

'I know it was you on Friday night. I saw you hit Maarten. I don't know why you did it, but I won't say anything. Was it you? Did you suspect Aksel then? Did Maarten see you do something? Was it you…'

But there's no time. Iqbal chokes on whatever he wants to say; the kitchen door opens, and an officer he doesn't recognise enters the room, wearing a full covered white suit, like the kind he's seen on the TV.

There's no time to say anything at all.

PART THREE

56

Filip

'Filip, I'm scared. Do you think they know?' Sophie holds his hand and her palm is warm; she pulls into his shoulder, turning her back to the rest of the room, where low chatter mixes with the sound of teacups clinking and the noise of the search above them: footsteps on the stairs, the bark of a dog; doors slamming outside as the vans from SOCO unload and reload.

He tightens his grip on her hand, leans down and kisses her head. He feels sick this morning. His stomach is lurching, but then he hasn't eaten anything. Drunk nothing since the coffee in the kitchen earlier. It had been bitter, but he was polite, didn't want to refuse.

'No. They don't know. We need to sit here, look calm, drink tea. We have nothing to worry about,' he whispers, but he *is* worried. They burned the evidence, but even he knows that forensic examination is likely to find some traces in the fire. He hadn't factored in a police search, and so soon. Once again, instead of actually looking after her, he'd gone for gesture.

Grand gestures are how he's composed himself in his head. He had wanted to seem determined earlier, in charge. But he'd been stupid. He'd been the fool he was always so worried he would seem. He should have gone straight to Maarten. Now what are they left with?

And a whisper, at the back of his head: *Did she do it? Had she tried to kill Marieke and killed Aksel instead?*

Rounded up in the dining room, they sit waiting. Tense. Expectant. The occasional bark of a dog or a shout from the SOCO team reminds them of the greater powers at play. Maarten enters and looks tired. He touches the side of his head where he was hit on Friday.

Friday, Filip thinks, feels like a lifetime ago.

Maarten begins, and there's a scratch to his voice, of lack of sleep and dehydration. 'We would normally interview you down at the station, but the press is starting to gather, so we'll stay here. It will protect your privacy as much as possible.'

'I can't believe Aksel is dead,' Marieke says.

A hush falls. Filip sees Lois reach out a hand to Iqbal, and Ebba, standing close, falls into an overstuffed chair, leaning her head back and closing her eyes.

Marieke is shaking her head. 'I just can't believe it. I never expected... I just thought he'd always...'

Marieke must be scared, Filip thinks. If someone tried to kill her and got Aksel instead, then she must be more terrified than ever.

The hairs stand on his arms. He thinks of Aksel's clutch, of the taste of his breath. The kiss of a dead man.

Maybe it's that which has taken hold of his stomach. The room is fuzzy for a second, and he feels himself sway.

And the whisper, *Is it her? Is it Sophie?* But no. It can't be. She might occasionally rank car brand above kindness when choosing friends; she can be rude to waiters, rude to cleaners. She listens only to the parts of conversations that interest her, tuning out the rest. And she's always late – like it's a policy. But she'd never kill anyone. She can't even kill a spider. She screams for him to take them away, but if he flushes it down the bath she's incensed.

There's no way she has killed someone. And he mustn't allow exhaustion to cloud his judgement. She had tried to frighten away Marieke, but there's no way she tried to kill her.

'How did he die?' This time it's Ebba who speaks. Her chair is by a table that is too small for all the teacups, but no one seems to want to sit at the dinner table, where they'd sat only thirty-six hours ago; when Aksel had played the piano, when Filip had cried.

'That is something we're looking into,' Maarten says.

'Surely he died in the crash?' Iqbal asks. 'And if it wasn't the helicopter that actually killed him, I thought he had a heart attack?'

There's some muttering.

Marieke says, 'Those are sniffer dogs.' She looks out of the window. 'What are they sniffing? Are you looking for drugs?'

'Oh God, it's not poison!' Sophie's face is pale and she grabs a chair. 'Oh my God, you don't think he was poisoned?'

Ebba stands slowly. 'Marieke gave her drink to Aksel. Was something intended for Marieke? And Aksel got it instead?'

Now the muttering becomes loud, chattering; someone half screams. Filip's head is aching and a blond officer has run towards Sophie, to allow her to lean on him. She's swaying. 'Oh God,' she says.

'It could just have been a heart attack!' Lois says loudly.

Filip wonders why he himself is so doubtful about this, why he actually believes it to be something else. Maybe it was the helicopter that had triggered a heart attack. Had anyone actually said anything other? He tries to remember what the police had said last night. He thinks of himself, Ebba and Lois, looking at each other. Thinking of murder.

'Please, calm down. Please.' Maarten raises his hands. The room falls quiet.

'Well,' Maarten says, 'we will know much more very soon. If I can ask you all for your patience. The search won't take long, then you can return to your rooms. If you wouldn't mind, DS Atkinson and DI Verma here will take your statements in the study, which leads just off the top of the room.

'Filip,' he says, and Filip finds himself the focus of the room. He knows he didn't kill Aksel, but he feels a flush build in his cheeks. That morning he had burned evidence of the letters Marieke had received.

'Of course,' he manages, and Sophie's grip is tight on his

arm. He gently removes her hand, kisses her and follows the two officers that flank Maarten. 'Back soon,' he says.

The room is silent.

57

LOIS

There is rain again. Lois listens to it, holding Iqbal's hand lightly and finding she is unable to let go.

The other hand holds a mug of coffee. The large cup is made with a thick clay and looks hand painted. She can't remember buying it, but then Ebba is a whirlwind, and sometimes things arrive in the house. They'd employed an interior designer, she remembers. She examines the mug without really looking at it. She thinks of the dark warm Friday night. Of seeing Iqbal raise a stick, hesitate, and whack Maarten over the head. Then he'd stood for a second. She'd frozen. She'd watched him throw the stick away, glance once in her direction and run full pelt up the lawn.

She squeezes his hand. Marieke sits opposite. They're in the armchairs near the fire, set aside from the dining table. There is a rug in front of the fire, but she does remember where that came from. She'd bought it in Dhaka. She'd paid what had been asked – she'd heard a few Western voices at the market, pushing for a bargain in their pale chinos and expensive sunglasses, proud of their skills. She'd talked to the man selling the rugs, who had been full of questions: *Where are you from? What do you think of Bangladesh?* She smiles, thinking of the warm air, drinking sweet cha. She'd browsed in bookshops, taken a river trip. All the day before the factory visit.

Marieke pours another tea and pushes it into Ebba's hands. Their brief conversation allows Lois a moment.

'I'm sorry,' she says, speaking as low as she dares. She's turned to Iqbal and he dips his head, doesn't quite meet her eye. 'I threw it at you, that I'd seen you hit Maarten. I haven't had a chance to ask you about it. It wasn't fair of me.'

'Lois… I,' he says, his voice quiet. 'I saw…'

'Lois, would you like to go next?' the female officer calls over.

'Of course,' Lois replies, sending her answer loudly across the room. As she stands, she clutches Iqbal, leans in to his ear. 'What did you see?'

Finally, he looks up, his brown eyes kind, wet. His lips are near her ear as she leans down on his shoulder, as though she needs help rising.

'I saw you. In the dark. I thought you were meeting… I thought you were meeting *him*. I saw Maarten follow you and I didn't want—' He stops, and Lois can feel the officer's eyes on the back of her neck.

'Meeting who? Meeting who, Iqbal?'

'I thought you were meeting Aksel. I thought maybe *you* knew. That maybe the police had wind of what had happened, with all the eyes on Marieke and Archipelago.

Maybe Maarten was on to it, and was following you. Despite it all, I couldn't let him… I had to protect you. I had to stop him.'

There are few moments where breath is really taken away, despite all the talk of it. It is, Lois supposes, how some people feel after a marriage proposal. But in this moment, where someone had protected her and thrown himself against every instinct he held, her breath is nowhere to be found.

'Iqbal,' she manages.

And he shrugs, looking down, not proud of himself. 'I'll tell him. I'll tell him later. I'll tell him I thought I was chasing the sender of the letters, and then when I saw it was him, I was afraid. I ran away.'

'Lois?' There's a change in tone from the officer now, and Lois makes her way across the room.

58

MAARTEN

'How are we getting on?' Maarten asks Adrika. They're all tired, including the guests. They've been going for a few hours now.

'I can't say we're miles further forward.'

Maarten thinks of the earlier interviews from the catering staff: *That dark-haired woman talking to Filip Schmidt. Really angry, almost passionate.*

Maarten thinks of Filip's discomfort when his wife had arrived, of Sophie's hands, clenched tight.

'Ask Sophie Atwood. If her husband *is* having an affair with Marieke Visser, she has a motive.'

Adrika nods. 'Anything come back on the search yet?'

'I'm stepping outside for an update now.'

Looking round the room as he weaves his way through the chairs, hands twist, eyes glance back and forth. They all sit with secrets, he's sure of it. Secrets they believe are worth protecting, with the lives of others.

Thinking of a possible affair, Maarten realises there had

been undercurrents. He could feel it in the room: the taste of jealousy, of something festering.

And Sophie hadn't been on the helicopter. They hadn't really thought about her.

Maarten glances out of the window. There are dogs sweeping the grounds, sniffing for clues.

He stops and shuffles the statements around, rereading comments relating to Filip and Sophie Atwood. Filip's statement was interesting, or rather, the figures were: 'I'd found out that Aksel was getting much better terms – millions. I know that makes it sound like I might have a motive. I know people have killed for less…' and they had, Maarten thought. But there had also been tension between Filip and Aksel over Sophie Atwood. He remembers their piano duet.

Jealous of money, jealous of love.

His head is thick. He picks up the coffee, which left untouched has gone from hot to warm to cold, and drinks it quickly.

Looking for Niamh, the CSM today, he asks, 'How's the search going?'

'Interesting. We've just finished in the bedrooms upstairs. A mess of DNA. But we did find this.' Niamh holds up a bag of evidence. She's new as a crime scene manager but she's worked for the Hertfordshire police force for longer than Maarten has lived here. He feels a prickle of anticipation. She wouldn't highlight something unless it was promising.

'It looks, from the remains in Sophie Atwood and Filip Schmidt's fire in their bedroom, as if the letters sent to Marieke Visser came from their household. Someone has burned the evidence in their room, and we have a fingerprint match for Sophie Atwood in Marieke Visser's room. It looks relatively fresh.'

Maarten allows a whistle through his teeth. 'You think she went to Marieke's room to get rid of the letter? Surely she'd have guessed that she would have handed the letter to us?'

'She might have just been sneaking around, looking for evidence of an affair, if that's what you're thinking of. Either way, she's looking likely, Maarten.' She holds up a finger. 'Wait for it – big news to come...'

'Go on.'

'We've got a match on the toxin in Marieke Visser's glass with the toxin in Aksel Larsen's blood. You were right. He drank from her drink, and it probably killed him.'

Pushing open the door to the room that leads off the back of the dining room, where the interviews are being held, he enters quietly. Sophie Atwood is sitting, white as a sheet, fingers tightly pulling her wedding ring on and off, quickly, roughly. Her ring finger is red and looks sore. Her eyes are blood dark.

'You suspected, didn't you,' Adrika is saying, 'you suspected Filip was sleeping with Marieke. You suspected, and yet you came here. This weekend. Was this the showdown weekend? Did you come here to kill her?'

Pale, still. The only thing moving is the wedding ring: on, off, on. She says nothing.

'You suspected, and what, you came here to bring it to a close? To end things, once and for all? Come on, Sophie, talk to me.' Adrika sits back.

'You can have a lawyer, if you like,' Maarten says, and Sunny stands up and exits, leaving the third chair for him.

She shakes her head, still not speaking.

The small room is warm, intense. He leans in, placing his hand on the table gently, watching his fingers curl down flat, giving her a moment. There is fear in her eyes. It rattles out of her, like the windows rattling on a shaking building. Her foundations are loosening. Her left eyebrow lifts and falls.

He likes her. He has liked her from the moment she stood on the step, collecting herself, when everyone else sat inside drinking. He liked her when he gave her his arm.

Did she try and kill Marieke?

'Sophie. We found the remains of the letters in your fire grate.'

A small sound, a whimper, passes quickly from her lips.

He feels Adrika beside him stir only the slightest bit. This evidence is the biggest find they have.

'Was it because you thought they were having an affair, Sophie? I don't know how I'd feel if I found out Liv was with someone else.'

Sophie sits up slightly straighter. He watches her pull her shoulders back a fraction, and her eyes close, then a second later open again, and she takes a deep breath.

'Yes, it was me.' The wedding ring comes off, slips back on. Her fingers shake. Her eyebrow lifts again, just the one. She must be tired, Maarten thinks. It's that kind of twitch lift that pulls when you're so tired you can't think any more. And a flutter of relief passes over her face, mixing with the fear like sugar falling into a hot drink. The swirls of sweet relief ease the tension around her eyes, her mouth. Her voice warms as she speaks, and she settles, the telling of the story flowing like hot sweet tea, spilling from a mug.

'I saw all the usual things. I saw a change in his manner. He had mentionitis: you know what I mean, brought up Marieke's name a few times more often than normal. And then after a month or so, nothing. He stopped mentioning her completely.'

She lifts her hands and scoops her hair into a ponytail, then lets it fall down her back, swinging her head a fraction to the left to lift it all back. She rolls her shoulders.

'That's worse, you know? I knew there were still meetings; tweets about conferences; photos of them all together, pushing ahead with this deal, making a difference, proud of themselves. And I knew. He changed colour occasionally when I mentioned her name. Our conversations, already so stilted, almost stopped...' She catches her breath, closes her eyes again. Her hands clench and unclench.

'We had something so special. But on honeymoon, it changed. He was always on his phone. His business was busy; busy business. All the time. I pulled away, made him try to work for it. Tried everything.'

She shrugs, glances down. Maarten looks to Adrika. The tape is running but she has made a few notes. She raises her eyebrows a touch, and then, as Sophie's head comes back up, she slips back to neutral. The heat of the room makes Maarten's head spin. So little sleep.

'Pulling away didn't help. He just got nervous around me. Tongue-tied. But, fuck, I loved him. Occasionally, we got it just right. And I knew if I managed to convince him we were worth it...'

There's a laugh from outside, and it dies quickly. Sophie glances at the door to the dining room.

'You know I slept with someone? I slept with my agent. Just once. It was when it was really bad with Filip. When I first saw him out for a drink with Marieke. He was laughing like he never laughs with me. Her hand was on his. He told me now he never slept with her, but what does that matter when he trusted her but didn't trust me?' She shrugs. 'I did a "fuck you" fuck. Fuck him.' She turns her palms face up, then down again. 'But it was crap. *Kak*, it was worse than that. So that's when I decided to try a different tack.

'I knew sending the letters was stupid. But I was angry. It was primal, like something I couldn't control. I could *taste* it. So, I sent a couple of notes. Just telling her to back off, to step away. I couldn't be specific. I copied much of the language on Twitter, on Facebook. I thought... She was a public figure. I guessed she'd get a lot of bad press, trolling.' She looks at Maarten. Her eyes are clear, her face so pale her skin almost melts away, transparent. 'I love him. And I knew he loved me. I just needed her to back off.'

Maarten nods at her, reassures her with his tone that telling him is the right thing to do. 'Sophie, did you try to kill her? Did you try to poison Marieke? And did Aksel drink it by mistake?'

A tiny shake of her head. It's not strong enough to be

believed as a denial, but it's too weak to seem like a false protestation of innocence. Too weak to be a lie.

There's the sound of a dog barking. It's loud. And Maarten wonders if that means they've found something. A few shouts follow. His ears listen. If he were a dog, they'd be standing on end now.

'Did Filip know, Sophie?' This time Adrika asks, and her voice is soft. She speaks gently, and Maarten likes that she gets her tone just right. Every time.

She looks up again. 'He loves me, you know. He loves me. He just doesn't love himself enough to have me. But after the crash yesterday, I could see it. The belief was back. And for a moment...' She looks at Maarten. Her eyes plead with him.

The dogs are barking again. Maarten watches her.

Is she lying about something? He feels suddenly nervous. What if her anger extended all the way to her husband? There's a flash of fear, for Filip. If she's lying now, does that mean Filip is in danger?

'Just out of interest, if Filip died now, what would you be worth?'

'I'm not...' – her gaze is stony – 'going to kill my husband.'

Maarten considers it for a second. Then pushes on. 'But what would you be worth? Hundreds of millions? A billion?'

She says nothing.

'By bringing down the helicopter, did you hope to get rid of your husband cleanly, and his mistress? You wouldn't have to fight a messy divorce.'

He pushes hard.

'Did you put poison in Marieke's glass?'

Still, she says nothing.

'Sophie Atwood. I'm arresting you for the murder of Aksel Larsen, for the crime of Malicious Communications, for sending letters to Marieke Visser. You do not have to say anything…'

59

FILIP

Filip sees a cluster of officers outside and heads are bent in discussion, some pointing at the house. He can sense it. There's a regrouping. He knows they've pretty much finished – he heard someone outside say it. But they've got hold of something and they're going back in. With new information. A new direction.

He hears crying from the interview room. Sophie's in there.

Fuck. The letters. The letters in the fire.

The room swims. The hold on his stomach is strong now, and there are stabbing pains running upwards, zipping over his head. This must be an anxiety attack. His heart beats quickly.

He leans his head against the pane of glass. The cold is sharp on his brow, and he closes his eyes, opens them again, hoping his vision has settled, that he's just fuzzy with confusion, lack of sleep.

He can hear words floating through the air. They're muffled, like word bubbles popping before they get to him. Some make it all the way: 'fire', 'the victim's room', 'fingerprints', 'Sophie Atwood'.

What does it mean? Lois stands nearby. He can feel her watching him. She must know what's going on because she doesn't come straight over. Like when you've heard someone's had bad news, but you don't know what to say.

This weekend. From jealous and suicidal, to hero, to husband again. Now about to lose his wife. After a year of pushing her away.

'Lois?' he whispers, trying not to attract the attention of the room, but he doesn't know why he bothers. They are all silent. Sophie's tears from behind the door are clear, and it's like no one can even breathe.

'Filip?' She crosses to him swiftly. Standing by him, with her hand on his arm. 'Tell me what I can do.'

'What's going on? Do you know?'

Her face is tight with confusion. 'I think…'

'Lois, please. You need to tell me. I'm going mad here.'

The whisper in his head is a roar now. *Sophie could not have killed Aksel. She could not have done it.*

'Filip, they've asked for the master key to the guest safe installed in your room. I don't really know, and I don't want to guess and get it wrong…'

'You know something, please, just tell me.' There's a roaring so loud in Filip's head it's like his skull is being crushed. It's sound alone, but a force. Like the ricochet of the sound barrier breaking, sound so loud it makes houses vibrate, bones shudder.

'I…' She looks at the floor, rather than at him. 'I heard them say "the suspect", and then I heard them talking, while I was getting the key. They said "the suspect has prints in Visser's room", they said they must have been left when we were all in hospital. And poison. They found a plastic bag with suspected poison. I heard them say the dogs found it.'

She could not have killed him. She is not capable.

Lois is still looking at the ground.

The roaring in his head threatens to topple him. He can barely open his eyes.

'Where did they find it? Where did they find it, Lois?'

'I think… I think it was in her make-up bag. I'm so sorry, Filip. I'm so very sorry.'

60

LOIS

Sophie comes out, led by Maarten, and Lois stands next to Filip, wanting to hold on to him. He looks like he needs tethering; he sways.

But Lois can't touch him. The room swirls and she herself feels unpinned. She looks for Ebba, but she's by the fire, not looking at anything, just staring forward, and her blue eyes are empty. She watches as Sophie is led by DI Verma, her brown bob holding still, like the very air in the room.

Filip crosses quickly to her. He takes her in his arms, holds her. The officers move to separate them, but she hears him: 'I am yours. Entirely. I love you, Sophie. I am sorry. It's all my fault.'

Lois can't breathe. She swallows hard.

As Sophie passes Marieke, she looks at her, and says, 'I'm so very sorry. You must have heard. It was me who sent the letters.' And DI Verma takes her arm, gently leading her out, not allowing her to remain.

Marieke, the colour of dust, lifts her arm, and as it hovers in the air, she raises her fingers to her lips, and kisses them, then holds the kiss aloft, turned towards Sophie.

As Sophie is led towards the door, just before she disappears, she halts.

With one last cry, Sophie turns and shouts, 'Filip!'

He takes a step towards her, but the officer holds up his hand.

Marieke staggers backwards, against the back of the overstuffed chair, and it is Iqbal who reaches out to her.

So, is that it? But why was Sophie trying to kill Marieke? Lois's brain crashes with questions, looking for answers, sorting data, flipping through the binary possibilities.

Lois looks to Marieke, then Filip.

Human affection. The power to destroy.

'Christ, is it all over, then?' Marieke begins in a laugh, but as she finishes, she doubles over, her head on her knees. The sobs arrive first in vibrations, soundless, but in pulls of air so deep, and expelled in ragged spurts, that even without sound they are piercing.

Lois looks to Filip, but he is watching out of the window. He speaks as though to himself, and he raises his palm high and flat on the windowpane.

Sophie looks back once from the gravel outside.

61

FILIP

I need to go to her, he thinks. *I need to go to her.*

His brain isn't seeming to function, and he waits for it to catch up. He can usually rely on his brain.

Slowly, the shock begins to feel like shock, instead of simply paralysis, and he pulls out his phone and calls Ruben, the person he relies on most in the world. Even as he is dialling, he has faith this can be sorted.

'I need a lawyer,' he begins with. 'We usually use Bakker, don't we, but I need a criminal lawyer. It's a murder charge.'

Ruben is silent down the phone for a second. And it's not like him. Filip is irritated. 'Ruben, can you hear me? I need your help.'

'Filip? Is everything OK? You're not making sense.'

'I know it's confusing, but we need a lawyer.' His head feels as though it's splitting in two.

'Filip, is there someone else there? Can you put them on? You're not making any sense.'

Rage, nausea, pain sweeps Filip, and he shouts down the phone. 'Ruben, will you listen to me!'

Gentle now, Ruben says, 'Filip, you're slurring, I can't make out what you're saying. Is there someone else there? I need you to ask them for help.'

Filip watches cars and vans pull away from the house. He's exhausted. He will need to go to the station later, but he won't have any access to Sophie just yet. And they will need to wait for the lawyer to arrive. Ruben will take care of all that. If he will only listen.

The phone is very heavy. His hand fights to hold it. Fights to keep it in his grasp, but it's too much. His fingers relax. Defeat comes quickly.

The phone falls, and it lands hard, shattering; and turning, like Ruben asked him to, he faces the rest of the room. They're all looking back at him. Marieke takes a step forward, and he can see from her face, like from Ruben's voice, that something is wrong. And he is so very tired. Standing is so very tiring.

The coffee had been bitter that morning. He'd drunk it, not wanting to make a fuss. He tries to think of who gave him the cup, and he remembers Sophie next to him, pouring in his milk, smiling at him.

No, not her. Who else?

He smiles. Vomit spews from his mouth, and he tips, feeling lost in his sway.

He needs to trust his wife. If it wasn't Sophie, then it was someone here.

What had Aksel said to him? Those last words. It's his nugget.

Clearing his brain, he forces himself to think of it all at once, like he might think of a crossword clue.

Those words float upwards, swim. *It was never meant...*
Then they fall.

Can it be?

One last glance round the room.

They had all been so very wrong. About it all.

Maarten. He needs to speak to Maarten. Before anything else.

And he can feel himself falling, free at last.

62

LOIS

'Filip!' Lois screams.

Iqbal bends down and places a hand on Filip's face, leaning his head close. Maarten kneels too. But it's clear Filip is still breathing; it's loud. Like a heave.

Pushing them aside, Lois gets to him, and his eyes are fast dimming. The heave, like a mechanical pump failing, is coming from him. This must be what they call the death rattle, and she screams again.

Through the window, she sees Sophie turn. Climbing into the car, the screams must have pulled her out. Sophie yanks hard against the officer holding her arm.

Breaking free, Sophie runs back into the house. Dogs are barking, and Lois hears one of the police officers swear loudly as he runs in and sees Filip, the vomit, hears his last few breaths. Sophie howls.

Running feet crunch the gravel. Someone shouts for an ambulance.

Lois can't make out much, movement is fast and blurred around her. She bends like she'd seen Filip bend over Aksel, and she bangs his chest with her fist, like she'd seen him do. And she thumps again, hard.

But she's not the first person, and Maarten is already leaning over Filip's face, his cheek close.

A gasp from behind is loud, as Iqbal shouts, 'Has he stopped breathing?'

'Yes,' Maarten says. He bends and breathes full into Filip's mouth, and the blond DS kneels, beginning CPR.

Like déjà vu, Lois watches as police take over the pounding on Filip's chest.

But she knows. She knows like she knew when Filip worked on Aksel.

Filip is dead.

63

MAARTEN

Dust flies, refusing to settle. Maarten's hands shake as he struggles to compose himself. He'd liked Filip, trusted Filip.

More than that, his flash of fear that Filip's life could be in danger had proven correct, and he'd been unable to stop it. If only he'd worked faster.

It's not the first time he should have moved faster. It's not the first time he tastes regret like sour milk.

He's stepped outside for a second. The ambulance is still busy.

'Sir?' Adrika says quietly. 'They're still in the hall. I don't know...'

'Take them outside.' He looks through the window. The sun is making a courageous return. 'The dining room is a crime scene. Get them all out. We'll need drinks, food... They need looking after. We can take them to the station and do interviews in a few hours. We need to feed them first. They'll all be in shock of some kind. That was...' There aren't words. He closes his eyes.

'Good plan. Niamh isn't finished with the house. I'll order food.'

Nodding, Maarten picks up the phone. He will have to let the super know. This isn't going to be easy.

Her anger rattles down the line: '…and get her lawyer in and get going. We need a statement for the press, this is…'

Maarten looks out at the lawn where the guests are moving. Many are crying.

'…At least we've got her. We can focus on that in the statement…' She sounds as though she's calming down. 'When you write it, make a big deal of the fact the suspect is in custody.'

'Ma'am,' Maarten offers in agreement.

'Keep me updated. What a shitshow.'

Ringing off, he looks at the dining room door. The ambulance had taken Filip but Maarten knows there's no coming back from that. He's already alerted the pathologist.

He will need to look at Filip's body again at some point. He feels sick at the thought. He calls to Adrika, tapping at a food delivery app. 'Let's head down to the garden table. See how they're doing. Could you feel the relief in the room once Sophie Atwood was taken out?' He couldn't work out where it came from, but the relief had been like ice in the air. 'Someone is pleased she's being taken away. Why? That house holds its secrets in the walls like cement. Let's find out what else we don't know.'

★★★

Walking down into the pale November sun, arriving after the rain shower, Maarten sees Lois and Iqbal talking, standing underneath a tree.

'Meet you there,' he says to Adrika, and he makes his way over to them.

They don't see him coming and he hears Lois talking, catching the word 'Dhaka'.

It keeps coming up, and he pauses. They are intent in their exchange and they don't see him for a second.

'Aksel is dead now. We don't need to report it, Lois.' Iqbal sounds stressed. 'What good will it do? Let's just pay him properly for what we took. Otherwise we'll lose the whole franchise deal if this comes out...'

'Not us – not what *we* took!' Lois is almost crying. 'Aksel!'

'But they won't make that distinction! The moment you're worth what Archipelago is worth now, no one makes that distinction...'

'We have to confess! We'd be as bad as him...' Lois is sobbing now.

'Aksel is dead. He's gone. Let his mistakes die with him. We're all better off...'

'Maarten!' Lois jumps, seeing him.

They both turn, stare at him. Red-faced and startled.

'How are you feeling?' he asks. What do they have to confess to? He wants to ask now, but from their faces, he wonders if they'll tell him anyway. Lois looks distraught.

Neither of them were on the helicopter, and he wonders briefly at their relief in Aksel's death. There's no way Sophie can be innocent, surely?

'Maarten.' Lois takes a step towards him. But she sways, and Maarten grabs her arm.

'When was the last time you ate?' he asks. 'I want you both to sit and talk to me about this conversation, but first, go and eat something. We'll get nowhere if you all start fainting on me.'

Lois clutches her stomach and Iqbal jumps. 'Is it the baby?' he asks. 'Shall I call a doctor?'

More information, Maarten thinks. *It just doesn't stop coming.*

'No,' Lois says. 'I'm going to be sick.'

'Eat,' Maarten says. 'You need to eat. I can call a doctor?'

'No. I'm fine.'

She looks anything but fine, he thinks, looking at her pale skin, the shadows under her eyes. He wants to push with questions, but they must eat first.

The table is laid out in the sun. Adrika has got water for everyone, and Sunny has driven to a coffee shop for hot drinks. Food is on its way. It won't be long before they can start with the statements.

Maarten thinks of the momentary hesitation, his doubt about Sophie. He's still thinking about suspects. Why? He was willing to think about Lois and Iqbal – but surely he's happy with Sophie.

There's a spare seat near Marieke, but before he takes it, he steps away from the table and calls Niamh.

'Maarten?'

'Anything odd about the glasses?' he says, thinking

things through. Remembering the chain of events. There's something niggling him. The sudden doubt about Sophie has unnerved him. She sent the letters, but could she kill?

'Now you ask, yes,' Niamh says. 'I was going to report at the finish, but the stem to the broken glass is part seared away. It looks like it's been done cleanly. Strange – why do you ask?'

Maarten thinks of Aksel holding the glass, making the toast. Then he runs through the afternoon again, events ticking over. The order of things.

'Thanks, Niamh.'

Interesting. Like three cherries in a slot machine, pictures fall into place. Who had been where. Who had done what.

If this is true, he must move fast. It's one thing to have a theory, but this will need some careful evidence.

'Maarten! Come and eat,' Marieke calls, and gestures to the spare seat next to her.

He smiles, heading over. She looks older than she had on Friday.

'So, it's over?' Marieke asks.

Voices swirl round them. He can't hear what the sisters are discussing, and he doubts they can hear him.

'Yes. Looks that way,' he says. 'I think you can stop worrying now. There will be no more letters. No more threats.'

'I can't believe it, Maart. Sophie sent the letters to me? Tried to kill me? Killed Filip? If I'd have known... It's all my fault.'

'How is it your fault?' he asks.

She shakes her head. 'Oh fuck. I've just pushed on. I've

not let anything stop me! I always do this. I just push on. I decide and then off I go. We all got on that helicopter even though I'd had that letter. Sometimes it works well. Sometimes I don't think of the fallout.' At this point she looks at Maarten. 'Twenty years ago, I didn't think of you.'

So, it's that time. She looks at him. Waits for him to say something.

A plane sketches its way through the clouds; a tractor is still, unoccupied, parked in a field nearby.

No one else seems to be listening. They've retreated into themselves and of the original eleven for dinner, it seems crazy that two are dead, one is unconscious, another sits by a hospital bed and one has been arrested for murder. With Liv at home, it's eleven down to five. In two days.

'It's been like a dream,' she says, speaking in Dutch. She looks out down the lawn, towards the Roman theatre. 'These last few days, like a rush of everything at once. Beginning with the shock of seeing you,' she says, her eyes softening. 'But that was the only good part, Maarten.'

Maarten thinks of the Marieke he knew when he was young.

'I can't wait to get back to my daughter,' she says, and Maarten is surprised.

'You have a daughter? How old is she?'

'Twenty,' she says, staring out across the lawn.

Maarten does the maths and feels the air in his stomach contract.

'Wait. Is she…? Shit…' His head spins.

And another thought. Liv's anger the other night. It

wasn't just about him being outside with Marieke... She'd half said something, and he hadn't listened.

Marieke speaks quickly. 'No, Maarten. She's not your child. But I do have a confession. All this time, without him knowing who you were, I've told Aksel you were the father. Not your name – but when you knocked on the door, and found me half dressed with another man. You saw him, he was there. That night.' She shakes her head, looks to the ground. 'I've been on and off in a relationship with Aksel for years. It's been *destructive*. To say the least. I've never wanted to tell him he was the father.'

She looks out across the fields. 'All this time, I let him think you were. That night when you came round.' She goes to touch his hand, but pulls back. 'Maarten, I messaged you about the car, I set you up to come. I wanted him to see you. I *needed* him to see you. I was pregnant before we got together, Maarten. All those fucking raw eggs in the zabaglione? It was a relief not to have to think of a reason not to eat them.'

Maarten feels like stone. That night comes rushing back.

'It's been so hard – my God, the guilt! Should I have told her? Should I have told her who her father was, when I could? But Maarten, you met him. He was so controlling. I couldn't let her be victim to him, the way I was. Getting away from him. It's been the hardest thing I've done.'

All this time, all this guilt and pain. She'd used him as a foil? Maarten stares at her. She'd played him. She'd used him to deflect Aksel. And he's lived with what happened that night, for so long.

'Your face.' She shakes her head. 'You meant something

to me, Maarten. It wasn't nothing. Aksel is destructive. Debilitating. For a while, I thought with you I'd get myself away. But he pulled me back in. He always pulled me back in. I've been free of him for a while now, and the *relief*!'

Maarten can taste the beer he'd been drinking, feel the steps beneath his feet as he'd climbed to her apartment, twenty years ago. He looks at her now; and then.

He'd left his car at her apartment the night before, at her suggestion. He hadn't been planning to see Marieke, but she'd sent a reminder, and it had made him think of her.

He'd been due on duty, so he'd only had the one beer with a friend that afternoon. And as he climbed the stairs to her apartment, he'd felt desire for her. If he was a little late for his shift, would it kill him? He'd knocked on her door and when she'd answered, he'd swept her up, buried his head into her, into what had come to feel familiar.

There had been a dry laugh from the back of the room. The laugh is tight in his memory box, locked for when he wishes to run himself down, when he wants to think less of himself. To feel small. He'd seen this weekend how Aksel excelled in making others feel small.

'Maarten!' Marieke had half shouted. And her face. Christ, her face. He's never forgotten it. He'd almost dropped her.

'I'm so sorry, Maart. I wasn't expecting you.'

And as he'd put her down, he'd taken in the candles, the music.

'Fuck,' he'd said, backing out. And he'd been so embarrassed. 'Fuck.'

And he'd fled, running down the steps and towards the car.

'Maarten! Stop!' she'd screamed at him, running after him. She'd pulled on a coat, and by then it was raining. The wet was thick, heavy in a sudden downpour, and his hair was soaked, water running down the back of his neck.

'Maart! Maart! Stop!'

But he'd carried on. He'd flung himself into his car, feeling stupid. Feeling small. And he was angry. Angry with her.

'Get back to him!' he'd screamed, slamming the door, glancing once in the mirror. She'd stood in the rain. And he'd powered away.

The car's wheels had turned, skidded beneath him. The car ricocheted off a wall, spinning in the wet. Her face was stark in the mirror. He'd started again, driving away, angry. He had spun the car wide, getting it back on the road. The wheels lifted on the water like they were gliding, and in slow motion the car had turned, in a pirouette, Marieke's face, carved with pity.

Driving back to his flat, planning on throwing a sickie, the call had come in. Backup was needed. A robbery. He was close. Actually driving past the jewellery shop at the time. He should have just stopped the car.

Instead, angry, he drove on. Flying fast through the traffic. Almost home, he thought better of it, and he swung the car round, going back.

He'd entered and the officer who had made the call was already dead.

Once he'd found him, his rage turned against himself.

He'd run in, tackled the gunman. It had been his duty to answer the call, and he had left another officer to die. Whether he could have made a difference, if he had got there sooner…

He'll never know. He'd received a medal for bravery, which he'd given away almost as soon as he was able.

Aksel had known it was him. Aksel told him he'd seen the articles about the death, about the medal, Maarten's face in the newspaper. He would have known when Maarten left the flat.

'Do you ever think of it? That night?' Marieke says.

Maarten's phone rings and he rises with relief. He can't speak to her right now. He made his own decisions that night. But all he can think of is Liv, of how soon he can go home and tell it all to Liv. Then all their secrets, frying in the sun, can be aired. It's no longer a secret, if everybody knows.

Moving down the lawn quickly, he rubs his face with the back of his hand.

Someone says, 'Lister Hospital', and asks him to hold. Then Sarah Arkwright's voice sails down the line.

'Maarten? It's Richard. He's awake! He's OK! Thank God.'

'Oh, Sarah, I'm so pleased!'

'Listen, he wants me to tell you. When Aksel was stumbling into Filip, he said something. And Richard thinks it could be important. I think I've got it right.'

Maarten's mouth parts slightly as he listens to her speak,

and it takes him a second to say, 'Thank you for that. And Sarah, that's such good news.'

The line clicks off, after Sarah offers a goodbye. Maarten glances back at the table.

Filip hadn't heard it right. What he'd said he'd heard. But this. This ties in with his theory. This will help enormously.

They're almost there. This weekend. A little more evidence, and it will be complete.

64

LOIS

Torn between grief for Filip and terror for her sister, Lois hangs on to Ebba's hand as though she's afraid she'll drift away.

'Please, eat something,' she says, but Ebba stares at her, vacant. It's almost 3 p.m. now and Ebba's eaten nothing all day, as far as she knows.

'Please,' Lois repeats.

Slowly, Ebba lifts a sandwich and takes a bite. Lois sees Maarten talking on the phone, walking in the gardens.

'Will we have to go to the station?' she asks the police officer with the brown bob, who nods.

'Can we take a walk first?' Lois asks, feeling the pressing weight of people, everywhere, for three days.

'If you like, but not up to the house,' the officer says, but she smiles, kind.

Looping arms, they walk down towards the trees, towards the amphitheatre.

'It's still standing,' says Ebba. 'I'd imagined it flattened after yesterday. All those years, and then it would burn to the ground.'

Lois takes in the scene. She thinks of how scared she'd been. Of how scared she is now.

'I'm pregnant,' Lois says. She looks down at the ground. She loves this place. She remembers them playing when they were young. Before their father had died and they'd lost everything they'd known. They'd climbed trees here, played hide-and-seek. Their birthday parties had been on this lawn: balloons, cake and their father, playing the part of the clown.

'Lois!' Ebba's face lights up, and for a second she looks like herself again. 'Lois, this is amazing! Who's the father?'

'Let's do all that later,' Lois says, not ready to confront the guilt, the sadness, wrapped up with the father. 'I'm scared. I am so scared we're going to lose all of this. Lose it all again.'

'What do you mean?' Ebba says. 'Why will we lose it all? We've worked so hard to keep it. To get it back.' Her eyes cloud again, and Lois wishes the weekend away, like a bad dream.

Looking up, the sun is breaking through. The light is cold. 'I was speaking to Iqbal earlier. He's heard from someone he knew in Dhaka. It sounds like we could be involved in some kind of IP theft from a factory worker; you know we've embedded clauses everywhere to force our contractors to minimise slavery and exploitation. If we're found guilty of doing the same thing, we could lose millions.'

'What do you mean?' Ebba looks confused. 'Who stole the IP?'

'It sounds like it was Aksel.' Lois wraps her arms around her, shivering. Her stomach growls, but she's still too nauseous to eat. 'He was in Dhaka when we were. He paid Iqbal's friend a pittance for the idea of moving the viewing lens closer to the eye in the way we did – what let us launch our VR sets with a splash.'

Ebba looks out over the theatre ruins. Lois glances at her profile – she looks tissue-paper thin in the light. Her hair is scrambled into a knot on her head, and it fades into the pale sun, sitting behind her. She's drained.

Before them, there are still signs of the crash. They will pass in time. The grass, blackened, is thinning anyway with autumn. Orange, red, yellow leaves have already part-covered the crash site.

'I knew Aksel was there. He was the one who paid for the trip.'

'What do you mean?' Lois says, amazed. 'You knew Aksel was there?'

'Yes, I knew. I was the one who asked him to help us.' Ebba shakes her head. 'We had nothing when we started this company. Once we lost the house, once we lost all the money in Dad's firm, we had no chance of starting out properly. You know Aksel and Dad were friends, worked together. I went to Aksel and I asked him to help.'

'But why would he help you?' Lois says. 'Aksel is vicious. Why would he bend over backwards to help you?'

Ebba looks down at her toes. Her eyes fill and she starts to cry quietly. 'I never told you, Lois. I never told you what

Dad said, when he was dying. He was in his office when the press ran that article, about the fault with a product, and within half an hour all his shares were worth nothing. I watched his face: he turned green, and then he clutched his chest. I phoned an ambulance but by the time it arrived, he was dead. There was nothing I could do. Lois, it was horrible! But before he died, he told me only Aksel knew about the possible flaw in the product. It had never even been confirmed!'

Lois can taste bile in her mouth.

'Aksel saw an opening and moved in for the kill. Once he thought he could buy the stock low...' Ebba shakes her head. Lois reaches out for her, partly for support. The ground she stands on feels as though it shifts.

'Oh my God,' Lois says, dizzy, her head spinning. 'Oh my God. Ebba, why did you go to him? How could you look him in the face again?'

Ebba waves her hand away, her face screwing up, spitting out the words quickly. 'It's easy for you Lois, with your ideals, your morals, your *goodness*. You don't have to deal in the real world! It's all men and egos, and power. How do you think we got our foot in the door? I went to Aksel and I told him I had proof he leaked the report. I told him we'd lost everything, and it was his turn to make it up to us. Otherwise, I would expose him.'

She shakes her head.

Like the house is crumbling down, Lois wants to run. Her foundations are shaking.

They'd grown up in this house, and they had lost it once. She understands why Ebba fought to keep it. She remembers wondering where funding had come from, when they had first begun making the devices. But she'd assumed it must have been part of Richard and Sarah's investment, or that Ebba had secured a loan. They had been loaned money from the bank at various stages. She'd never really gone into the details of which parts of the business had been funded from which source, always leaving the business side of things to Ebba. She'd been so busy with the creative side.

'So Aksel suggested the factories in Bangladesh?'

Ebba nods.

'And I'd insisted on seeing the conditions. Whether or not we we'd be happy to go ahead with them.' Lois thinks back to that time. 'When we came back, that was when we had the breakthrough with the sets, and it all started to happen.'

Ebba interlaces her fingers with Lois's. 'Don't throw it all away now, Lois.'

'Oh, Ebbs.' Lois thinks of the millions on the table at the moment, of the deal with Hollywood, of the huge factories in Rotterdam and Bergen, waiting to take their products, to ship them out to the whole world. And one man, who sold his idea for less than the price of the bottle of champagne Aksel had brought with him that weekend. 'We'll need to go to Dhaka, to compensate him for his invention. Give him what he's owed. What Aksel stole from him.'

Ebba nods, looking outwards. She speaks carefully. 'But let's do it quietly. We don't want to scare away the franchise. IP theft would take us down completely. And then all of this, this whole weekend, would be wasted. A waste of time. A waste of…'

Lois nods. 'A waste of life,' she says. She thinks of Filip. 'I still don't really understand why Sophie killed him. I thought they'd sorted it all out – it seemed that way. To think we had a murderer at our table, under our roof. That Filip spent his last hours here. And the crash, Aksel's death. All in our home.' She puts a hand on her stomach, her tiny baby. 'Life is so fragile. I'm not sure I'll ever trust anyone again.'

'People are strange, Lois. You know that. People are the game changers. To play and be played.'

Lois thinks of Obaidur and of Aksel. Was his death karma? Aksel hadn't got away with anything.

'I'm sorry, Lois. I'm sorry I didn't question Aksel. He told me of his idea for the lens and said he didn't want to take the credit. That after what happened to Dad, he wanted us to benefit. I believed him.' She shrugs. 'He could have brought us all down. He could have brought the whole thing crashing down. Just like Dad.'

Lois is cold now, spent. A bird swoops low; the day has a chill to it. A gust of wind feels like ice, and it blows straight through her.

65

MAARTEN

Leaning back in his chair, Maarten takes in the fields. Autumn is a funny time. A waiting time. The earth has a mini death in winter, comes back to life in the spring.

One word difference. It's all he has. One word. There's no way he could build a case around just that. And who is to say who heard what? Filip said it was something different entirely. No one is convicted on one word, heard differently by two different people.

'Sir? Shall I get the cars ready? Shall we go to the station?'

'I'll need a bit longer,' he says, picking up another sandwich. 'Adrika, in a minute I need to run through something with you. First, I need to check with Niamh. See what they've found.'

'Maarten.' Niamh drinks from a bottle of water. 'That was one big house.'

He smiles. 'Anything?'

Nodding, she swallows and gestures to the kitchen. 'Same poison. In a milk jug and in a coffee cup. Did you say Sophie Atwood poured the milk this morning?'

Maarten nods. 'Yes. Three witnesses for that.'

'So, there you go. Same poison found in her toilet bag, same poison found in Aksel's blood, and I would guess, Filip's.'

Looking up the stairs, Maarten sees SOCO heading down. 'You all done?'

'Yes, they can go back in. If you dare let them! I'd be running from this house if it was me.'

Maarten laughs hollowly.

'You need to get changed,' Niamh says, walking backwards, swigging the water. 'Is that Schmidt's vomit? Snappy.'

Glancing down, Maarten takes off the jacket. His stomach turns.

Adrika enters the main door. 'Ready?'

Nodding. 'Go and tell them to head in, and then I need to talk to you. We've had a game plan change.'

66

LOIS

Dusk is setting in early. Lois glances at the kitchen clock and it's almost four. It will be dark in half an hour. The day has almost passed. This weekend is almost over.

Marieke, Ebba and Iqbal all sit. There's a jug of water on the table, and no one speaks.

It's over, Lois thinks. *Everything's over.* She can see it in their faces. They are done.

Maarten enters, talking to the other officer with the shiny dark bob.

'So, if you can get a statement?' he's saying.

The officer nods, glancing at a pad. 'And he heard what Aksel said, on the helicopter?'

Maarten stretches, looks tired. 'Yes. Sarah said we'd find it interesting. She didn't want to say over the phone.'

'I'll get right to it, sir.'

Pulling out a chair, Maarten sits down. It's like he's waiting for something. There's a fruit bowl in the centre of the table. He pulls out an apple and holds it. Something about this bothers Lois. She's desperate for everyone to

344

just leave. She thinks she will scream if he starts to eat an apple.

'The cars are arriving to take you all to the station for the final statements,' he says. 'Before we all head off, I just wanted to say a big thank you to Ebba and Lois. I know it's not the weekend you had planned.' His smile is real.

'I've just got one last question. Dhaka. I know most of you were there at the same time – when you and Iqbal met?' Maarten looks at Lois.

'Yes,' she says, surprised. Then she tenses. Is he going to charge Archipelago? Will they lose it all? Hurriedly, she lists: 'Ebba and I went to see the factories. That's where I met Iqbal. And I found out that Aksel was there too.'

'And Richard,' Iqbal says.

Lois wonders what is coming. Something is coming.

Ebba frowns. Her skin is practically translucent now. Bloodless.

They just all need to leave, Lois thinks. *They are killing Ebba.*

The doorbell rings. 'That might be the first car,' Maarten says, standing up. 'I'll get it.'

67

MAARTEN

Walking across the wide hall with its thick rugs, its bright velvet curtains, Maarten opens the door to Sunny. 'Great. Nearly done. Can you stay here?'

'Of course. I won't move.' Sunny nods, flicking his hair.

'Thanks, Sunny. Any news on Sophie Atwood's lawyer?'

Sunny shakes his head. 'Nah, nothing. They're coming from Holland. It'll be tomorrow at the earliest.'

Nodding, Maarten thinks of her in the cell. If he's right, she might be out by tonight.

The sun has dimmed. The well-lit reception hall is darker now, and he flicks on a light.

'Stay here,' he says. 'We'll need you in a bit.'

Walking back into the kitchen, the sun falling outside, the air is tighter. Maarten looks from Iqbal to Lois, to Marieke.

'Where is Ebba?' he asks, glancing round the room.

'I don't know.' Lois stands up. 'I didn't see her leave. She must have gone to the toilet.'

There's a scent change. Maarten sniffs again. He's been waiting for evidence. Stirring for evidence. Some kind of evidence.

Smoke.

68

IQBAL

The smell. The smell is back, and the taste of pennies floods his mouth.

'Fire!' he shouts. 'There's fire! Quick, everyone out!' He runs to the door that leads out to the garden, unbolts it, and it flies open, banging hard on the stone of the house. He shouts louder, 'Now, out!'

'Ebba?' Lois calls, looking round. 'Where's Ebba? Has she gone upstairs?'

'Lois, out!' Iqbal repeats. He is sweating, and the dizziness is back.

Maarten calls, 'Iqbal, I've got this. You go out with everyone. I'll look for Ebba.'

But Iqbal can see Lois running into the house, not out of it.

'Lois!' he screams.

'Iqbal, please. Can you look after everyone here? Get them away. I have officers inside the house. You can go.' Maarten's hand is on Iqbal's arm, and it's his height more than anything. He is persuaded. The dizziness is all-consuming.

The guests run out. Marieke trips and falls, and Iqbal pulls her up.

'Iqbal, what's happening?' she screams.

The factory walls are back. The heat of the burning fabrics – cheap material, the plastic polyester that catches like dry timber, like fire starters.

69

Lois

'Ebba!' Lois shouts as she runs towards the hall, past the snug. She glances through doors as she runs – no sign of Ebba.

She hears a cry, back in the snug, and she runs.

Ebba stands, her hands up to her face. She screams again, staring at the fireplace.

It's been set every morning. And now it blazes upwards, outwards. Flames have leapt and caught the kindling, which burns. The sofas, soft and velvet, smoulder. The rug is on fire, and the flames stretch towards the curtains.

'What's happened!' Lois screams. She runs and grabs Ebba's arm. 'Come on! Let's get out!'

Ebba holds some papers in her hands. She steps forward and throws them in the fire.

'Ebba, come on!' Lois pulls her arm, hard and firm.

But Ebba doesn't move. 'I think there are more upstairs. I need to check… I took his briefcase… It's in my room. I hid it in our secret panel.'

'What are you talking about? Come on! Get out of here!'

'No. Lois, I need to go upstairs. I told the blond officer in the hall that Maarten wanted him. We have to be quick. There's not much time!'

'How has this all happened?' Lois looks round the room. Tiny trails of fire burn in lines down the centre of the rug. They spring outwards.

'The whisky,' Ebba says. She grabs both of Lois's hands. 'Then I threw the match, and a box of firelighters—'

'The whole box!'

'Yes, I need it all to be burnt, Lois! We only stand a chance if they can't read it!'

'What are you talking about, Ebbs? What's going on?' Staring, aghast, Lois sees the decanter on the floor. Its crystal lid is flung close to the logs, and it's empty. 'Fuck! Come on, Ebba!' She pulls again.

'I had no choice. He knows. I hid the letters here, in the gardening book. It's only me who likes gardening. I knew no one else would ever open it. I stuck the edges of a few pages together to make a pocket. No one would ever find it. Even the police. I put them in there. But I haven't had a chance to go through his briefcase. I hid it in the wall panel, the one we used to hide our treasures in. There's no way they will have found it. I need to go! Quick!'

'What letters? Ebba? Come on!'

But Ebba has fled the room. Lois looks round, sees the water jug and throws it at the fire. But the whisky must have splashed everywhere, and the flames are too hungry.

The firelighters have all caught. The whole kindling box, the magazines on the coffee table…

It's spreading. It curves up and out of the open window. The wooden sash, the wisteria… Lois can't breathe. The panic sets in. She's tumbling.

No. No one will rescue her this time. She can get herself out. She needs to save Ebba.

70

Iqbal

There is heat behind them. The back of the house has caught, and the wisteria that climbs up and round the brickwork is flaring quickly, searing up and over the window frames, reaching the roof where moss hides in the guttering. The flames leap from the building like they're trying to reach the moon.

The clouds are dark now, and an explosion blisters overhead, rockets reaching for the heavens. Piles of colour thrown, heaped into the sky. Fireworks have begun early at the Rugby club nearby. The whole sky is burning.

He looks up. The sisters' rooms are above them. If Lois can't use the stairs, she could always jump. He starts pulling cushions from the garden chairs; he searches for anything that might break her fall.

'Help me!' he shouts. For the second time that weekend, the fire crews are on their way. But they might not be fast enough. 'Help me!'

And they need to fight the fire. Not just run from it. He needs to face it.

'Come on!' Iqbal shouts, and he can hear the distant sound of sirens as he runs for the hose. His hands tremble. Flames shoot from the roof. Colour bursts in the sky above them. The world is ablaze.

71

LOIS

'Ebba!' The main hallway is clear – the front door is closed and the hall empty. Ebba had looked like she would fade away. And smoke is already seeping towards the stairs.

'Ebba!' Lois screams again. The curtains on the main stairs are lit. Velvet – catching the sparks from outside. Tiny flames. The window in the hall is open. The wisteria must have caught.

On either side of the huge window on the curving staircase the heat is growing by the second.

She doesn't know where Ebba has gone, but she knows where the secret panel is. She runs upstairs: Ebba's room.

The heat beats as she rises. She knows already that she will struggle to get downstairs again. The velvet has welcomed the flames. Allowed them to settle in, take hold.

The fire rises upwards quickly, like a snake, darting its head, its tongue.

'Where are you?' she cries. Not again. This can't be happening again.

There's a shout below her. 'Lois! Come down! We'll take care of it!' It's Maarten. 'Sunny?' he's shouting. 'Where are you?'

Lois makes it to the landing. Up here is barely smoky, the fire from the main curtains, ablaze below her, hasn't yet caught. She will trust Ostle House to protect them. She runs forward, to Ebba's room.

'Ebba!' she screams, pushing the door open. It rebounds off the wall and the bang is loud. She pulls it shut, to keep out the flames, the smoke at bay.

'Ebba?'

Ebba stands by the window, looking across the lawn.

'What are you doing?' Lois says. 'We've got to get out!'

'It's empty.'

Lois stares at Ebba's feet. A briefcase has been upended. Pens, papers are strewn on the floor.

'He said he'd made copies. But I think he was lying.' She rubs her head. 'I think that's all the evidence now.'

'What are you talking about, Ebbs? We need to get out!'

Ebba talks as though to herself, rubbing her hands up and down her face.

'Richard is awake. He must have heard what Aksel said on the helicopter. I heard it. Filip got it wrong. It won't be long. I need to plan.'

'Ebba, what are you talking about?' Still thinking of the fire, rising, Lois isn't really listening.

'I killed Aksel, Lois. It was me. Don't you know that by now?'

Lois stares. Frozen.

'I had to kill him, Lois. I just had to. It was the only

way to save our company. To save us! It's the only thing we have.'

There are so many things to say, and Lois can't think where to begin.

72

MAARTEN

'Sunny!' Maarten roars. 'Where are you?'

'Sir?' The voice comes from the hallway.

'I told you to stay near the front door!'

'Ebba Munch said you'd asked me to wait outside. I only stepped out for a few minutes. Oh my God, the fire!'

Christ. 'Where is she?'

The hallway is hot now. The flames rise on the outside of the building.

She must have lit it from in here. He has officers outside, had Sunny in the house. He hadn't thought of this. He hadn't thought she'd be capable of this.

'I've phoned it in. Fire crews are on their way.' Sunny is red, realising his mistake, red with heat.

'The sisters must both be up there!'

Maarten runs, Sunny's footsteps loud behind him.

73

Lois

Lois leans back against the thick door to Ebba's room. She had lain on that bed two days ago, planning the weekend. She's lain on that bed more times than she can count. How can her sister have done what she says she's done? Her head spins.

'But Marieke... It was Marieke who was supposed to be killed. Not Aksel? You said so yourself. We were all there. Aksel's glass broke, and Marieke gave him hers...'

'Lois, will you stop it and just wake up? No she didn't. Marieke didn't give Aksel the glass. I gave him the fucking glass! I gave Marieke's glass to Aksel. I asked him to make the speech. I'd tampered with Aksel's – it was going to break. It was barely holding on. I was so nervous it would break too soon... But it worked.'

Lois needs to sit down. Sliding down the door, she slips to the floor, knees up, resting her head back against the thick wood. She needs support.

'But the poison...'

'I put it in Marieke's glass. I brought the cocktails out.'

'They were on the table. It could have been anyone.'

'Oh, for fuck's sake, Lois. Get out of cloud cuckoo land. I'm telling you what happened. I had to kill Aksel. He was blackmailing us, and he was about to take over the whole company. His distribution terms were daylight robbery.'

The information crushes Lois's brain. It's all too much. 'What?' she says. 'What are you saying?'

'Aksel helped us from the start – don't you remember? He helped me structure the deal, flew us out to Dhaka to see the factory. And it wasn't until later that I realised he'd set the whole thing up, so he could take it off us, right at the end. All the liability ours. And all the profits his. He was going to steal it from us, exactly as he tried to steal from Dad!'

The smoke smell is stronger, and because Lois is already burning inside, she doesn't move. Not right away. It leaks in under the door, pools around her feet.

'Why? Why wouldn't you tell me?'

'Because you're always so fucking perfect, Lois! You'd never let us get off the ground, if you knew what it took! For fuck's sake! You live on the moral high ground. Nice up there, isn't it? Not so fucking nice down here. Where the men are in charge and if you're clean, you get nowhere.'

Lois stares at her. The roar of the fire not as loud as the roar in her head.

'So you knew the VR tech wasn't ours? You knew that Archipelago was built on a stolen idea?'

'I knew that Aksel bought the idea cheap from a factory worker. He asked me to write a memo and leave it on a desk in your team. It allowed us to launch our company, Lois! I never looked back. We never looked back.'

Ebba moves, but Lois is light-headed. All the secrets. She'd been so naïve.

'And the distribution? Was Filip right? Was Aksel getting a much better deal?'

'Oh, Lois. Of course he fucking was. By then, Aksel knew too much. He was blackmailing us. I had no choice.'

'But you could have told me? We could have gone out to Dhaka, sorted it out. We could have brought the factory worker on board – paid for the IP properly. It wouldn't have been too late. For God's sake, Ebba, why didn't you tell me?'

Ebba looks up. Her face is blotchy, tears falling. 'Because you would never have forgiven me. You would never....' She cries again. 'God, Lois. You have no idea how insanely hard it is trying to measure up to your exacting standards of near fucking perfect righteousness all the bloody time!'

'But I... You're my sister! You just needed to tell me. You just needed to say.' Lois, heavy with the weight of it all, struggles to understand. 'You should just have told me, Ebba.'

'But you see, he was going to tell you...'

'Tell me what?'

Lois knows there's something big coming, but she can't think of anything more than this. 'What, Ebba? Just tell me, tell me, please.'

'Oh fuck. It's not just about the IP theft. It's about what happened afterwards...' Ebba's head drops to her hands, hides away. 'It's the fire. He was going to tell you about the fire. He'd written it all down, in a letter. Like the one he sent to Richard. He might have been done for IP theft, but me… People died, Lois! I killed people!' She cries, loud and raw. 'All those people. I'm not a monster, Lois. You think it hasn't eaten away at me?'

Almost crawling, Lois makes it to Ebba's bed, sits next to her, puts her arm around her.

'Go on,' she says.

'The meeting with Obaidur, when Aksel was posing as a researcher… He made me go. He said he needed to know if the product idea was viable. So I sat in, and we looked at the headset, the positioning of the lens. His drawings were technically perfect. Such a simple, ingenious idea. And then Aksel sent his car and driver with Obaidur back to work, and told him that now we'd paid him for the idea, he had to burn his drawings. He told him to put the stuff in the waste unit, and burn it.'

Lois can't speak.

Ebba carries on. 'I went with them. Aksel said he needed me to check the evidence was destroyed. But when we got there, Obaidur was late… He could have been in trouble if he'd been late for his shift…'

She leans forward, rocking.

Lois's mouth is dry, her tongue tight, immobile.

'Obaidur ran for his shift; I ran with him. We took it to the waste burning room, and he gave it to me… Told me what to do.' She looks up, holds Lois's gaze. 'I threw it all in. I put them all in there, but I couldn't close the unit properly. Someone was coming. I knew I couldn't be found there. I threw it all in the burner, and I ran. I shut the door but I didn't hear it click shut. Lois, I had to leave!'

Lois stares at her.

'I was sure whoever was coming in would have done it properly, but within hours, the factory was burning. There were no real fire safety measures in place. And you were in the factory. You'd gone back. To see it again.' She shakes her head.

Lois thinks back. She and Ebba had visited the factory on the first day, and Lois hadn't been able to speak. She'd been so frightened – the horror of the whole thing. People working, like ants, like slaves... Then Ebba had gone off for a meeting, and Lois had returned on her own. She'd walked through the factory, and then the sound – like the ground itself might swallow them up.

'Aksel tracked down Obaidur later. Made him write a statement, saying what I'd done. His driver wrote one too. I killed those factory workers.' Her cries are louder. 'I know Iqbal has been angry with Obaidur for disappearing, like Rajita. But it was shame, Lois. I'm sure of it. His drawings lit the fire. He was powerless to challenge Aksel. And he'd accepted money.'

Lois stares at her hands, limp in her lap. So many deaths. So much guilt.

'All those deaths, Lois. Almost your death. That's what Aksel threatened to tell you, if I didn't do what he wanted. I knew you'd forgive me for most things, but not for silence about that. I never had any choice. I had to kill him. I had to.'

74

MAARTEN

'The door is locked!' He runs into the next room. The darkness is softened by the red glow from the window. The fire has hit this wing of the house. The smell of smoke makes his head spin.

'Sunny, get out. The smoke is getting bad. I can't have you in here.'

'I'm not leaving! Anyway, the staircase is out. Is there another way? Is there a way into the next room from here?'

'I was hoping… *Kak!*' Maarten swears as there is no adjoining door. He pushes open the window in the room, leans out. It's not so far down. He will not let Sunny die.

They run back out into the hall. The sound of fire engines arriving is distant over the rage of the fire.

'Can we break the door down?' Sunny asks, looking round for something to use.

The crackles are loud.

'It's so hot! Let's just get out. The crews will be here…' Sunny's voice is fading, as Maarten feels dizzy.

He thinks of Lois in the room. Filip had heard, '*It was*

never meant...' But Richard had heard, '*It was Ebba, meant*...' The dying man had named his killer. And now she's locked in a room. The lab was still determining the poison. It looked plant based, possibly from a poisonous flower. Most people don't know how dangerous plants and flowers can be. He doesn't have enough to bring a case against her – he needed her to give herself away. Liv had said Ebba had been good with flowers, it was a hobby. But he'd had no idea she would do this...

The window frames are now ablaze. How quickly it spreads.

Sunny falls against the wall. His blond hair damp against his brow. Maarten strikes pointlessly at the smoke, trying to clear a path to him. He lifts Sunny from beneath the shoulders. Inching backwards, his chest screaming, Maarten pulls him towards a door that is open.

Sunny is out cold. *Kak*. Once he makes it into the room, he slams the door closed, and runs to raise the old sash window.

Air rushes in, cooling him. He grabs the quilt from the bed, and he pushes it up against the space beneath the door, trying to slow the smoke.

He drags Sunny to the window.

Sunny's cheeks are pink, and Maarten lifts him up to the air, the oxygen.

Fire flicks from the rooms nearby.

These walls are thick. These doors are thick.

Verdomme.

He will *not* let Sunny die. He *will* save a life.

He just has to hope that there's time.

75

Lois

Part of her still doesn't believe Ebba could have killed anyone. If Ebba turned round now and said she didn't do it, she knows she'd believe her. She wants to believe her. She struggles with the details.

'How did you do it?'

'I used aconitum – wolfsbane. It's a hugely poisonous flower. It's one of Sophie's favourites. She liked its power. Those are the flowers I put in her room. I think it's a close enough link to stand up in court.'

'But what about Filip?'

'He was on to me! You heard him. He said it was like Aksel had been poisoned. It was only a matter of time. And I know he heard what Aksel really said on the helicopter. He heard, *It was never...* but Aksel said, *It was Ebba...* Aksel knew I'd passed him the drink. And he knew what I stood to lose.'

Lois feels stunned. 'But... but the police said Sophie killed Filip?'

'Sophie poured the milk for Filip's coffee. I had the

poison in my pocket to put in his coffee, but I put a few drops in the milk jug afterwards and swirled it round. Forensics should pick it up. We should be OK.'

'We?'

Ebba nods, coughing now.

Lois thinks of Maarten, talking about what Richard had said earlier. 'Maarten knows. He knows it's you.'

'Yes, he fucking thinks he does. But he'll find proving it harder than thinking it. I made the poison and put it in her make-up bag, the flowers are in her room, she admitted she sent those letters – she let something slip recently, after drinks. Sophie will go down for this, not us. We can still get away with it, Lois!'

Lois is aghast. The gulf that lies between them is made up of more than right or wrong. Iqbal stands there, Sophie… Obaidur. But they're tied in blood. Lois could no more deliver Ebba to the police than she could strike her dead.

'But why, Ebba?'

'God, Lois, you have no idea! You have no idea how hard it is to break your way through. Your ideas were so perfect, so bright! But if we couldn't compete financially, then how would we ever get off the ground? You want to be like Dad? A failure? Dead before fifty-five?' She shakes her head. 'He trusted someone, he worked hard. It's not enough. There are Aksels everywhere. Morals might be good enough for you – but I wanted us to win! Now we're almost worth millions. Millions! You could see it through. We'll do it for Dad. Prove ourselves to him. Prove Aksel hasn't won.'

'I thought you were having an affair with Aksel! I thought you were in love…'

'With Aksel? He was threatening me. Us.'

'And you were meeting him, on Friday night?'

'He told me I had to pay Filip the same distribution rights, even if it bankrupted us. Otherwise he'd expose us. Either way, we'd lose everything. He needed the agreement to go through.'

'Was it you, outside?' Lois can barely speak through tears. A life without Ebba opens up. She can't be alone. She can't be.

'In the garden? Yes. I'd gone to meet Aksel. I knew someone was following me – I was nervous it was Maarten. That's when I decided to use the flowers on Aksel.'

'But you could have died too? On the helicopter?'

'God, I didn't know it would happen like that! I thought he'd just keel over later – much later. I thought it would look like a heart attack.'

With the sadness of a lifetime, Lois realises that the loss that swamps her now is bigger than her ideas, bigger than Archipelago. If she could hand Archipelago to Aksel, alive, and keep her sister and Filip, she'd do it in a flash.

Coughing, her throat raw, Ebba is hard to see now. The room is filled with smoke. Dense. Acrid.

Everything is already lost. The heat is intense. The room swims.

Crawling, she makes it to the window, pushing up the sash. She sticks out her head, and Iqbal stands below.

'Jump, Lois! Jump!' he screams.

But she's too tired. She can barely lift her arms.

'Lois!' It's Maarten. He leans from the window to the right. 'Lois, jump. Ebba will be OK. The fire crews are here.'

Nothing is clear now. The night air smells like a burnt firecracker. And Lois has nothing left. She turns to look for Ebba, but all there is behind her is a blurred figure in a smoky grey sea.

'Ebba. Come!'

Ebba shakes her head. 'I need to think. I can't face anyone now, Lois. I can't face it all.'

Iqbal stands below, arms outstretched. Will she make it?

'Ebba, we have to jump. We have to.'

But her sister shakes her head. 'I need time to think. I'm not going down until I've worked it out. I started the fire, Lois. I just need time to think.'

Too dizzy, Lois leans out. There are sparkles in the sky. The world is dancing with light.

76

MAARTEN

Maarten inches along the window ledge. He has lowered Sunny down. Iqbal had pushed over the iron table, built it up with all the garden cushions he could find. Sunny is out, and he can hear the engines, but Lois and Ebba do not have long. He clings to the brickwork.

He thinks of Liv. His face burns and his throat is clogged. He thinks of getting home and telling her everything, all of it: Marieke, attending the call too late, the death... Holding her.

'Lois!' he shouts. 'Lois!'

The sash window lifts, and he pulls himself into the room. Lois is unconscious, heaped up against the wall.

The room spins. The engines' sounds are louder now, but the smoke is dense. He can't see anyone else in the room.

'Ebba!' he shouts.

There is nothing.

Lifting Lois, he manages to get her up to the ledge, and he looks down for Iqbal. The smoke pours out of the downstairs windows now. It is impossible to see clearly.

Dizzy, he sits on the ledge. The cushions are somewhere down there. Somewhere. He can't lower her; his hands shake and his visions swims.

Judging where he thinks Iqbal is, he wraps his arms around Lois, and turns backwards. She is pregnant. He can protect her fall.

The fire crackles above him in tiny flecks of flame, fierce and bright. The heat is tremendous.

'Ebba!' he shouts one more time.

Then he allows himself to fall, holding on to Lois tight, arms crossed round her. He thinks of her baby. He holds the two of them.

Liv's face is the last thing he sees, as he falls into nothing, into blackness. There's a shooting pain in one leg, and then the sound fades away.

77

LOIS

'Liv!' Lois wraps her arms around her. 'How is he?'

'He's OK,' Liv says. She holds a balled tissue in one hand. 'It's just a broken leg. He's inhaled smoke, but they said he's fine. And he's been on the phone to work.' She half laughs, half sobs. 'I never thought I'd be so happy to hear him chat to his boss on a Sunday night!'

'Oh, thank God.' Lois collapses into a chair. The hard plastic offers no comfort, but she's exhausted. She'd heard Iqbal telling Maarten about hitting him, apologising, over and over again, as they waited for the ambulance. But Iqbal had watched for him, softened his fall.

'And how are you?' Liv sits next to her.

'Fine, I'm fine. Maarten saved me, you know. If I'd been in there any longer, I'd be in the same state as Ebba; the doctors said it was the smoke... He got me out. He fell on the cushions Iqbal had put out, but I was on him, so I'm OK. I've been given the all-clear. The baby is fine – they scanned me, checked its heart rate. My chest still hurts...'

Cries rise up in her in a wave, and she breaks down. Her whole body shakes.

'Oh, Lois. Do they know yet?'

'She wouldn't come out!' Lois fights to breathe through the sobs. 'She wouldn't. I really think she meant to die in there. I don't think she could find her way out... Even if I'd dragged her. I always knew she was fragile. I know what she's done... God, I know it's terrible. But I can't hate her. I just love her. She is all my family. All of it. Why couldn't I save her?'

Liv shakes her head, puts her arm around Lois and pulls her in tight. 'We can't save everyone, Lois. We have to realise we can't do it. We're not super-beings. We're just human. We just do the best we can do, most days. And some days that best is better than others. Ebba wasn't yours to save. No one is. You tried your best. All of us try, and sometimes we fail. We just have to get up, and try again.'

Epilogue

Just after Christmas

IQBAL

Iqbal's palms sweat. There is a lump at the back of his throat he can't swallow. His body is warm and his toes are cold. His blood races round his organs.

'Is it hot in here? It feels hot.'

Lois laughs. 'Iqbal, it's freezing. The heating system in this building must be crap.' She puts her hand on his shoulder. 'It will be OK.'

His hands are shaking. 'It's been such a long time. What will I say? Lois, what will I say to her?'

'You'll think of something. I know it.' Lois's phone beeps. She looks down at it.

'Is it Ebba?'

Lois shakes her head. 'No. I'm due at the hospital again later. The nurse said she'd let me know if there's any change, but I don't think there's going to be.' She flexes her hands, her fingers. There are a few scars on there. The ledges had been hot.

She shakes her head. 'Even if they did get her off the

ventilator, they're not sure… And even then, she'd have a whole court case to face. Then prison, realistically. The consultant doesn't think it will be long. I spoke to her this morning. She's been kind all the way through, but it's been two months now. And no change. She suggested we talk about the next step. About…'

Lois pulls out a tissue and blows her nose. 'I will not get upset, not today. Today is your day. You've waited long enough.' She smiles and Iqbal pulls her in, holds her close.

'Lois, without you…'

'None of that. I'd be nothing without you. You saved my life in the factory. And then again at the house. I wouldn't be here without you.'

Lois's phone beeps again. 'It's Marieke. She's arranging another meetup. She's very keen.'

'How's it going?'

'So-so.' Lois shrugs. 'It's been tough. But I admire her – she's still fighting the fight. Her daughter, Norah, is lovely. And I want this one in here…' – she pats her stomach – 'to have a family. I want her to have a sister.'

Iqbal nods. 'Any names yet?'

Lois shakes her head. 'Thinking maybe Pollyanna? We could do with a bit of gladness.'

'Who?' Iqbal says.

Lois laughs. 'Oh, I don't know. Think of one for me? I spoke to Sophie the other day.'

'Me too – no trial date. She's OK, though. It's not looking too bad for her.'

'No, and I saw Maarten! I meant to tell you. He visited the other day, with Liv. There were a few updates on some of the details of the investigation, but with Ebba at the end… His leg is out of the cast now. He seems to be doing well.'

Iqbal covers her hand with his own.

A woman wearing a blue suit enters the room. 'Mr Bari?'

Iqbal leaps to his feet. Sweat pours down his back. 'Yes.'

'We've just had word. The raid was successful. The police have pulled out five victims. Two from a house in Mayfair. Three from a nail bar run by the owner of the house. They're on their way here. We need to process a few details, but if it's her, and if she wants to, then she's free to come home with you almost immediately. She's free. She's free now.'

Iqbal starts to cry. His shoulders shake. It can't be true. 'Is it true?' he asks, his words breaking through his tears. His throat chokes. Tight. 'Can it really be true?'

'Yes, yes it's true. And I'm just so sorry for all of this. The investigation has been ongoing for a while. We've still got a long way to go to bring her the justice she deserves.'

Iqbal thinks of the photo he'd been shown – it had been her. He'd wanted to run there, immediately. To shout that he'd seen her. To see her; to free her.

The sound of a van.

He runs to the front of the building.

'Stay back, give them a minute.' The woman in the blue suit is calm. 'It will be overwhelming.'

Climbing down the steps, helped out by an officer.

Rajita. His very soul.

Will she want him? Fear, love. He is choked. He is choking.

And walking in, eyes looking everywhere at once, she catches his eye. She smiles. She runs.

Rajita.

Acknowledgements

As always, I couldn't do this without my agent Eve White. She and Ludo Cinelli are the best in the business.

A huge thanks to my publishers, Head of Zeus and their team, who have worked this year under circumstances unplanned for and unprecedented. Laura Palmer, my editor extraordinaire, deserves a medal.

The research for this novel began some time ago. Thanks to Felix Dodd of Felix Dodd Studio, for his instruction in VR and for helping with the technical detail of the novel. Also, thanks to Isobel McFarlane of the Salvation Army, for her help with research into modern slavery. The Salvation Army work tirelessly to battle modern slavery. Thank you to all the freed slaves who have told their stories. You are inspirational.

Many thanks for all the accounts of life in Bangladesh from all those who have shared your experiences.

Special thanks to Victoria Quinney for providing research trips support.

For procedural research, thanks to police officers and former officers David Newsome, Richard Johnson and Jason Dawson. Their advice is invaluable. For all of this advice, I may have twisted procedure for the sake of the novel, but this is all me.

I'm lucky with the best writing friends. Thanks to Ella Berman for reading, Jodie Chapman, Clare McVey, Helen Treacy and Louise McCreesh. And huge thanks to all the informative and supportive Criminal Minds.

As always, thank you to my family.

Finally, thank you to Iqbal and Oxo, who began this story years ago.